Jane Austen out of the blue

Property developers are erecting sea-side apartments in the village of Sanditon, for people who may prove winners or losers as lovers or money-makers.

Towards the end of January 1817 a lady novelist, less well-known then than she is now, begins a novel on those lines – a setting and theme very different from anything she has previously attempted. She has written less than a quarter of it when she becomes too ill to continue. At the end of April she makes her Will, and on 18 July she dies.

Jane Austen out of the blue is about those three months – from the writer's point of view. What could have been going on in her mind? What would have happened next in the story?

In seeking answers to these and other questions, the present work provides a lively account of the rise of a sea-bathing place in Regency England; and an inventive extension of Jane Austen's fragmentary final novel. Of her world, too: Sanditon is a place where anyone – whether based on fact or taken from fiction – may go in search of sea air.

Life and half-life, reason and the surreal, social history and magical realism, fact and speculation are all to be found in the pages which follow. Yes, it's a novel, but one which has been described as 'also a subtle and felt form of literary criticism'.

Donald Measham lives in Derbyshire, England, and knows 'Pemberley' and its gardens well. Most of *Jane Austen out of the blue*, though, takes place in 'Sanditon', in the county of Sussex, where the book was researched and partly written. It first took shape as a novella, with a more restricted range of characters: Angus Wilson very kindly read it in typescript and provided a detailed commentary.

The author also has a special interest in the life and work of John Ruskin. He devised and presented a major exhibition for the centenary of *Praeterita*, Ruskin's autobiography – and has written a novel about him. Entitled *A Dream of Fair Women*, it is currently being revised with a view to publication.

Previous published work includes: *Fourteen* and *English Now and Then* (both Cambridge University Press); *Ruskin: the Last Chapter* (Sheffield Arts) *Lawrence and the Real England; Twenty Years of Twentieth Century Poetry* (ed. with Bob Windsor – likewise 60 monographs, collections, issues of *Staple New Writing* 1983-2000).

Pending is *The Jane Austen Puzzle*. It is scheduled for 2007. See page 222, below.

Jane Austen out of the blue

A NOVEL

By

DONALD MEASHAM

Donald Measham
26th September 2006
For Janet, with love and
best wishes — colleague and friend,
Don.

First published 2006

Copyright © Donald Measham

The right of Donald Measham to be identified as the author of this work has been asserted by him in accordance with the Copyright, Designs and Patents Act 1988.

All rights reserved. No part of this publication may be reproduced, stored or transmitted in any form or by any means, electronic, mechanical or otherwise, without the prior written permission of the copyright owner.

ISBN 978-1-84728-648-2

For Joan and Caitlin

To read something uniquely interesting like this out of the blue is so strange –

        Sir Angus Wilson, in a letter to the author.

✷

…recovering my looks a little, which have been bad enough, black and white and every wrong colour

        Jane Austen, on her illness, March 1817.

✷

Part One: SALT

1

It is April 1817. Miss Jane Austen is half lying on a couch: her eye-sockets are black, and her skin has a strange bronze sheen. She has Addison's disease. It will kill her, because Dr Addison is still a young man, and forty years short of identifying the condition which bears his name. Miss Austen has a deficient adrenal system, which means low blood pressure and the secretion of salt.

This loss of salt has drawn her to write about the sea. A seaside place called Sanditon – the setting of her final work. She writes about brine: writes about it in an unfriendly way. Writes of taking the waters: of drinking salt water, bathing in it. She is sceptical of what some part of her mind guesses her body may need. Convinced of the quackery of all that.

So she remains beached in Winchester, and will die there. Recumbent, supine – secreting salt – she can write no more. Papers are within reach, but she cannot raise herself. Cassandra, her sister, is her patient nurse.

Her work is beside her. Her characters are stopped. They stay where she left them. So far.

Not yet. Yet it is a truth far from universally acknowledged that Jane Austen's characters cease to exist, or cease to develop, when their author passes them to her public. She is on record as frequently speculating about their future lives.

She lies there – secreting salt – beside her papers, a spinster of sound mind.

JANE AUSTEN OUT OF THE BLUE

✱

Elizabeth is alone at Pemberley. Though she feels easier without Darcy's eyes upon her, she is out of sorts. A letter from Jane Bingley, her favourite sister, arrives opportunely.

> Northampton
>
> 15th May 18–
>
> Dearest Lizzy
>
> Such news! We are not, after all, to be gypsies at Nottingham Fair – or outlaws in Sherwood Forest. Instead we are to be settled (commodiously) by summer – and for who can tell how long beyond. The works we left behind us multiply and grow more urgent daily, the surveyor tells us. (Bingley maintains it will be the Abbey's first lick of paint since the reign of good king Harry – the monarch whom you called an Executioner and Butcher in the school room!)
>
> B– (Bingley not butcher) was travelling in these parts and looked to see an old acquaintance, but found his house shut up and the remaining family still in half-mourning for dead sons and sires and fortune: of which I don't make light nor does Bingley. He is, as you know, a gentle soul; and, wishing to afford some help to the afflicted family, took on this half-empty Mansfield Park as our Northampton home during the Nottm refurbishment. All agree that old Sir Thomas Bertram, who had the sorrow of outliving his sons, was a just (though strict) master. The few staff remaining with him in his last days will be kept on; as well as several nursemaids and women able to make pretty

things. They are greatly relieved by their prospect of being in Bingley's employ.

I find that the counties of Northampton and Derby are a hundred miles apart (I hoped they'd be nearer!). Dear Lizzy, it saddens me to think of such a distance, though it gives even more reason for your dear letters. The last with its hint that all might be well *this time* – unlike the previous (letter, I mean) in which you fear you'll fare no better than before. And before-and-before-and-before, as you put it. Alas, Lizzie. But since petticoats can't inherit – put your trust in the present. I do. Do for you, I really do. Trust me. And, Dear Lizzie we can continue constructing our causeway of correspondence – eight years in the building. Eight married years, isn't it, now?

To ameliorate our situation further, I have a proposal for an emissary: I refer to Mrs Fanny Bertram whose person and parts I have mentioned previously. Brought up in Mansfield Park itself, you may recall. You would find her a very sensible companion – learned, I fear! – But in a droll, modest way. Her accomplishments arising out of sad adversity etc are exemplary. (I do not say this Lizzy in that tone of voice which we sometimes used to amuse each other!) She tells me that she was brought up to be very quiet – 'insignificant' is the word she uses. 'Born for dependency and domesticity', she says, raising pretty eyes with a wistful glint in them. In spite of which she has become known as a blue-stocking lady – but a far from over-bearing example of the kind! – who still modestly averts her eyes, those pretty eyes.

Dear Lizzy, I do believe her company would delight you and *her* fortitude strengthen *you* during the months that you await – you await Mr Darcy's return from abroad. She is a lady whose life has taken a very different course, not merely from our own, but from that of any of our acquaintance;

and all the more interesting for that. As I say, she has had much to bear and might have been content to be pitied; whereas, intended commiserators find their own hearts lightened. I, for one, have become dependent upon Mrs Bertram, and only now find myself able to spare her; with so much to do at Mansfield and tasks that I do not wish to inflict on her – for she has her own proper work, as you will discover – whenever it is that you make her acquaintance (for I am determined on it!), whether it be soon at Pemberley or later at Mansfield – when you and your *happy* family are able to visit.

I believe you will find the lady, as I have done, agreeable and instructive company –

But here come Bingley and the boys, so I must break off, and end my letter – so as to ensure that it is ready for the post.

If when you write you wished to enclose a note for Mrs Bertram, I would of course take care she had it without delay.

I remain &c your loving sister,
Jane Bingley.

✱

Some characters shift willingly, others refuse to budge. A little to the west of Kingston-on-Thames, Emma's father is a case in point. Mr Woodhouse has for several years determined not to set foot beyond Highbury, or even outside his old home there. From his standpoint rather than his daughter's – or even his author's – he has decided that there is life in the old dog yet; life of a sort.

SALT

✲

Far beyond his biblical span, Mr Woodhouse was making clear to those about him that he was simultaneously alive and close to death; though the latter was retrievable, given good management. The years had made him increasingly querulous and child-like – and not always able to identify Mr Knightley (himself beginning to age) as the husband of Emma, his favourite daughter; seeing him rather, which indeed he also was, as brother-in-law to his other child Isabella; and as a species of imported guard-dog whose purpose was to keep his poultry yard safe from intruders. This function had been urged upon Mr Woodhouse when he reluctantly consented that George Knightley should join his household as Emma's husband.

Mr George Knightley's habitual courtesy and respectful demeanour were becoming difficult to sustain. The second-childishness of Mr Woodhouse increasingly drew attention to the fact that none of Knightley and Emma's children had survived for more than a day or two. It was as if there would not have been room for them had they lived. Mr Knightley had begun to regret moving from Donwell Abbey, and having made it over to John and Isabella (his brother, and Emma's sister) to use as their own during Mr Woodhouse's life-time.

The old gentleman's manner was as sweet as ever, but it seemed to Knightley, who spared Emma this thought, that he could perceive in Mr Woodhouse the beginnings of wilfulness and cunning.

Either it was: 'Emma, my dear, will you introduce me to this gentleman whom I do not recall having met before?'

'Why, father, it is Mr Knightley.'

'No, my child, if that gentleman were Mr Knightley then you are my daughter Isabella and I know full well that you are my daughter Emma.'

'I am sorry to contradict you, father, but this is your old friend Mr George Knightley. His brother to whom you referred is

Mr John Knightley, who is, as you correctly state, the husband of my sister, Isabella.'

'I had not thought that you would seek to confuse your old father so, to take advantage of him with such talk of people who can be nothing to us,' knuckling away a tear and pushing away whatever food or drink was before him.

Either it was behaviour of this kind or a garrulous recollection of the previous decade; apparently purposeless, but within which Mr Woodhouse's chatter would soon find its bearings – with this end, to discourage Emma from marrying if the ceremony lay in the future, or to extricate herself from the arrangement if it lay in the past:

'I have been thinking, my dear, why do we need gentlemen in the house? We managed well enough in the past without their presence, did we not? We never did have gentlemen. Suppose, my dear, we were to get our eggs and fowl from Mr Weston we would no longer trouble Mr Knightley or his brother. Perhaps Miss Taylor would return.'

(Miss Taylor, Emma's companion and protectress of the household poultry, had left the household some dozen years previously to marry the Mr Weston whom Mr Woodhouse now saw as an alternative source of poultry provision.)

'We need,' said Mr Knightley, a shade grimly one day, 'we need, my dear Emma, a change of air. I concede,' he added as Emma looked perturbed, 'I concede, my dear, that your father is in need of a change of air too.'

Emma feared that Mr Woodhouse would neither be likely to agree to accompany them to any place whatsoever, nor have them leave him behind were they to seek to travel.

'Perhaps,' said Knightley, ' Mr Woodhouse would find it acceptable for Isabella and John to live in the house with him for a short period in our stead.'

'Perhaps,' said Emma uncertainly, 'I'll do my best to prepare my father for what may seem to him a cataclysm.'

But when the proposition was put to him with much gentleness, he began, equally gently, to cry.

Emma had always had more cleverness than her life required; but not always enough sense to see what was plain to simpler souls. Neither her brightness nor her blank spots were of help to her now; she was sustained only by the real affection she had for her old father – even for what was irritating in him. As for Mr Knightley, although discomfited by his father-in-law, he was incapable of wishing the old man dead. Emma herself was fully capable of entertaining such a thought, but, to her credit, never permitted herself to do so.

✴

Less complex were Elinor Ferrars and Marianne Brandon (the former Miss Dashwoods, who through nature and nurture had typified sense and sensibility respectively). The matches they had made – seemingly inapposite for their dispositions, the rational lady to a first son with a second son's income, the romantic one to a gentleman twice her own age – had modified the bias of their characters. Marianne had a more practical appreciation of autumn fruits (while retaining her mournful pleasure in fallen leaves); while Elinor was less dismissive of personalities which differed from her own. However, the latter lady (though now with her own portion of sensibility) remained the one to turn to in practical matters.

Marianne had never acquired a head for figures: it is fortunate that as wife to Colonel Brandon she had little need for computation. The secure income of the Delaford estates meant all she needed to be was a neat copyist, and to look pretty in that activity. Elinor Ferrars, on the other hand, as the wife of a parson who had quixotically relinquished the better part of his fortune in favour of his younger brother Robert, found as much utility in totting up her cash book as Mr Richardson's celebrated Clarissa Harlowe.

But Death was the constant creditor of that heroine; and – an arbitrary accountant. So while Emma's father, Mr Woodhouse, lived on, Rev Edward Ferrars and Colonel Brandon (neither of whom had ever met Mr Woodhouse or would have been remembered by him had they done so) had been both struck down in the same fatal year.

The widowed Elinor Ferrars joined the widowed Marianne Brandon at her marital home Delaford House, where they and their children lived together amicably. For a long time they saw nothing of Robert Ferrars who had gone through a form of marriage with an adventuress. Much improved by being rid of her, he resumed his acquaintance with what had become a largely female household. Within it there were three little boys, one of whom was Colonel Brandon's heir.

Young Brandon was not strictly Robert Ferrars' avuncular business, but he gave the lad much attention. He did indicate to Elinor that it was her children – his true nephews and nieces – who would be remembered in his will. So she thought no worse of him for playing with Brandon in the here and now; recognising in his comparative shyness with her Ferrars children the old awkwardness that his riches had been acquired at their dead father's expense.

She and Marianne did not see him as a family man yet, but they liked his capacity for playfulness. He would skylark about the corn stooks with Brandon, or disguise himself as a scarecrow in a field: behaviour regarded as not quite fitting by the bailiff, Mr Robert Martin, who dealt very soberly with the young squire. Martin was a yeoman farmer who had married a wife with a little education and been urged by her into estate management. He proved good at this work, never adding unnecessary worries to the Brandon and Ferrars families, who lived very quietly; careful in case fortune should deal them some further blow.

Then one day the morning sun, in its dispersal of the cool of the previous night, brought about a kind of fragrance that made those who are receptive to such sensations feel they could live for ever. Only mortals need be cautious, so before breakfast Marianne called out: 'Let us do some thing special, Elinor. Some excursion, some quest...'

    Elinor smiled at her sister's choice of phrase, but was quick to accede: 'The children would benefit - and now may be the best time – before the summer grows too hot.'

    'Which, then, shall it be,' said Marianne, excited to find they were agreed, ' – distant vistas or the salt sea sand?'

    'Maybe both,' said Elinor. 'You may recall that there is an invitation to Norland, but I fear it may have been sent as a matter of form –'

    'I would like to see Norland again,' said Marianne, 'though I'm not sure I should care to stay there for any length of time. I suspect you have feelings similar to my own in this regard?'

    'Indeed I have,' said Elinor.

What once had been unthinkable was now possible and even desirable: that they should take a place for the summer within easy reach of Norland Park, Sussex – the childhood home, from which they had been unkindly expelled ten years ago in favour of their half-brother, John Dashwood, and his unpleasant wife.

    The ladies were of one mind, Marianne having supplied the general notion, Elinor having a securer application of smaller matters:

    'There is perhaps a way of seeing the old place,' she began, 'and getting sight of the ocean (that is to say, the English Channel). I have been speaking to Martin, as you asked me, about the new schoolroom, and he mentioned again his former employer.'

    'I recall but little of that,' said Marianne, 'something about a man who vacated his family acres in Sussex, I seem to remember, because that was the reason Martin left his employ.'

    'And do you not also recall,' said Elinor, 'that the name of the gentleman was Mr Parker?'

    'No, I must have been thinking of something else by then,' said Marianne, 'why not?' – a little of her girlish impatience persisting, 'I was interested only in how Martin came to be with us.'

'You're right, my dear Marianne,' replied Elinor evenly, 'The gentleman's name doesn't matter at all, save that – ' And she told how Mr Parker had erected, by his own (according to Martin, vainglorious) account, commodious dwellings for the discerning traveller in a picturesque and quiet location – handy for Norland, but sequestered from its estate, if concealment should prove the better part of convenience.

They resolved, discounting Martin's disapproval of Mr Parker's enterprise, to draw him out further on the subject of Mr Parker and his sea-bathing place.

Part Two: **NEW SANDITON**

1

A kind of magnetism must be supposed to draw people to the ocean. Captain Wentworth, for example, having given up the navy, could have no further relinquished contact with the basis of his former profession than he could have gone without his breakfast.

He and his wife Anne lived on the coast of Sussex; by nautical or land measures well distant from the large house in Lyme which he had taken on marriage to Miss Elliot; and from which he was recalled to command a ship of the line. It was to that house he had shortly returned, invalided from the service he loved. Though wars had threatened, his own incapacitating injury had arisen not in some high encounter for national advantage, but in coming to the rescue of a fellow officer set upon by a drunken rating.

That the felon was hanged on Wentworth's evidence was no satisfaction to him. More in accord with his good nature, though sad and unconnected the occasion, was his ability to settle a large sum upon the family of an old service acquaintance; who plagued him by dying – while another, foolishly matched (and his wife in raw health) had composed quantities of miserable and incompetent verse, which Wentworth was obliged to endure. Small wonder Dorset became for Wentworth less of a haven and more of a sand bank. Leaving good works and best wishes behind, he headed East – but not for the orient.

Sea wanderings finished, those he made about the land were but those of a good dog settling his bed. A lesser house than the one at Lyme he had first shared with Anne had been followed by a smaller one, a cottage almost. But all and always in sight of the sea, and mostly, too, within its sound. They were happy in their seclusion, having one daughter Agnes, a favourable girl of seven, and seeing very little company. Wentworth walked at set hours with his telescope; Anne drew and pressed flowers; Agnes was compliant.

Years had passed peacefully for them, until Wentworth one day returned home from some family business in what for a man as calm as he would pass for a state of agitation. His quietness was threatened. The captain had previously heard talk of a gentleman who had given up a decent house for a gimcrack one, but it was only now that Wentworth realised what it was that this gentleman – this Mr Thomas Parker – was up to, at a place barely half an hour from his own front door. Or a quarter of an inch on a favourite map; the name of the place still printed very small. A modest place, as Wentworth preferred places to be: Sanditon.

✷

'Sanditon' seems to have been located near modern Seaford, which has a Willingdon on the Hailsham road, and a Thomas Parker interred in the local church. The dying author of the unfinished *Sanditon*, as it came to be called – seeking, secreting, hating salt – sought or thought it out as a setting, a subject. The heroine's first name was to be 'Charlotte', after Miss Austen's acquaintance Charlotte Williams, whose 'large dark eyes always judge well.' On the page, she has become Charlotte Heywood of Willingden, who is awaiting events in Mr Parker's sea-bathing place.

✷

'Pemberley is so distant from the sea,' complained Elizabeth to Fanny, gesturing, as another landscape feature came into view: 'I suppose that's why the ancestors of Mr Darcy – or, rather, his uncle's line – were so busy for so long – raising the river-level with dams and weirs; planting the grounds with pools and ponds and puddles and fountains and falls. But, these water-works are nothing like the sea, for all their diggings and diversions. No tide, no gulls, no salt...'

'I was brought up by the sea,' said Fanny, slightly out of breath, 'but – no – our situation wasn't at all picturesque. This was a dark little house in a narrow street in Portsmouth. On a clear day it could be pleasant walking along the ramparts. But that was all – that and the dock-yard. As I think of it now, Mr Price, my father – his house seems smaller than that enjoyed by the least of your tenantry – tinier, certainly, in relation to mother's quantities of children than even your smallest gatekeeper's cottage – and far less charming...'

Pausing at a viewpoint, Elizabeth made gentle inquiries which drew from Fanny the satisfaction she felt in her brother, William Price – full lieutenant since Trafalgar and now commander, with prospects of rising further in the service.

'We were poor relations,' said Fanny, as they resumed their walk. 'All this space about us here reminds me of how, as I say, stifling and cluttered were my earliest years. I owe everything to Sir Thomas, the late Sir Thomas Bertram, who brought me to Mansfield. How lost I was, too, a very little girl, in that great house! Set in Mansfield Park – a considerable estate, as Mrs Bingley will have told you.'

They both smiled at the thought of Jane.

'I did grow accustomed to life there – but my happiest times, by far my happiest times – were to come. Those were in a small house, once more. Not, of course, the Price house in Portsmouth, but dear old Mansfield parsonage with its cheerful conversation and quiet occupation...No,' Fanny assured Elizabeth, 'I prefer to speak about it. Three years have passed since my Edmund's death – and, as to Sir Thomas, he was old – and I have become attuned to my new circumstances... Would Edmund be surprised at what I have become? At what occupies me? Probably he would. Fond as he was of me, I believe he would have preferred me to re-marry.' Fanny blushed and broke off. 'Really I have talked enough, have not breath for much more. I can hardly keep up with you, in spite of -'

'In spite of my advanced years?' Elizabeth replied teasingly. 'I do of course know what you mean. I absolve you from any reference to my matronliness. It is, we know, the progress of that other thing, which we have in mind. But that has still some way to go.'

The sun was already proving too warm, the ascent they had undertaken too considerable; so the ladies gave up their intention to walk to the stand of trees by the old hunting tower on the craggy height which overlooks Pemberley. Instead of leaving the gardens by an upper gate, they were drawn to the little temple at the head of the great cascade.

'Stand back, Fanny,' said Elizabeth, 'for the breeze coming to these arches as it passes through the *torrente* can drench you to the skin, chill you to the bone, before you've even noticed. Very well, it is in that respect a little like the sea – and you'd think I could be cool and easy here, yet I cannot. This Derbyshire air is harsh...I don't want to think about it. I'd rather that you told me some more of your life with Edmund.'

Fanny hesitated. 'Are you sure?'

'Certainly,' said Elizabeth.

The two ladies moved to the stone seat of the temple out of reach of the spray, refreshed by the sound of the waters. The scene before them seemed like something in a great arched mirror, or as seen through a Claude-glass; bright and unreal.

'This is an idyllic spot,' said Fanny, 'though I can understand why you are out of sorts with it. My own married life in the parsonage was also idyllic – though not everyone's – no, not *anybody* else's – idea of an idyll.'

'And why was that?' said Elizabeth, sensing that what Fanny was hesitating to put before her was neither unpleasant to recollect nor in the usual sense private. Fanny was anxious not to concern Elizabeth with trivia; Elizabeth whose responsibilities – particularly in Darcy's absence – were considerable. Also she did not wish to appear odd, though at the same time she was not averse to appearing different. So in the end she said:

'I made progress with him. Edmund drew me to him. I transcribed with him, and finally learned to translate. This was also true of the way he was to me and of me to him: it describes the progress of our loving companionship. And of the pages before us – not between us. These were pious texts, of course – seen at first solely through my husband's eyes.'

Elizabeth smiled in turn, in part because she was reminded by Fanny's earnestness of her own solemn sister, Mary Bennet – still on her father's hands and still, by his account, uttering quantities of sentiments which she copied into notebooks without the capacity to distinguish the acute from the vacuous, or to develop her personality in anything like the way which Fanny had begun to describe.

Poor Mary was both owl and parrot, though able to impress Mrs Bennet still with what could pass for learning. Not so her father, whose indulgent smile in this daughter's presence was made possible by increasing deafness. Old now, Mr and Mrs Bennet still lived in the family home in spite of the entail which would put it in the hands of odious Reverend Collins on the husband's death. (The latest news Elizabeth had from there was that Collins was like to lose his wife, her poor former friend Charlotte Lucas, worn down by this boor.)

But any comparison between Mary Bennet and Fanny Bertram was, Elizabeth saw, unfair. Earnestness without judgment is mockable, whereas Fanny brought intelligence and engagement to join those twin attributes. For instance, Fanny had become gently silent now, so that Elizabeth could be the judge of whether she had spoken too long.

Not so. Elizabeth, recognising that there was more of interest in Mrs Bertram's preoccupations than the lady would display unaided, set to draw her out; eliciting an unaffected explanation of how she was to take over from the poetess Laetitia Barbauld all the preparation for publishing anew and presenting to a forgetful public the works of Mr Fielding, Mr Richardson, Mme D'Arblay and others.

'That I should move from my prose transcriptions – and my husband's kindly teachings – to the supervision of lively narrations, some pages of which would bring (though not without moral purpose) blushes to a young girl's cheek, was not to be looked for.

And yet to have the capacity to blush is dependent on having the knowledge that what is written merits a blush. Better that the young lady should experience such blushable occasions in phantasy, encounter them in the care of one who has experienced and thought many things – do you not think, Mrs Darcy? – than stumble across them alone and unaided?'

Fanny looked Elizabeth straight in the eye. Then, without waiting for an answer and without apparent cause, Fanny gave a start as if challenged – recollecting some thing in her life or some thing she had read. She turned on her heel as if she would escape, but the wall behind them was blank.

'No, my dear Fanny,' said Elizabeth, 'your way is barred. Yes, I agree this is a Gothick place for all its baroque trimmings, but it lacks a massive sliding door or hidden apse to swallow up its heroine. Don't deny it,' she continued, 'you have been a heroine in a haunted Abbey. If not, it was someone very like you when you were very young.'

They had been leaning, with at first a frisson and then laughter, upon the wall which had proved to be no less immovable than a wall should be.

'Solid as solid can be,' said Elizabeth. 'But the place does have its secrets, as you will see.'

'Really?' said Fanny.

Rested, they moved towards the stout front frame of the temple with its shifting inner mount of spray. As they did so, the point of Fanny's closed parasol caught in a curious little hole or slot – one of a series cut in the flagstone floor.

'There,' said Elizabeth, 'that is one of the secrets. But you are quite safe, dear Fanny.'

'Safe, Elizabeth? Who would doubt that?'

Elizabeth laughed. 'I see you have no idea of the purpose of these secret crannies, each of which contains – see – a small leaden tube. No, they are not gothic keyholes to some Stygian underworld – merely the hidden water-spouts or spurting-places designed to catch young ladies of a former time unaware. Darcy's grandfather –

or was it his great-uncle? – had the trick of withdrawing to the thicket behind the Cascade House. In it are concealed the means of driving water through hidden pipes into occasional indoor fountains to shock young ladies with their sudden force; for they were lured to stand at this midpoint in their innocent summer frocks and petticoats. You smile,' said Elizabeth, 'yet you are concerned that these poor things should be drenched for gentlemen's sport. That was the age of sentimental toasts. You will have heard of them.'

'Indeed. Madame D'Arblay – Fanny Burney that was – tells what an ordeal they were for young ladies. I was reading some of her letters in Mr Darcy's library only yesterday.'

'Well, Fanny, the library is the place for such things. We live in more civilised times. There'll be no cause for you to drench your neat costume or to repeat dubious maxims at dinner to help old men wet their whistles, as the vulgar put it.'

'Indeed not,' said Fanny, 'though I am an interested bystander of such curiosities.'

'Mr Darcy has no time for what he thinks tomfoolery, I'm afraid,' said Elizabeth.

The two ladies had proceeded to the very edge of dryness overlooking the cascade with its frothings from tufa rock on either hand; and the outpouring from cups, horns, mouths of mossy river gods; beyond, the predictability of the watery stairs receding before them and disappearing beneath the sward: a haze of heat after, with the great house lit by the south, and screened by a rainbow from the spray and the spume – like unexplained fire.

"This,' said Elizabeth,' must be our sea. But there's no taste to it. No salt, just the smell of old limestone or whatever it is.'

'Calcium carbonate,' said Fanny quietly, automatically.

Elizabeth, not hearing, continued:
'Except for the respect in which he holds the work of his forebears, Mr Darcy would have it re-fashioned. He finds this piece of work irrational – Pemberley's celebrated cascade – whereas he accepts the Canal, by the south front, which I find too tame. He sees this

watery display which gives a sparkle to our eyes as no more than a series of declining weirs; makes serious inquiry whether these subsiding waters could not be made to serve some practical purpose.'

'And in the gardens of Italy,' said Fanny, 'he wishes to find an answer?'

'Yes,' said Elizabeth, 'such is his stated purpose. To see whether comeliness and industry can combine their identities in a given work or operation. And yet –'

Elizabeth paused and Fanny did not like or wish to prompt her friend to proceed. In a little while Elizabeth took up where she had broken off:

'And yet, it has been a sad time for us – that Fitzwilliam still lacks an heir, has no living male child. I blame myself: my mother's side of the family always made a sad shot at delivering boys. But excuse this maundering – I can understand that he needs the solace of a change of situation during the coming months.'

'It is natural that he should prefer you not to travel abroad,' said Fanny, putting a kindly construction on Darcy's absence.

'To be sure,' said Elizabeth, 'and sometimes I hope.'
'There must always be hope,' said Fanny

'I suppose so,' said Elizabeth, 'but there have been so many disappointments – I was going to say so many daughters, but such disparagement is unworthy.'

'I expect,' said Fanny, 'you were just led on by alliteration to what you were thinking of saying.'

'I expect I was,' said Elizabeth, adding – 'alliteration is a dangerous thing. I used to have a wit, but I know no longer whether what I say is my own or borrowed.'

'*Mine* is all borrowed,' said Fanny, 'and there is a place for that. As there should be for a lady with many daughters – or with none at all.'

'My dear Fanny,' said Elizabeth, 'have I been insensitive?'

'Not a bit,' said Fanny. 'The thought of my mother's life makes me shudder. Besides, childlessness is convenient for the kind of work I do.'

NEW SANDITON

They gazed into the water, over the parkland, beyond the stands of trees, up to the escarpments beyond – and slowly back down again.

'I understand,' said Fanny uncontroversially, 'that Italy has many fair mountains and lakes as well as fertile plains.'

'I believe so,' said Elizabeth, 'yet Italy is not an island; and the English are used to an island. It remains a pity that Pemberley is so far from any coast.'

*

It was from the safety of the land that Anne Wentworth had grown to love the sea. At first this affection was for her dear husband's sake; even as he had put solid ground under his feet for Anne's comfort of mind. Anne, though a shore-based spirit, was a courageous walker: the wildest weather would bring a healthy glow to her cheeks and to those of little Agnes. Nor did the heat of that early summer of 18– prevent their daily walk: the nearness of the sea ameliorating the ardour of the sun. It was upon one such that she first encountered Miss Charlotte Heywood, resident at Trafalgar House in New Sanditon.

In spite of Captain Wentworth's misgivings about the press of people from the sea-side speculation, Anne was both charmed by the young lady and interested in gaining her impressions of life at the sea-bathing place. To this end, Miss Heywood readily allowed access to a long letter to her parents who lived at Willingden, which – in accordance with Jane Austen's instruction in the seventh of the surviving twelve chapters of Sanditon – she had recently written; and of which, as young ladies will, she had retained a copy for contingencies such as her present pleasant encounter with Mrs Wentworth, in whose parlour she now sat.

JANE AUSTEN OUT OF THE BLUE

Trafalgar House, New Sanditon

3rd June 18–

I had every intention of writing, my dear parents, as soon as I arrived. To my shame I find that what was then the morrow has become another yesterday! I beg your pardon if this delay has caused you anxiety. You may suppose that the kind importunity of our new friends has afforded me little leisure in daylight; and to settle down to my letter in my bed chamber that first evening (having been commanded by Mr Parker to sleep!) would have been to set myself up as a heroine who corresponded secretly by rush-light – though kind Mr Parker has, as you may expect, the most modern of appliances including a species of mechanical lamp whose operations I am unable to describe, but which he is anxious to demonstrate to you personally at the earliest opportunity. In short, enjoined – ordered – to sleep after my busy day, sleep I did; a victory for the Sanditon air which Mr Parker was quick to seize upon.

Thus the pleasant task of writing home to Willingden has awaited the morning light of Mr and Mrs Parker's Venetian windows: they overlook (in accordance with Mr Parker's promise) a noble expanse of Ocean; and (a foil to set it off?) a foreground of sundry unfinished buildings, canvas awnings, exposed mansards and chimneys. I am enclosing at Mr Parker's behest his paper descriptive of Sanditon's scenic attractions. I know you would wish to see it. You will recall that he very much regretted not having a copy to hand during his enforced stay at Willingden. The printer had evidently misdirected or he would have had it long ago.

Much of the pamphlet's content will be familiar to you from Mr Parker's conversation - though the condemnation of the rival enterprise is less specific than in the spoken declarations he made to us! (Nevertheless more severe than his strictures on the equilibrium of carriages! For his upset, after all, brought about the acquaintance of our respective families.) Can this other sea-bathing place be so very uncongenial? Whether or no, like a naughty child I long to visit it, though I certainly ought not to do so unless I can be quite sure that Brinshore (Mr Parker cannot bring himself to use its name) will displease me very much.

(There is no opportunity of a post today, I learn to my chagrin. My company is required – I will resume as soon as I am able.)

Taking up my neglected pen: obedient to Mr Parker, I have slept. *I* do well here. However, Sanditon, I fear, prospers only moderately: there are not so many people as I was led to expect. The Terrace as it is called (the Mall of the place, though strangely near to the edge of a cliff that, I think, crumbles) is smart-looking; but I detect a shortage of decent houses and a plethora of poky lodgings – some in what were until now fishermen's cottages. Mr Parker is much cheered by news from his sister Miss Diana, who (one gathers) is a very active invalid. She has great hopes that a whole seminary from Camberwell (where she, Miss Parker, resides) will lodge here six weeks of the Summer.

This possibility has much interested Lady Denham, who is the great lady of this place – she heads the library subscription list! Lady Denham is taken by the likelihood that some of the young ladies from Camberwell will, chancing to be consumptive, need quantities of asses' milk (which her own two milch beasts can supply). But in the matter of remedies, here lies dissension; Lady Denham having spoken against Mr Parker's ambition to introduce a surgeon into the neighbourhood. Her first husband (a rich Mr Hollis) had been rapidly consigned to his eternal rest by his doctors, but not before they had beggared him with their fees.

So home-produced asses' milk is the only sure remedy – particularly for young ladies in decline. But even Lady Denham could not suppose me (with my *nowadays* healthful countenance, and *elderly* at twenty-two!) to be consumptive, so – being of little interest to her – I was handed over to her ward, Miss Clara Brereton. Seeing that I was charmed by this young lady, Mrs Parker (who had accompanied me) sought permission to bring her back here to tea. To Trafalgar House, that is: an elegant building (though I have seen more solid structures) with about it a very young plantation, whose inclination before the determined winds indicates the exposed nature of this vantage point.

I do not recall that Mr Parker, while he was at Willingden, mentioned the substantial house of his forefathers situated a little inland, in sheltered Old Sanditon. For all Mr Parker's advocacy of balconies and viewpoints, he cannot disguise an abiding affection for this old home. The disregarded love he bears it is not unlike that which he more readily reveals, his feeling for his dear dead father; the Thomas Parker after whom this Mr Parker (our Mr Parker) is named. Our Mr Parker (whose energies you came to know at Willingden, in spite of his injured ankle!), our lean Mr Parker, would never be confused with the corpulent younger brother, Mr Arthur! (There is, I gather, a more interesting middle brother, who lives elsewhere, whom I have yet to meet.)

Mr Parker (our Mr Thomas Parker, that is) has put a tenant in the family home, which is the reason why Mr Arthur and Miss Susan – a second sister whom I've barely seen owing to her sickly constitution –- come to be living here too. Do not worry about me on that account – Mr and Mrs Parker are very hospitable and Trafalgar House, though newly erected, is spacious. (I learn that the middle brother whom I mentioned briefly is unmarried and lives somewhere in town in a bachelor way. He made no claim on what Mrs

Parker describes as the 'dear old place', so the letting went ahead.)

Mrs Parker does her best to conceal her misgivings about its abandonment; but Mr Parker remains convinced that the family's moving one mile in a southerly direction and a hundred feet in a vertical one will effect a wonderful transformation of both Mr Arthur and Miss Susan. But transformed as they might be by all the waves and vistas in creation, I cannot see this pair of Parkers as either hero or heroine in any one's book – Mr Arthur, too plump and too young; Miss Susan, neither plump enough nor young enough!

Miss Clara Brereton, though, of Sanditon Court (at tea with us here today) is another matter. She has come straight from the nicest pages of the better sort of novel: but if she is a heroine – and appearances declare she is – she's a rarely unaffected (indeed sweetly modest) example of the kind. As heroine, she is helped by the fact that one can – just! – visualise her as the object of barbarous persecutions. For the proper display of such notable Poverty and Dependence joined with Beauty and Merit, difficulties and dismays may seem a necessary corollary.

Certainly, Miss Clara's situation is promising, though not necessarily enviable. She – a poor cousin – is the sole admitted representative of Lady Denham's blood relations, those who see past impoverishment by the old lady's Brereton dowry as certain security for future enrichment from the same source – thirty thousand pounds brought to Mr Hollis; whose kin have not set foot in Sanditon House since Lady Denham took on her present name and title. The dead Sir Harry does still have family hereabouts: Sir Edward Denham and his sister, Miss Esther, gentlefolk who live frugally near by. (Until Clara Brereton's arrival last year they had been seen as most likely to succeed to the property.) One wonders whether Sir Edward is as plain a case of Hero as Miss Clara is of Heroine, because, if so – But 'if so' s affirmed would impel their story (hardly begun) to a premature completion.

Having mused a moment on heroes and heroines – as non-heroines (yes, dear papa) as non-heroines will – I was about to take my leave of you (with much to distract me) only to find Mr Parker's paper on the attractions of Sanditon omitted. I haste to enclose it; should have hated to disappoint my kind host. He – they all – are so good and send their respects to every one at Willingden (News now that Sir Edward and Miss Esther Denham have driven over!) – to add to my own affectionate duty.

I have done it the honour of refraining from annotation – an intrusive habit which I am trying to put behind me, in spite of my known predilection for filling other people's margins!

Sanditon

Equally favoured by Nature as by private families of gentility and character; poised above a sweep of waters as aquamarine and as saline as any in these islands; romantically situated on the salubrious coast of Sussex between those popular, some would say over-populous, bathing places of Hastings and Eastbourne; yet a full measured mile nearer the metropolis than the latter: such is New Sanditon which witnesses the unimpeded grandeur of the elements, though safe from all hazard; which is precluded from urban evils, yet preserved (by due amenity) from the shades of incivility. Its climate is the most genial; its sea breezes the purest in these latitudes: here is excellent bathing with fine hard sand (with none of the mud, weeds and slime-covered rocks to be encountered by the unwary at a certain nearby brackish settlement of transient character). Sanditon, in short, is palpably designed as a place for bodily restoration and uplifting entertainment.

NEW SANDITON

Neither is the pastime and promenade of those restored to health neglected. The Terrace of Sanditon with its broad walk has just claim to elegance. There active lady visitors may equip themselves with straw hats and pendant laces at Mrs Jebb's; calling next at Mrs Whitby's well-stocked library shelves, so allowing the gentlemen to repair to billiards next door.

Opportunely, one may put up at the pleasingly appointed hotel and equip oneself with daily necessaries from nearby Mrs Stringer's. From the hotel begins the Descent to the Beach and Bathing Machines. It may be supposed that hereabouts is a favourite resort for Beauty and for Fashion.

The foremost of the buildings of Sanditon and the nearest of any consequence to New Sanditon (or Sanditon proper) is Sanditon House, principal residence of the Lady Denham. Of the recent architecture, the visitor may observe on a high eminence above the Terrace, Trafalgar House (erected for and after designs of Thos Parker Esq), while on the slopes itself the picturesque cottage ornée of Sir Edward Denham should be noted. Similar plots of ground are available to gentlemen of taste and sense who wish at modest cost to erect such another dwelling in this healthful other Eden.

The fares of the different conveyances &c are deliberately omitted from this slight description. A visit is a necessary prelude to an experience for which these casual jottings are no substitute. You will be received cordially and accommodated hospitably by Mr Woodcock, proprietor of the hotel: alternatively, attractive lodgings are to be had in New Sanditon. **NB There are family houses available.** The new Wellington Crescent will be found to command a specially fortunate prospect.

✳

Anne Wentworth handed the above papers back to Charlotte, having studied them with quiet animation. Every so often she had showed the twinkliest eye when looking up from her reading, but she was well past the age for girlish cries of delight. Nor did she congratulate Charlotte on the facility with which she wrote, nor would Charlotte have liked to receive such a compliment: she had presented Mrs Wentworth with the papers as a short cut between the paths of several possible conversations. Thoughts having been in this manner shared, very few further words would be necessary to make them firm friends.

Charlotte detached Mr Parker's encomium and returned it to Anne's hands, beginning to say something.

'Exactly so,' said Anne; and the understanding between the two ladies was such that it did not need to be stated between them that Mr Parker had many, many copies of his paper and that he would much prefer that it should lie in a friendly parlour where visitors might see it than be kept with the selected correspondence of Miss Heywood – who would, in any case, be taking back to Willingden a gross of his pamphlet, together with a range of other printed curiosities devised by Mr Parker.

The ladies sat comfortably, with beside them not just Mr Parker's pamphlet but (in spirit) Mr Parker himself, smiling, re-introducing them to one another; conscious of his own enthusiasm – conscious even of his over-enthusiasm (for he was nobody's fool), taking pleasure even in sensing that others felt he overreached his intellect. He knew he was not as practical a man as he some times thought himself to be – but this reservation about himself (which he happily overrode) was part of his great good nature. Both ladies were happy to have him conjured up between them in spirit. Both – one on short acquaintance, one on no acquaintance at all – realised he was the kind of gentleman whose quickness of recovery was part and parcel of his capacity for error.

'But he made no mistake in being the means of bringing us into a full understanding,' said steadfast Anne, with no words having been spoken to lead to this position. (Anne had been fully twenty-seven when Wentworth, her rejected first love, had returned.)

'It is almost,' said Charlotte, putting her letter away, 'as if I have been exercising my invention.' (Charlotte, twenty-two, had suffered in much the same way as Anne – but with no possibility of redress.)

'Your invention?' said Anne, 'Oh, your account of Sanditon, you mean. And have you? Have you made it up?'

Charlotte hesitated: 'No,' she said, 'no, I don't think so. Not made it up. Rather, I have –'

'Interpreted?' suggested Anne.

'Just so,' said Charlotte, 'how did you know?'

'I know,' replied Anne, 'because we are two of a kind. Readers both, for one thing – and –'

They compared their impressions of various works; and Anne produced an old notebook (for Charlotte had been very sure such a thing existed); and they talked of Captain Wentworth's poetic friends (with a preliminary word about Sir Edward Denham); and how Wentworth himself was better than a poet, with his sturdy regularity, yet withal having a rush to do the right thing, and a love of little children, and of strong images in art and life.

Captain Wentworth returned with little Agnes. Though he would be sorry to see less of his darling child, he and Anne suggested – and Charlotte agreed – that, if the Camberwell seminary should become a settled fact at Sanditon, she would sound out its provisions, inspect its premises, consider its suitability as a place in which their daughter should spend some time.

Agnes clapped her hands, Anne and Wentworth offered theirs, Charlotte Heywood took her leave; insisted on walking back to Sanditon – with a visit for Agnes to Mrs Whitby's library in mind, and an open one as to what the visitors from Camberwell might bring.

✳

It was Camberwell, when the John Knightleys were in London, where Isabella attended Sunday service. But on weekdays she consulted Aesculapian oracles. Isabella Knightley's liking for the company of apothecaries and physicians was matched by that of Miss Diana Parker, Thomas Parker's elder sister who lived nearby.

Isabella was calling at Miss Diana's lodgings for urgent advice after conference with Emma about her father. She came direct from Hartfield, uncomfortable and inclined to faintness by her journey. She was immediately introduced to, and put in the care of, a decently-dressed gentleman who had a habit of clicking his fingers, suggesting either great activity of mind or some incipient nervous complaint which his own best efforts had been unable to remedy.

The gentleman bowed in several directions.

'Ah, but my dear Miss Parker, I am already acquainted with Mrs Knightley; know her very well indeed. Mrs Knightley's respected father, Mr Woodhouse of Hartfield is a most valued patient in my Highbury practice. Tell me, Mrs Knightley' (who was considerably soothed by this familiar medical presence) – 'for I understand that you have come directly from Hartfield (though not, I hope, from any particular urgency) – how is Mr Woodhouse today?'

Isabella proclaimed that Hartfield was afflicted with a general malaise; that the condition of Mr Woodhouse was as bad as polite description could convey; that she was pleased to see Mr Wingfield not only on her own account, but so as to secure his further advice regarding Mr Woodhouse's decline. She feared, though, that seeing him so busy in Camberwell meant that her poor father would have fewer opportunities to benefit from his ministrations in Hartwell.

'For,' she concluded, 'I have heard, Mr Wingfield, – as everyone but my poor father has heard – the rumour that you are to entrust your work at Highbury to a locum tenens.'

Mr Wingfield, surgeon, clicked his fingers with pleasure at his fame in that community, but instead of answering directly – told how some while back he had met a chemist from Westcliff who had made an analysis of the beneficial elements contained by the sea water of Essex. He had been on the point of entering into a partnership with this gentleman to bottle and market the commodity, when he was shown by Miss Parker – a respectful gesture and a click – a paper by an apothecary of Brighton, which Miss Parker had had of her brother Mr Thomas Parker (himself a student of natural philosophy), wherein were enumerated the toxic effluvia of the Thames Estuary. As a consequence Mr Wingfield had revised his plans.

He was about to continue when Miss Parker – transported mentally to the southern climes (fifty miles off as the crow flies) from which her poor sister Susan and brother Arthur were deriving such benefits – began to testify to the abilities of her clever brother Thomas; who read quantities of scientific writings with true understanding; how it came about that Mr Parker had met Mr Wingfield, who – both gentlemen now being convinced that Sussex sea water was the best that was to be had, and – Brighton being too populous, too developed, too expensive – had agreed to work together for the public good and as a private speculation in the summer months of 18– in New Sanditon.

Mr Wingfield, thus prompted, unassumingly removed an unassuming cloth which had been covering an unassuming bottle, the contents of which resembled ginger ale or some other small beer. Some of it he transferred to a smaller container, which he then strained through a funnel with a philtre into a phial. From this receptacle he subtracted a large spoonful which he skilfully presented to Miss Parker, retaining hold himself for she seemed suddenly too weak to manage the utensil unaided. She smacked her lips over the beverage and pronounced herself restored.

Isabella who enjoyed the same delicate health as had enabled her father to outlive his spouse by two decades was eager to try the remedy for herself. Mr Wingfield was very obliging, but conceded that water which had been taken from even the best of seas some little time ago was, even when dispensed by his own practised hand, somewhat less efficacious than that which had been, as it were, snatched from the ocean's lip.

Nevertheless, Isabella took some brine and declared that it much cleared her head; thanking Mr Wingfield for that. She would, if her health permitted, travel to Sanditon very soon to take the water in its pristine condition, but what of her poor father? She feared that Mr Wingfield would not be able to visit Mr Woodhouse personally during the coming months.

Mr Wingfield clicked his apologies. His temporary replacement, however, was however entirely to depended on and had been authorised to administer stagnant sea water in the manner which he, Mr Wingfield, had personally instigated.

Isabella found little comfort in this provision. She knew that her father would not take to a stranger in charge of his remedies and said sadly:

'But that wouldn't be at all the same or as good for my poor father, would it Mr Wingfield?'

Mr Wingfield, with a click for the professional pride which overcame professional prudence, agreed that Mrs Knightley's perception was in all probability a sound one, and while regretting, he hoped &c.

Isabella made her way back thoughtfully to the John Knightleys' London house feeling fortified and set to convince her husband that they must travel to Hartfield immediately.

✳

Isabella strode into Mr Woodhouse's library: 'Damaging humours, father,' she cried, an opening which immediately engaged her father's sympathy. He put down the book which concealed his face, concealed in fact his doze. He was immediately alert.

'Mr Wingfield, father,' she cried.

'Wingfield,' he replied, 'couldn't do better.'

'Ah, but father,' she cried, 'there's more.' And she pulled down her lower eye-lid to reveal the clarity of the white and the blackness of the pupil; a manoeuvre lost on the old man whose own eyes were not equal to the perception required of him. Mr Woodhouse's hearing was another matter, Mr Knightley privately suspecting that the degree of impairment fluctuated according to whatever was convenient to the old man's purposes.

'What does the child say?' asked Mr Woodhouse of Emma (as interpreter of Isabella) 'and who are these gentlemen? Are they physicians?'

The Knightley brothers were not physicians, not even barber-dentists, but sons-in-law of long standing, whose silent diagnosis of the situation was that it might develop helpfully for their domestic concord.

'Isabella,' said Emma, 'believes, father, that you might benefit from the regimen advocated by Mr Wingfield.'

'Wingfield's regimen,' said Mr Woodhouse, retentive of such information, 'Yes, Wingfield – a good man.'

'And that good man, that Mr Wingfield,' said Isabella with the fervour of one who shared the other's infirmities and foibles, 'holds that spa treatments are outmoded. There is a new and invaluable way to take the waters that ensures relief of all rheums and distempers. So much so that Mr Wingfield is to take up the offer of a Mr Parker to reside for the season in Sussex as medical adviser to this gentleman. There Mr Wingfield will' (already she had got this by heart) 'prescribe and introduce into the patient's digestive system measured quantities of pure sea-water extracted from a particular area of our native shores, the which, regularly taken, neutralise all toxic matters.... See, father, sea-water – and I have it here somewhere – and Sanditon!'

Isabella waved a piece of paper: Mr Parker's descriptive leaflet. Sections of it, together with some hastily-printed medical topography from Mr Wingfield, were read aloud by Isabella.

'But,' said Mr Woodhouse uneasily, 'you are asking me to undertake a great journey. Cannot Mr Wingfield attend me here with his new remedies?'

'I am afraid not, father,' replied Isabella. 'My understanding is that it is imperative the water be fresh.'

Mr Woodhouse looked confused.

'No, father,' said Isabella quickly. 'The water is, of course, salt – that is the virtue of it – but it has to be freshly taken from the sea. It cannot, therefore, be transported any distance without loss of efficacy. Moreover, its external use is also highly to be desired, in which case very large quantities are required.'

'A whole seaful, father,' interposed Emma.

It was further explained that, as Mr Wingfield was to be resident fifty miles from Highbury, there would be no possibility of his visiting Mr Woodhouse on a regular basis (and that if he did so visit on occasion he could bring only an inadequate quality of the less effective standing water with him); that the only means of bringing together all three parties, i.e. curer, cure and cured, was that Mr Woodhouse must travel to Sussex.

Mr Woodhouse looked sad and emitted uncertainly the syllable 'wait', whereupon his daughter Isabella looked sincerely sadder and intimated that time might be too short for that. This sentiment Mr Woodhouse could not fail to apprehend, so it was resolved that provided some substantial old house could be found for the summer, Mr Woodhouse would be brought to dwell not merely in a land of milk and honey but of medicine and poultice.

2

A personable lady of twenty-two who is unmarried will have her reasons. In Charlotte Heywood's case the circumstances of her first attachment – which had occupied the greater part of her heroine years – were painful and irremediable. Since the detail of these events could no longer (for her health) be contemplated, she had replaced them with a set of alternative particulars and generalities. Viz: that she was not of the marrying kind; that there were young creatures, younger than herself (the Clara Breretons of this world) in whose imminent prospects of marriage she could lose any claims of her own; that the right gentleman had not presented himself.

Charlotte Heywood kept a series of commonplace books (grown-up looking commonplace books, befitting the reflections of a lady who will not see eighteen again). Her present volume began with the coach accident which had brought Thomas Parker to her family home, together with his immediate offers of reciprocal hospitality at Sanditon. She had known Mr Thomas long enough now to have formed an affectionately sceptical view of his enthusiasms. She was proceeding, in this respect, with what felt to her like caution.

Being non-committal, though, was foreign to her nature. Thinking back to the letter which she had shared with Mrs Wentworth, Charlotte wondered at her boldness; not in showing the letter (though she blushed still a little for that), but for the way in which she had turned events into herself, or herself into events. The line between description and ascription is a fine one; a question of including or excluding a word; of paraphrasing a banality when it is on lips of a person whom one favours, of giving that same banal phrase verbatim, rendering it in its full fatuity, in cases where the speaker has earned the writer's disapprobation.

The notes in the commonplace book were, then, uncertain in purpose: partly descriptive; partly towards, as it were, a construction. Was it folly, Charlotte wondered, to move from being a writer of letters who shared what she had written with others (and angled those writings to such readers' expectations) into one who made notes towards – towards turning (could it be?) the lives about her into – into some species of romance; and her own into that of a closet Novelist. Charlotte opened her book and wrote:

> Where's the harm in it? But Memo: I am neither my own heroine nor any one else's. That way sadness lies.

Yet it was with something of a sense of guilt that Charlotte regarded her reversion to private scribblings. Certainly, it could all be locked away; any foolishness she might write. It could even be ripped out and burnt; or, it could be weighted and dropped into some especially private part of that deep blue ocean which lay behind the moving curtains and the dusky sea-view.

Whatever Charlotte's uncertainty about the purpose and future fate of the book, the handwriting and layout, with little by way of erasure or insertion, suggested that here was a person who knew her own mind. Perhaps temporarily. She turned back several pages and reminded herself of the positions she had taken up:

> Sir Edw. remains a mystery. His sister, Miss Esther Denham taciturn. He not. But what he discloses about himself – and he is voluble – confuses. His air and his address seem at odds with his capacity. Perhaps a man of sense, in spite of conversation at our second meeting. The first – that which made a foolishly dramatic drop-curtain for my letter – was mere formalities. The second: If Clara Brereton isn't allowed to be a heroine, then Sir Edw. is no hero. Attentive to the said Clara on nearer of two Green Benches beside the gravel walk by the Terrace. Yet Sir Possibly-a-hero abandons Miss Perhaps-a-heroine and sprinkles me with quotations (from irregular Mr Burns – I

do not refer only, or primarily, to his numbers). Such conversation is good for neither one of us – nor for the writers Sir Edw. inaccurately invokes.

Lady Denham observing some attention of this kind, states baldly to me that both Sir Edw. and his sister must marry money. I receive this dictum with equanimity. Lady D– not displeased, becomes confidential: she sees him as a rich widower, has already caught sight of his bride, a sickly heiress! In short, Lady D– is *mean and calculating*. Sir Edw. and Miss Denham being rarely received at Sanditon House (to obviate the miniscule expense of their reception? – or to keep the penniless Sir Edw clear of the indigent Clara? But, if the latter, why did Lady D– choose to take her under her roof? Perhaps she plans to dismiss a servant or two and have Clara take on their work. *Perhaps – though here I am in Gothick vein – Perhaps there is some darker purpose.*

Arrival of Mr Parker's elder sister, Miss Diana Parker, from Camberwell. Miss Parker, it appears, is not so much an invalid herself as dedicated to the invalidism of others – of, within the family, Mr Arthur and Miss Susan Parker; and, beyond it – yes, this is evidently Lady D's choice for Sir Edw – one Miss Lambe, a West Indian heiress; who has arrived in the company of Mrs Griffiths as advance party of the Camberwell Seminary, the complement of which is keenly awaited by Mr Parker.

Why is it he and only he amongst the Parker brothers and sisters that seems impervious to the effects of damp and has no need to regale himself with herb tea? Yet whether Miss Diana – for she can display startling energy – suffers from any indisposition is dubious; Miss Susan, too, is not always feeble; while Mr Arthur – were it not for his nerves – one would judge to be a lusty young man in need of fresh air and exercise.

But I am forgetting the brother younger than Thomas and older than Arthur; the mysterious Mr Sidney whom I have yet to meet: I would suppose him to be of a suitable age. 'For what?' I ask myself. 'For nothing,' I answer – simply that he will be, judging from the rest of the family and his place in it, of about my age, with the addition of five years or so.

Intimations of imminent arrival of medical man to be resident in Sanditon. A Mr Wingfield – about whose credentials I am not yet clear, though Mr Parker is all enthusiasm – when he thinks of surgeon-less Brinshore, he triumphs!

Alas! – Mrs Griffiths has had to confess her Seminary complete – the expected hordes have been reduced to a total strength of three! Disappointed Thomas Parker and abashed Miss Diana have found them temporary lodging at the Hotel. Only Miss Lambe has shown herself: she is about 17, half mulatto; but with a maid of her own, and – it is said – school and board fees payable to Mrs Griffiths of a magnitude equivalent to the total of all that which had been anticipated from the four-and-twenty other young ladies who have elected to remain in Camberwell. Mrs G– settled by Miss Diana into the corner house of the Terrace adjoining the Hotel. Mr Arthur Parker observed (not aspiring to the West Indian) to look up at the rest of the Seminary, at the two Miss Beauforts – though, since they are the possessors of a telescope on their balcony, they have the ocular advantage.

*

Shortly after the above lines had been re-read, the gentleman 'of a suitable age' arrived in Sanditon. Mr Sidney Parker was, as Charlotte had supposed, about seven or eight-and-twenty. He put up at the hotel, though called often at his brother's house where Charlotte was to remain for some weeks yet. But his presence was unacknowledged by her diary: its confidence had lapsed. She found him difficult to write about, difficult almost to think about – or not to think about: it was almost as if he reminded her of a previous error of judgment. And yet there was no resemblance either in the gentleman's appearance or in the circumstances of the encounter.

No, gentlemanly, unaffected and easy, he had much to commend him as an escort for any lady. Why not then as a subject for Charlotte's disquisition? It was less that she needed to be cautious in writing of him – though there was a caution there – more, a diminution of power; a want of spirits which was affecting them all. Could it be that Sanditon was the antithesis of every healthful thing that was claimed for it? Or was it that the present company in Sanditon – or that the combination of the two, people and place – was amiss? Collective activity was suspended; or, if there had been activity, Charlotte could recall nothing of it beyond the weakening jottings of her diary in the handsome notebook. Little enough to lock away there! A growing sense of unreality behind it all.

If this were a dream or a fiction, then it was a dream or a fiction consistent within itself. To Charlotte it seemed as if the immobilised active Parkers and the silent or silenced Denhams had projected themselves inwards upon her consciousness. The vital members of the party seemed touched and held by the ailments, real or imagined, of the others; by an invalidism no longer ameliorated by the brisk contrivances which Miss Diana Parker made for her brother and sister, the over-eating Mr Arthur and the bloodless Miss Susan. It hung unhealthily over the room.

A sudden clarity, a remission of pressures within, an act of will: Charlotte rises from her chair in the Parkers' sitting room (shielded from the heat of the still glowing fire that unusually warm day by the bulk of Mr Arthur Parker), relinquishes the book of Psalms which is somehow in her hand, and, striding to the heavy and drawn curtain – on day like this! – pulls it back with a swish. At the edge of the misty bay a faint line of foam; where the horizon may be, a faint light as of a ship; a lifting of the mist. Charlotte reaches for the catch and draws up the sash. A slight breeze and with it for the first time a little freshness; a smell of pinks and seaweed and the sound of shingle.

A heavy stormy evening with the curtains closed in Winchester; but with them open here, or with the act of willing them open, the storm receding. A calm evening, even a clear one, in Sussex. Not obscured.

What has happened becomes obvious to Charlotte. The right people are gathered at the wrong time and in the wrong place. It is not at the Parkers' house above the Terrace that they should be. It suddenly becomes a fine morning and as the party is making its way to Sanditon House, Charlotte fancies she sees bold Sir Edward start up from a secluded spot in the grounds like a timid, surprised little creature.

✱

It could only have been some trick of the light, some image from the unhealthy past, some remembrance of two figures on a green bench by a gravel path; only a phantasm of Sir Edward that the horses' hooves had disturbed behind the palings of the Park... For here was the real Sir Edward Denham with the pale Miss Esther and Mr and Mrs Parker in a solid enough, if rather cramped, conveyance; Miss Diana Parker, who loved to be first, having joined them. Mr Sidney Parker (the interesting middle brother) sat beside Charlotte, as if by right, in the second carriage: opposite were Mr Arthur and Miss Susan, to the left of whose bonnet varying segments of the first coach could be seen. Now Charlotte lost the coach for fifty yards as it turned into the drive to Sanditon House.

NEW SANDITON

The journey was a more enjoyable one for those in the second coach than the occupants could admit: both of the invalid Parkers were in better spirits from applying their contrasted remedies to their contrary ailments; verbal leeches cooled Mr Arthur, spoken port wine fortified Miss Susan. The upholstery was too warm to be thought comfortable, but the sky was a cool-looking blue – without the brassy glare of excessive heat. The new summer foliage rocked a little in the breeze counterpointing the motion of the coach.

(Charlotte feels well and happy again, if slightly apprehensive; is relieved to find that it is not she herself – as in her sick phantasy – who is expiring, who has been allowed to melt away before the unseasonable fire. It is that consoling presence, someone else.)

As to another personage (who it has suddenly been decided should depart this life) Charlotte regarded with equanimity the loss of Lady Denham and her austerities. She was sorry for Clara's sake, as that young lady had perhaps regarded the rich old tyrant with disinterested affection. It was to be hoped that Lady Denham had made adequate provision for her young companion. No, *ample* provision: Clara was deserving.

'Let me assist you, Miss Heywood.'

Mr Sidney Parker, though as decorous as the news from Sanditon required, would have been a more than satisfactory companion for a longer journey than this.

Miss Diana Parker – acquainted with Lady Denham only slightly – had been the first to hear the news: after which the dead lady's niece Miss Esther – whom Lady Denham had formerly seemed to favour – had essayed a silent tear and good-natured Mr Thomas Parker blown his nose hard at the loss of an old adversary; his wife imitating this action in a minor key.

The Parkers and their party entered Sanditon House; were caught by the varnished canvas eyes of Sir Harry Denham in his stately frame over the mantelpiece, but ignored by a diminutive likeness of Mr Hollis on the other side of the room. Away from these representations of dead husbands lay the tidily arranged remains of Lady Denham. Charlotte experienced a momentary if regrettable vision of the translated dowager loudly counting out celestial dividends with a subdued husband at each elbow and miscellaneous Breretons (including poor Clara), the family from which Lady Denham had sprung, beneath her feet.

Mr Hollis had been devoted or submissive in letting his capital go out of his family; Sir Harry Denham had been indulgent or pliable in conferring a title at so little cost to its recipient. Miss Esther Denham having passed Sir Harry's portrait, suddenly turned on her heel to inspect it as if for some clue as to Lady Denham's intentions towards her family: causing Mr Sidney Parker to step to one side and give the late lady's chair and desk an inexplicably hard look. Miss Clara Brereton – not dependent on past marriages for her relationship with the deceased – stood in the middle of the room in a quick pause from all the activity which had suddenly been required of her: she had no clear expectations or any sense of injury or surprise that she had none. Clara was grateful for what had been done for her and if no more was to be done, then what had been done had been done and that was all.

It having been declared by the whole party that the demise of so very great a lady was an irreparable loss for Sanditon (Lady Denham's name could not decently remain on the library subscription list beyond the current season), Mr Parker, Sir Edward and Miss Esther brought their attention to bear on what might be thought to be the wishes of the deceased: in summoning Lady Denham's disparate family. Clara Brereton was the most conveniently-located example, and therefore considered to be in need of protracted conversation with the vicar, a Mr Balm, whose living was in the gift of Sanditon House. He addressed himself to her as either the person most in need of consolation, or the most likely inheritrix, and therefore his future employer:

'Trust and confidence, my dear Miss Brereton, love and sympathy too, by a reciprocation of beneficent offices, twists into a cord which binds good people to one another, and cannot easily be broken.' Such was his parting sentiment.

All the doctors who had attended Sir Harry (with so much pecuniary advantage) being themselves dead, a physician had been called from Eastbourne. Also, for good measure, one from Hastings. They arrived – and disagreed – together. Thomas Parker felt he was well rid of the two gentlemen; and congratulated himself that he had managed to postpone Mr Wingfield's arrival – stay even the rumour of his arrival – for fear his restorative reputation should become associated with the irrecoverable passing of Sanditon's great lady. Mr Parker had considered the different strategy of having Wingfield on the spot in order that he might inveigh against Lady Denham's unscientific view of medicine, but had decided that it was best to let her death stand as a lesson to others. He intended to provide hints to this effect in an obituary for the county newspaper.

Sir Edward was inviting Clara Brereton to join the group in the library of Sanditon House for a discussion of steps which needed to be taken immediately in connection with his late aunt's affairs, but Clara politely declined on the grounds of a headache. Her desire to be excused was sympathetically received by all, though Miss Diana Parker was eager to furnish a number of reliefs and remedies. 'Thank you, Miss Parker,' said Clara firmly, 'for your kind solicitude. I don't doubt but that I shall be right enough directly,' and was allowed to retire to her room unremedied. Sir Edward and Miss Esther Denham returned to the library with Mr Thomas Parker; but, after lunch, the day continuing fine, they took their affairs with them on a walk about the grounds. In the sitting room there remained, therefore, Mrs Parker, Miss Diana, Miss Susan, Mr Arthur, Mr Sidney and Charlotte.

'I suppose,' said Mr Arthur fretfully, for they were keeping him from his tea, 'Sir Edward and Thomas have much to discuss – but I had thought they would have been back before now.'

'Thomas's time is always full of business,' sighed Mrs Parker; 'he's seldom at home nowadays. And don't we miss him – especially little Mary,' who fidgeted on her lap; 'fretful and feverish, isn't she? – Never fear, my pet, Miss Esther will be back soon. We quite depend on her, our Miss Esther – though the boys are too rough for her – and I hope we don't put upon her. Yes, yes, my treasure, our help-meet is to come again. I fancy Thomas indulges Miss Esther (like a child herself, she is some times, that young lady which makes her so good with children), buys Miss Esther little things; as a token – for she's much too much of a lady to be anyone's governess. Don't you think, Sidney?' And so Mrs Parker prattles on, a counterpart to the dyspeptic squeaks of little Mary (her mother's namesake).

The others have little to say for some time. Then a conversation or, rather, a range of sentiments is brought forth for inspection.

Mr Sidney Parker addresses himself chiefly to Charlotte, with a formality suited to the occasion, albeit with a roguish tendency:

'Unusual energies are not infrequently occasioned by an inheritance; the which expenditure, as some would have it, is but part payment for that not otherwise toiled for.'

The conversation of Miss Susan (on Sidney Parker's other side) has, when there is no medicinal reference to render it precise, a tangential quality:

'I'm sure that there's as good a chance for happiness in marriage with a person of fortune, as with one who has not any,' she observes in her weak but clear voice.

Sidney Parker raises an eyebrow as if his sister has surprised him in a private thought – a disturbing habit of sisters – and then lowers it again. He exchanges a glance with Charlotte by way of a punctuation mark; seeming to indicate that some other possibility, indeed any possibility, is not ruled out.

'I hope good will come of it,' says Mrs Parker,' – of it all,' she adds, her generalised but deeper doubts becoming too much for her.

'Good will come of it for some, to be sure,' opines Miss Diana Parker, ringing for tea, to Mr Arthur's relief, 'and bad for others: the one quality carries the other along close behind it.'

'This is the one time of day,' asserts Mr Arthur (his sister's conversation much less interesting to him that her sonorous request for refreshment), 'when tea – or a little weak chocolate – does me no harm that I can detect.'

Miss Diana is of the opinion that it is undetectable damage that is the most damaging and, by extension, the most painless pain that is most painful. Certain drinks made from dried weeds are the best safeguard against unseen peril; and it is a worry to them that Mr Arthur has begun to declare himself at least once a day as not of their mind or party. Nevertheless, the sisters do not take him to task, as he is by way of being their pet.

Arthur Parker's tea has awakened his recollection – not merely of previous cups of Indian tea consumed, but of another gesture of independence. Two nights before, at one of the Miss Beauforts' invitation – the elder harp-playing Miss Beaufort, not Miss Letitia – he ascended to their balcony accompanied by Charlotte Heywood, by means of – the normal stairway. Mr Arthur has neither the frame for a spectacular fairy-tale ascent nor Miss Beaufort a head of hair likely to supply even the vestiges of a rope ladder. However, once there, the fact of being there and the telescopic views of the green bench near the Terrace and other maritime delights seemed to give him a new way of seeing the non-imbibable universe.

Mr Arthur's sensibility is at that stage, then, when an indolent young man begins to consider whether there is more to life than cups of tea. He would have done better to have put that thought into words and spoken them to the company. Instead, he repeats another polite ready-made sentiment:

'I have heard,' says he, with little relationship to any thing that has gone before, but some to his hopes for Miss Beaufort, ' that it is all over with reasoning ladies when once love gets into their heads.'

'And what of gentlemen?' counters his brother Sidney, seeking courteously to keep a balance, while asserting his seven years' seniority over Arthur. 'What of the gentlemen? Wouldn't we have the most reasonable man, in such a case, soften the severity of his logic?'

'Yes, if the gentleman wishes to be as soft-headed as our supposed lady is soft-hearted,' is Miss Diana's sensible old-maid's view.

Tea has come and the company settle to solid agreement that those marriages are generally the happiest where there is no inequality of birth or degree (inequalities of sense remaining un-discussed); that the Denham estate may either eliminate or aggravate existing tendencies towards inequality in possible beneficiaries.

Mr Arthur's sympathies are now so enlarged by quantities of tea and his reflections on Miss Beaufort, that he has begun to evince a curiosity about other possible matches. If Clara Brereton were to inherit the bulk of the Denham fortune, then Sir Edward would no doubt make advances to her openly? Charlotte's mind's eye sees things differently: Sir Edward might prove too proud to raise himself on Clara's fortune, if there was to be any fortune. Much better for the estate to be divided equally between those Breretons and Denhams resident in Sanditon – that is to say, between Clara, on the one hand, and Sir Edward and his sister, on the other.

How convenient would be a marriage contract which brought together the separated halves of such a great estate! This would be altogether the best, for it would confirm Sir Edward and Clara as the old-fashionedly sensible hero and heroine which Charlotte has looked for. Alternatively, if the Denhams were to inherit, it would be possible for Sir Edward to invite Clara to be endowed with his worldly goods: this too would have attractions of a novel-like kind, but the dependence would be less mutual, the outcome more arbitrary.

Tea being taken away, Mr Arthur Parker in an excess of his new-found confidence returns to his opinions; asking generally, or rather stated inquiringly, that he does not quite see on what grounds Lady Denham, from her complicated kinship, chose this one little Miss Brereton to be her companion. The three tribes of Brereton, Hollis and Denham in their entirety could have asked nothing more nor asked it more clumsily.

Charlotte Heywood blushes for Mr Arthur; feels for Clara; is about to give him the means of moving from the subject after three words on the absent young lady's charms, when she senses that Mr Sidney Parker is likewise attempting a change of conversation. The absent Clara Brereton has returned! – Quite suddenly, but no more so than might have been expected from her assurance that her indisposition was temporary. She could not but be seen to have overheard what has just been said and evidently means to answer.

Whether from nervousness or indignation, she is at first unable to find her tongue. Whatever the reason, the pause between Mr Arthur's indiscreet remarks and Clara's appearance in the room like a little ghost is long enough to command attention, yet too short to allow the conversation of others to make new beginnings (at first that would have been a series of quiet murmurs and then more open discourse).

When she is able to begin her response it is less diffident (for all its self-effacement) than might have been expected:

'I was chosen – or so I suppose,' says Clara slowly, 'and I am no less grateful that I was chosen, because Lady Denham being herself born a Miss Clara Brereton, bore that name until her first marriage and long before my family chose that same forename for me. I expect that I am called Clara – Clara Brereton – in her honour. She did not hold that against me, for she knew that an infant would be innocent of any conniving in its baptism. She chose me as her temporary companion because of that. Nothing more, I am sure.'

Arthur Parker awkwardly asks Clara Brereton's pardon; some of the others appearing shame-faced for seeming to be a party to what may have appeared more a public speculation than it was; but Charlotte cannot help being grateful for this piece of information. Was consonance in the matter of names to continue? Would – could – the present poor dependant called Clara Brereton become another rich Lady Clara Denham through succeeding first to the fortune, then to the name? The first possessor of the name began rich and grew richer before taking on the name of Denham, and the style of Lady – the present Clara's prospective match would have more to it that was spontaneous and transforming, less that was calculating and cumulative. The couple would – could – in such circumstances be very nearly a hero and heroine.

It should not be supposed that Clara's evident sense of wanting nothing for herself, nor expecting any thing for herself, is forced. Yet was it to be wondered at that her spirits were not high; or that the headache which had taken her away was genuine? Her brief retirement, however – why should we expect it? – has not been given up entirely to inactive repining and gloom; nor at all to running distracted (an activity not to be looked for in one who has known her protectress but nine months; though all that was loveable in Lady Denham could have been noted in a shorter space of time).

Something of Clara Brereton's state of mind will have been gathered from her response to Arthur Parker's conjecture. As further evidence that Clara is unaffected and sensible, the following letter is one of several which she managed to write in spite of her head-ache, in the calm of her withdrawal from company.

Sanditon House, 14th June 18–

I have to inform you, dear guardians, that Lady Denham, my kind benefactress, is no more. I know you'll be saddened by this news. She retired to bed in her usual health, though perhaps a little subdued, yesterday evening (13th June, and a Friday for those of superstitious turn of mind), but could not be roused this morning when I – for Alice has left her employ – took up her glass of asses' milk. Lady Denham led a most active and useful life and was greatly respected in this community. I owe her a great deal. Thanks to her care and trust of me while her ward I shall be able to get me a post of governess – or perhaps Mrs Griffiths who keeps a seminary at Camberwell and is now visiting Sanditon with some of her young ladies may be able to use me.

The funeral will take place in Sanditon church next Thursday morning; the service being conducted by the Rev. Mr Balm, vicar of the parish and Lady Denham's chaplain. There is a great vault reserved for her in the chancel, I understand, adjoining the tombs of Mr Hollis and Sir Harry Denham, her late husbands. Beyond that I know nothing of her intentions, though feeling sure Sir Edward and Miss Esther Denham, our relatives through marriage, would not allow me to starve if every other support were taken from me; nor would good Mr Thomas Parker. I am conscious of all that you have done for me, my dear uncle and aunt, over the past years, but am equally of the opinion that I cannot revert to being a burden upon you. I pray that Lady Denham has remembered you all at the last.

3

Some days after Clara Brereton's letter had been despatched, Mr Thomas Parker wrote to Mr Wingfield as follows:

> I am now able to give you a better account of why I asked you to delay (and yet I so eager to have you here!!). Thank you, my dear sir, for your tacit concurrence. Lady Denham is now safely buried and so presents no impediment (I mean by association of events) to your arrival at Sanditon. To reiterate: the sudden death of our great lady might have been seen by the unthinking as having a causal relationship with your residency here as medical practitioner and adviser to the Sanditon enterprise. *Post hoc, ergo propter hoc.*
>
> True, any that might have done so would have had only fallacy on their side.
>
> *De mortuis nihil nisi bonum* as may be, but Lady Denham was an ill-advised old gentlewoman; indeed, she took no advice. So it was her misfortune not to have experienced the benefits which it is my privilege to be introducing to the neighbourhood. The neighbourhood? – Rather, given your enthusiasm for the cause, sir, combined with your redoubtable expertise, I believe I might more accurately claim to have rendered some service, not merely to this portion of Sussex, *but to the nation as a whole!*
>
> Lady Denham left no will, probably because she was unwilling to pay the fee to have one drawn up. So none is like to be found, unless no lawyers were involved; and if no

lawyers were involved then who were her witnesses? And whether she proves intestate or whether somebody somewhere has some knowledge of her intentions, lawyers are involved now with a vengeance. The situation is meat and drink to them. They are eating up money from her estate, which might have been spent on New Sanditon. These legal parasites tell me – with smiles of satisfaction – that establishing whom she was related to, and with what precedence to inherit, will be a very slow business. *Ergo* there could and can be no knowing who if any would benefit amongst the conflicting array of Hollises and Denhams I observed at her funeral. *A fortiori*, none of them knew or know how to manage their countenances.

I will mention some Sanditon residents amongst the mourners (or doubtful celebrants): Sir Edward Denham displaying the public carelessness about his fortunes which befits a generous man with an empty purse; with his sister, Miss Esther, keeping her eyes discreetly on her finger-ends (though she's a good girl with my little Mary – excuse a fond parent his parenthesis!); Miss Clara Brereton, a poor relation and recipient if all's to be believed, of little but hard words, appearing sincerely touched by the suddenness of her mistress's going; while insisting that she has no right to stay under the roof of Sanditon House, even though it stands empty. She is an amiable young lady and I shall do what little I can to help her find employment – would have had her for my little girl, but I have a small arrangement (have I mentioned?) with Miss Esther Denham – again, please excuse fondness, but remember, sir, my little Mary and all of mine are to be your patients.

Sir Edward – did I mention his impecuniosity? – cannot afford to take on Sanditon House, so it is agreed that a tenant should be found, any sum resulting from this transaction to be added to the considerable deal of disputable capital left by the old lady. It would be excellent,

I hope you will agree, if the house could be taken by someone with the means to become, not a new great Lady, not a sceptical opponent – *rather, an active advocate of our sea-water system.* The place is old and solid and I am told comfortable enough. It would, though, need considerable refurbishment for any person of fashion.

Believe me, my dear sir,
Thomas Parker

PS I suggest that you hold your arrival for no more than a fortnight. By this time Lady D's demise will no longer be on everyone's tongues, and I will have set in place all the necessary support for your public-spirited work.

✷

Nothing could have turned out more fortunately! First – and without demur – Mr Woodhouse, Isabella, Emma and Knightley (Mr John Knightley having much business in London) were to take Sanditon House for the summer, during which season Mr Wingfield was to be constant in his attendance.

Furthermore, the transfer they had shrunk from was quickly fixed and effected in a manner which exceeded their best hopes: a supply of jolly inn-keepers and pretty chamber-maids appearing at every stop for Mr Woodhouse's pleasure. Such good cheer took care of what energies he had; the motion of the carriage lulling him to sleep through his family's company and the greater part of the travel.

Arriving at Sanditon House refreshed, Mr Woodhouse, supported over the threshold, turned and pronounced himself 'quite at home'. Upon which a bystander who had doffed his hat put it on again. It was Sir Edward casting an eye on those who were taking possession of his late Aunt Denham's house. But though melancholic verses re the Seventh Age of man were sometimes within his repertoire (for which species of composition Mr Woodhouse was a fine exemplar), his eye could not rest for long upon married ladies of – what? – they could be thirty, they could be fifty (he was unpractised in computation beyond the age of two-and-twenty). Ladies of uncertain years.

Sir Edward was not angry on his own behalf that the Knightleys (strangers to him) were taking over the fine old house. He was sorry – his generous side was sorry – that Clara Brereton was obliged to leave the protection of its walls. However, since she was eighteen and in bloom (like a red, red rose), it had crossed his mind that her situation might prove advantageous: that he might become her protector with the prospect of ambiguous delights.

Clara's view of her future was more straightforward. She was ready and willing to earn her bread in the Seminary on The Terrace. (The smells of new plaster and the bright paint of The Terrace were strong upon her senses.) Clara had been with Lady Denham for less than a year, but, despite the trials of life there, she thought of Sanditon House now as like some ripe old apple with its pips rattling at the core: she kept to herself a contrary observation, that Mr Parker's (to him) splendid new buildings resembled sour wind-falls. In the old house she had felt enclosed, if not protected; here she was exposed to cold air – chilled by the drying walls, or by some spring accidentally tapped when setting the buildings into the rock – even in the summer heat.

✳

There was no second Sanditon House for Mr Parker to offer to Mrs Elizabeth Darcy and Mrs Fanny Bertram after a long and broken series of journeys from Derbyshire in search of the sea. The east coast being too flat for Fanny's perspective eye, and Wales already too hilly for Elizabeth's condition, they had had no more original thought than to head for Brighton. But hearing that the Regent and his entourage were expected, they had pressed along the coast for a smaller, quieter place. (Though Fanny would have liked to talk to the Prince's librarian with whom she had corresponded, Elizabeth had been firm. 'My dear Fanny,' she had observed, 'I doubt whether there is much going on of a literary character in that particular assemblage!')

No sooner had they set foot in Sanditon than they were greeted by the owner and architect of Trafalgar House in person: enthusiastic about them, as the latest – and as *famous*, he assured them – visitors to Sanditon. Elizabeth and Fanny were directed to two possible lodgings, of which they decided to take the last-but-one of the completed houses in Wellington Crescent. They might have become neighbours of Clara Brereton in the vacant Terrace property adjoining the Seminary; but the ladies judged it too large for them, with their small accompanying attendance. The one fault with Wellington Crescent – which otherwise suited them – was its situation, for Elizabeth was beginning to be troubled by a swelling of the ankles.

Once they were on the cliff top the going was easy. It was there that Elizabeth and Fanny met Clara Brereton again. Again, because they had made one another's acquaintance while Mr Parker was demonstrating the picturesque virtues of his various properties.

They were strolling upon this high but level ground, when rapid foot steps – hoof beats almost – overtook them. Sir Edward Denham, for it was he, raised his hat to Mrs Elizabeth Darcy and Mrs Fanny Bertram, then diverging from his path, placed himself by the side of Miss Clara Brereton (his cousin, but withal a young lady with whom he still needed to make progression after his inconstancy at the green benches by the gravel walk). Clara understood too little what her kinsman supposed were his motives to be compelled, or repelled, by them. For the present she was equally content to retain the company of the young baronet, and to have in addition that of two such fine, older ladies; one of whom was saying, 'Miss Clara puts me in mind of my sister Jane when she was of that same age.' (Though the other, Fanny, was privately reflecting that Clara Brereton was too much of a mouse – though a nice little mouse – to grow up to be like Jane Bingley; that there was someone she more resembled: herself when a girl, little Fanny Price.)

Clara warmed to the lady who had paid her (not thinking that young ears were so sharp) what she knew be a sincere compliment; then, turning shyly to Fanny, who seemed well-informed, she asked for a word of advice about being a governess and instructing the young. She had earlier in the day made a similar inquiry of Esther Denham, but had received a cool response. Now the studious lady addressed was averring she knew nothing about children herself; and the grander one saying something to the effect that boys were unfortunately not her speciality, which Clara did not quite catch because Sir Edward was distracting her. A passing seagull had prompted him to assert, with a solemn kind of passion:

'I would to heaven that I were so much clay,
As I am blood, bone, marrow, passion feeling -'

(To which Clara made a little rejoinder, both appreciative and reassuring – whereas someone such as Charlotte Heywood would have had the quickness of knowledge to point out what Lord Byron, in the next couple of lines makes clear – 'but I write this reeling' – that this fragment is a drunken lampoon, his remarks mere tomfoolery.)

The brilliance of the day then put Sir Edward in mind of darkness:

'The bright sun was extinguish'd, and the stars
Did wander darkling in the eternal space...'

(Clara waited, arrested, for Sir Edward to continue, but for the present he could recollect no more: Fanny, leaning across – though she found the Manichee in Byron offensive – furnished Sir Edward with some of what came immediately after, but still he could not take up where she left off.)

There was then a pause from poetry; Sir Edward regretting that he had not brought a suitable text with him to which he could refer (as Charlotte Heywood had already noted, memory was not his strongest feature). For this reason – and having grown bored with his own remarks on indifferent topics – he raised his hat to Elizabeth and Fanny, smiled a special smile at Clara and was gone.

*

But a few days later Sir Edward had not only a pocketful of books but Clara to himself; the Thomas Parker family following – walking at a slower pace than the two cousins – and gradually being left behind, growing smaller. Further off, but growing larger – almost recognisable now – were two other, faster walkers.

It having been determined early on that Sir Edward Denham was to be a despot to all women, circumstances had disobligingly reduced him to a pauper. He was a man who needed to live inexpensively until he could marry money – which was hardly fair, for Richardson's Lovelace (he who had abducted, drugged and deflowered Clarissa) had had at his service a purse as bottomless as Eldon Hole: Sir Edward liked to believe that he also could pursue and contrive, and make provision for discarded mistresses, in the princely style of this great master. Instead of which, his ingenious spirit was cramped. Sir Edward was obliged to rely on vicarious exploits – reading, re-reading, misreading quantities of passionate literature; becoming as dependent on the exceptionable side of other men's imaginings as he was upon the stray coins which his late aunt had permitted to roll within his stooping distance.

His cousin, Clara Brereton was clearly of a precious metal, fresh-minted after an impeccable design. Furthermore, in spite of her natural graces, she was sweetly modest. These charms, together with her position as a doubtful dependant, seemed to call (in accordance with Sir Edward's canons) for her seduction. Such, any way was the best sense Sir Edward could extract from our more renowned authors.

That those whom he saw as heroes had been meant as villains was a contrary thought set aside as mere self-deceit and timidity; that the intention on the part of the writers was to extol virtue was still more emphatically dismissed as hypocrisy. It was the readiness to act; the lack of caution; the power of succumbing to feeling, that he admired; and, if in the end, one was to be seen as a villain for having pursued one's legitimate desires – well, that was the way of the world. An inner, pulsing egotistical heart was the only judge of truth. Happiness of any settled kind was not to be expected or looked for. Fleeting moments of passion, evanescent insights and an overall sense of random gloom were – whether true philosophy or no – inexpensive companions for an empty pocket. And words were a solacing stimulant:

>'He who hath bent him o'er the dead
>Ere the first day of death is fled,
>The first dark day of nothingness,
>The last of danger and distress,
>(Before Decay's effacing fingers
>Have swept the lines where beauty lingers)
>And mark'd the mild angelic air,
>The rapture of repose that's there...

'– What follows is perhaps less to the life, dear cousin, that I'll concede. But the first lines, to my ear, present not merely a just representation, but truth of an immutable kind.'

And Sir Edward again spoke those of the lines he knew well enough to repeat.

As he did so, Clara could not but think of Lady Denham's visage: the *look* of it; opinionated. But still keeping its counsel, even in death. (When the sheets were drawn back – as they frequently were at Miss Diana Parker's instruction.)

Sir Edward Denham had a fine deep voice and Clara Brereton liked to hear him read, though (because of Lady Denham's dead face) he was not on this occasion receiving her fullest attention. To his remarks Clara merely indicated a polite unwillingness to disagree.

She could not, however, repress anxieties for the safety of his footing; he glancing at the book to be sure of his lines, or gazing into Clara's eyes (forcing her eye-lids to lower), so as to put both Sir Edward and herself in danger from the cliff-edge.

Fortunately, Clara knew Miss Charlotte Heywood and Mr Sidney Parker – for it was they – would be catching up, first the Parker family, then themselves; and that they might be able to call out a warning before Sir Edward toppled into the sea.. Without which, unperturbed by ominous cracks in the pathway, stumbling over tufts and stones which he sent flying into the Channel, he continued sonorously:

'So fair, so calm,'

– making clear by a side-long glance that those epithets applied to the healthy young creature by his side. He had now just one dismal line to get through before arriving at his required point and purpose:

'The first, last look by death reveal'd
Such is the aspect of this shore-'

And he broke off the sense to indicate Sanditon's little bay and its canvas awnings as if he had produced the whole panorama out of a hat.

He had noted in a preliminary survey, taking a leaf out of Lovelace's book, a small cleft or chine with at its head a large rock, recently chipped away here and there to accommodate another green-painted seat. As they neared it, Sir Edward moved back to an earlier text, his voice becoming lower and full of meaning:

'And many a summer flower is there,
And many a shade that love might share,
And many a *grotto*, meant for rest,
That holds the *pirate* for a guest -'

Clara looked startled.

'Come cousin,' said he, 'here is a grotto. Now,' taking her hand. 'Let us be – pirates.'

Clara laughed and sat – relieved that the rocks suggested solid ground, and that this was evidently a children's game and not grown-up business. She sat with him happily for a while looking at the view, and occasionally at her finger ends to make sure that Sir Edward had given them (gently) back to her.

But now Sir Edward was striving to suggest facially the perturbedness of his thoughts for Clara's future. He sighed, looked at her feelingly, and with the inquiry, 'And what will you do now, cousin?' took her hand again, in what could still pass for a cousinly way. Clara allowed him this family privilege with little misgiving, though she could do no more than first shake her head and then, after a while, confess that she did not know.

Nor was she altogether clear how she should respond to Sir Edward as a kinsman with Lady Denham no longer there as the one living link – or barrier – between them. A long-dead great-aunt of Clara's had been the sister of Lady Denham's father. Sir Edward Denham's father had been the brother of Lady Denham's second husband.

So it was a fact that Sir Edward and she were, in common parlance – if not in the strict letter of the term – 'cousins'. Clara did not doubt that when he called her 'cousin', it was this tenuous piece of family history which he referred to; and when he took her hand – a protracted cousinly gesture – she was almost equally sure that that was how distant relatives behaved when they sat in a grotto.

In answer to Sir Edward's question, Clara was repeating that she did not know what she would do, with the same little shake of the head. As long as he held her hand, Clara – with nothing to say – continued to speak. As for Sir Edward, a little bored by this repetitious *tête à tête*, he might in any case have relinquished Clara's hand, for his own plans were equally indefinite and undecided. In fact, the pair had been noticed by Charlotte Heywood and Sidney

Parker who presently joined them on the green bench in the grotto.

In the world in which Sir Edward Denham thought he wished he lived, when two ladies and two gentlemen came across one another in a rustic setting (whatever its provenance) certain patterns of behaviour would ensue. One of the ladies would identify herself as the object of the seducer's designs; the other, her confidante, as the person to be circumvented by the second gentleman acting on behalf of the first. The first gentleman, of course, being the protagonist and seducer, in this case the Chevalier D*nh*m himself; the second gentleman – who? – the rakish Mr S*dn*y P*rk*r...

Sir Edward's musings upon what was taking shape as a deplorable History of *Cl*r* Br*r*t*n, in a Series of Letters* were interrupted by Charlotte Heywood. As not infrequently, Charlotte proved to be in touch with his thoughts – and at odds with his conclusions. She was making some light remark to the effect that if they – 'Good afternoon, Sir Edward; Good afternoon, Miss Clara; Fine day, Mr Parker etc,' – if they had all been characters in an epistolary novel, it would greatly inconvenience their author to have had the four of them sitting and speaking together, with no excuse for pen and paper.

Sir Edward meanwhile continued his invention of rococo correspondence, refusing to be drawn by Charlotte into any discussion of the relative outmodedness and absurdity of such works (and the attitudes in them); neglecting the real Clara Brereton for the asterisked creature of his fancies. He tried to give his design – his design for his *designs* – an exact formulation – but much of it stayed grey and misty.

A haze came over the sun, the sharp shadows lost their edge, and Sidney Parker (even S*dn*y P*rk*r seemed unlikely to become his aide in the abduction of Clara Brereton (with or without asterisks).

And there were always so many people about! Yet, even had he been able to affront Clara when solitary, an outrage against an unwilling victim was an unsatisfactory outcome – for one who would wish his despotism to be acknowledged and applauded. More civilised if *he* should think her a victim and *she* should find herself a willing party, and that both should have an intuition of the other's view.

Anguished words from a persecuted lady would have given rise in him, not rhetorical tears, but a desire for atonement; would have sent him off ready to search for and assail some other wrong-doer (provided he had the cost of transport). Did such inconstancies and inconsistencies make him a better or a worse man? Sir Edward, in so far as he could bring himself to bear on this question, felt committed to *feel* – thinking was to ask too much – that he was lessened because of it; others may see in his lack of resolution, in his comparative civility, evidence of the effects of intercourse with reasonably good society.

Perceiving that Sir Edward's attention had wandered, and unsure whether she preferred him lost in his own thoughts or chivvying her, Clara – unusually bold for one who was aware that she worked in a schoolroom – directed the conversation, without frivolity, back to Charlotte's remark about novels written in letters.

'It would be not unnatural for us to write – we *could* all four of us write,' she said, ' to some other person – to someone who is not here. *Who* is not here? Miss Esther Denham is not here. Why should we not, all of us, write a letter to Miss Esther? That would be probable enough circumstances, in a novel, don't you think?'

The suggestion was addressed to Charlotte Heywood, but it was Mr Sidney Parker who changed the subject, without naming Miss Denham:

'Ah no,' he said to Clara, ' don't introduce more ladies into the discussion – either by letter or direct conversation – for *that* is likely to turn towards poetry. I yield to female opinion there, on account of their direct acquaintance with a fine range of feelings. That will always give them too great advantage over us men – especially if we are outnumbered.'

Sir Edward thought this view worthy of serious consideration, Charlotte tried not to laugh, Clara took the words at their face value, which gave her the confidence to turn to poetry, to ask Charlotte if she were a devotee of Lord Byron.

'Not of the noble Lord himself,' said Charlotte; 'as for the work, I'm afraid (similarly to the case of Burns)', turning to Sir Edward in recollection of a previous conversation, 'that I find it difficult to separate what is written from my impression of the man who wrote it.'

Sir Edward was all impatience: 'But the work is the man. I'm sure Mr Parker would agree –'

'You have my declaration already. Consequently, I never,' said Sidney Parker, 'never intervene in a literary argument between a lady and a gentleman, save to commiserate with the latter.'

'That,' said Sir Edward with some degree of fierceness, 'is the kind of judgment which hinders the just progress of our national sensibility – confusion of politeness with passionate appraisal is unworthy.'

Since Mr Parker had silenced himself and Clara felt she had been too forward, Charlotte was left to reply:

'I have conceded, Sir Edward, that I am unable to distinguish such a man from his works. The life of Byron as it is commonly described – though it may be admired for its activity and variety – seems to me to be of a piece with the extempore, with the unreflective quality of his writing.'

'Well spoken, Miss Heywood,' said Mr Sidney, 'ah, yes, I am permitted to *applaud* – though not to intervene; save to urge that "unreflective" be here construed as *uncorrected.*'

'Perhaps,' said Sir Edward to Charlotte (ignoring Mr Sidney, though encompassing Clara), 'so far we may be in agreement. But the lack of reflection has as its positive side a – what? – a spontaneity. The vision of Byron and Wordsworth is a transitory thing, necessarily fleeting – which must be set down before it fades and dies! – "The rainbow comes and goes, And lovely is the rose, But these things are not " – whatever it was...The rainbow comes and – but you know these lines, Miss Heywood.'

It was clear that Charlotte Heywood did, but she seemed to defer to Sir Edward; making some slight sign, though, to Clara Brereton: who took up where Charlotte Heywood might have continued:

'Is there vision in the present scene, Sir Edward?' asked Clara – innocently or teasingly, Charlotte was unsure which.

'There is at any rate a sensation,' said Sir Edward after a little staring out to sea, 'an ephemeral quality: the feeling of,' after a little thought and standing up and stretching, 'wind on my cheeks and its sound.'

Is this not carrying temporariness too far?' asked Mr Sidney.

Sir Edward had only time to sit down, not enough to answer:

'On the contrary,' said Charlotte, 'it is not temporary enough. It will be there tomorrow and so is ineligible for this kind of consideration.'

'Not necessarily so,' said Sir Edward, inadequately.

'Have others not remarked its presence?' asked Clara.

'Its presence? Where?'

'Why here on Sanditon cliff-top,' answered Charlotte – 'when they might more usefully be taking sounding and measurements of the land as it crumbles. Do you not think, Sir Edward, that there is some danger of a landslip?'

But Sir Edward was not to be distracted from his Temporary Verities.

'We are speaking, Miss Heywood,' said Sir Edward, 'of poetry, and you would shift the discourse into the realms of hedging and ditching. Yes, many may have observed or half-observed the natural forces to which I refer – but, since they have not set down their sensations in the best and freshest language known to men...' He lost track of his argument at this point.

Charlotte was unwilling to let him escape:

'The wind on your cheek or my cheek, Sir Edward, of what interest is this to posterity? Why does it need recording? Cannot we take a walk here tomorrow if we wish to add to our information in a natural way about this natural force – if the cliff has not fallen away, that is. And, Sir Edward, does not the poet Wordsworth make much the same point – "One impulse from the vernal wood", as he puts it. *Shouldn't* nature be our teacher?'

'You must understand,' said Sir Edward, 'that the example of the breeze is a comparatively trivial one and arrived at on the spur of the moment.'

'Yet,' said Charlotte quickly, 'from your own principles, its unreflective nature, its being on the spur of the moment, renders it, therefore, of the highest order. Is that not so?'

Sir Edward felt some discomfiture at the way, as it now seemed to him, that he had been trapped:

'No,' said he, 'not altogether; you simplify. Of course, some spontaneous observations are more striking than others. You judged *spontaneously* that my poor thought was not sufficiently evocative. Perhaps (I am consistent with my principles here you must allow) it was not truly spontaneous. But now, a sudden fit what of this? It came into my head unbidden – flowers like flames, flames like flowers.'

'Good, Sir Edward,' said Clara, accepting his arm like a cousin. Upon which the four of them continued their walk together.

They looked at the sea, they picked a flower. Mr Sidney pulled off some of its petals and pretended to eat them as if they were fruit. Handing the abbreviated flower-head to Charlotte, he opined (of Sir Edward's similitude or of the flower):

'It's fresh.'

Charlotte refused to indulge him by laughing; insisted – to protect Sir Edward, teased as he was by Mr Sidney – insisted on taking him seriously:

'Fresh it may be, but doesn't one tire of freshness, of novelty?'

'One tires of all things,' said Sir Edward. 'One has only the option to flee – along with the best of the modern poets – from the verb *s'ennuyer*.'

'But,' said Charlotte, ' this argument depends, I believe, on our being bored by boredom.'

'Quite so, Sir Edward' observed Sidney Parker, shuttering one eye-lid, 'and, it seems our search for something preferable to that which we have is dependent on allowing that your poets bore us, isn't that so?'

Sir Edward was unwilling to reply to Mr Sidney directly, turning instead to a predetermined demonstration:

'Of course, I, you, we, any man or woman, can choose *ennui*; can be stolid and boring as cliff-stone' (kicking at what he supposed to be a chunk of granite and carrying off the fact that it disintegrated into shards); 'or,' – improvising – 'apparently lively, but in fact as obedient as a dog...and in point of fact *ennuyant*.' For effect, or from some unexpected urge, he emitted at this point a strange and distracting cry: 'That is a sound which Canines hear at a great distance.'

'You activate your idle dog in spectacular fashion, Sir Edward.' said Charlotte quickly, before Mr Sidney said some thing less polite on the same subject, 'If his qualities are such as you describe, mightn't you see him as Energy when he's active and as Ennui when he's unoccupied!'

Mr Sidney did not take the hint. He had to cap Charlotte's remark: 'From what you say, Miss Heywood, he sounds to me a cross-bred. *Cerberus* – wasn't that the name of the hell-hound? But, pardon me, Miss Brereton. I was too hasty. I think you were about to speak.'

Flippancy was not at the present time to Clara Brereton's taste. She felt protective of Sir Edward (not a role the chevalier had envisaged for his cousin): believed that neither he nor she would suffer *ennui* or the poor gentleman bother his head about such things were he to be less provoked.

'I cannot tell,' she answered. 'All I have to say is that this quality of which you speak – well, might not it be a less troublesome thing if it had a quieter name...?'

She broke off, fearing that Mr Sidney Parker was about to make some jest, but instead he gravely urged her on:

'Please, Miss Brereton, do continue.'

'It was nothing,' said Clara, after a short pause, 'nothing – merely that might not a quiet kind of what Sir Edward' (with a polite little nod to him) 'calls *ennui* bear a better name than that?'

'You mean contentment, Miss Clara,' said Charlotte with what seemed a sigh. Sir Edward began to walk up and down as if to guard against petrifaction of the lower limbs: 'Fungus,' he said, 'fungus may have such "contentment". Is it not better,' and he screwed up his eyes, his sensations turning inwards, 'to be a god in pain than a contented mushroom?'

Charlotte, who was conscious of increasing difficulty in following Sir Edward's elliptical cast of thought, made no claim to knowledge of or insight into mythological megrims, giving it simply as her opinion that some kinds of fungus, boletus and mushroom especially, did very well.

'Ay,' said Sir Edward loudly, 'in a rich sauce on a good stomach, but in themselves, Miss Heywood, in themselves: are not the culinary kind, the table delicacies, quite outdone by the villains, the poisonous varieties?', his theme bringing on a doomed facial twitch.

Sir Edward's ear caught a distant sound, he twitched alert – and clapped his hands noisily. Conjured thus from the air, a dog did certainly appear: though, to the diminution of Sir Edward's élan, it turned out to belong to Mr Parker. It was first heard, then seen and continued to be noisy. It was boisterous and quite unlike Sir Edward's large, compliant Bosun (not, of course, a Cerberus, but named after Byron's faithful Newfoundland). Further conversation being thus rendered impossible, Sir Edward was enabled to have had the last word.

The animal was just quietened when its owner appeared. Mr Parker was glad of the silence which greeted him, for he was full of news with which to fill it up.

'How convenient,' he dried, with great cheeriness. 'Convenience upon convenience. You are the first to hear of Sanditon's good fortune – that is, after my sisters and Arthur – and little Mary – who chiefly stand to benefit.'

He paused and waited for Charlotte – it was usually Charlotte's role – to request further information. She did so now.

'Yes,' was Mr Parker's predictable response, 'it is a great day for our sea-bathing place. You know I have lived in hopes – ever since our families met at Willingden in such fortunate-unfortunate circumstances, I being misdirected in search of a surgeon who might become resident here.' He paused and Charlotte indicated, as he hoped she would, her eagerness to hear much that was familiar repeated.

'And then a further mishap. Unfamiliar lanes…Carriage. *That* proved to be a most happy mishap. Not merely did our families come to know one another, but I was thereby prevented from doing any thing in haste; was enabled to delay a decision until the right man – perhaps a great man – should be ready to take up his calling on our shore. In short Mr Wingfield (of whose existence I have, I believe, given a previous hint) – *the* Mr Wingfield – is arriving this afternoon! Word was sent to me out here on my walk, and I hastened to tell you the good news before returning to greet him. A red-letter day! Mr Wingfield is to begin his – I was about to say, ministry; and indeed that is almost the word; very probably is the best word – *forthwith*!'

The ladies and gentlemen, uplifted by Mr Parker, gave a little cheer; and Mr Sidney patted his brother on the shoulder.

Mr Parker re-orientated his dog for the return to Sanditon. The rest of the group turning likewise, moved on, talking lightly of Mr Wingfield; until Sir Edward dug in his heels and stood still. He did not wish to think of the restless ocean measured out in medicine bottles and hip-baths. He did not wish to discuss the salt-water cure with Mr Thomas Parker or to put up with further raillery from Mr Sidney Parker. Facing them in valedictory fashion (though he was staying and everyone else going), he searched his memory for some soulful quotation.

Finding none, he said something about the vantage point and the beauty of the scene at that time of day; and indicated his need for solitary reflection.

While the others moved off – Clara slowest to do so, he noted – Sir Edward remained, motionless at first, but soon nodding his head in time to the sound of waves as they hit and undermined the cliffs. He had got by heart, but found insufficient confidence to recite in company, an Albanian rhyme collected and published by his master, Byron.

He found himself now beginning to commit its lines to the air like an incantation. The wind picked up his words and carried them on:

> 'Bo, Bo, Bo, Bo, Bo, Bo,
> Naciarusa, popuso.
> Naciarura na civin
> Ha pen derini ti hin.
> Ha pen uderi escrotini
> Ti vin ti mar serventini.
> Cariolote me surme
> Ea ha pe pse dua tive.
> Buo, Bo, Bo, Bo, Bo ...'

And the already distant dog of Mr Parker took up the refrain:

> 'Bo, Bo, Bo, Bo, Bo, Bo.'

4

Below the Sanditon cliffs, walking along the shore, Elizabeth Darcy and Fanny Bertram fancied they could hear the measured tones of someone – Sir Edward? – declaiming blank verse by some blanker poet, with the rhythm of the tide as counterpoint.

'So, then, the sea-side is the realm of poetry today.' said Elizabeth, shifting her gaze from where she thought Sir Edward might be to the English Channel in general: 'As, for example, "Water, water, every where Nor any drop to drink."'

A certain lilt to Elizabeth's voice made Fanny suspect that there was some prankish purpose behind the familiar lines. So she kept a friendly silence and Elizabeth completed the thought herself:

–'Save at Sanditon, where every drop provides a dose of Mr Parker's elixir.'

Fanny, though knowing she was intended to be amused by this sally, had never learned to be frivolous:

'I have heard Mr Coleridge speak of a distinction between the classic and romantic poets – as, on the one hand Pope; and on the other, in our own time, Lord Byron and Mr Wordsworth – '

'I think I perceive,' said Elizabeth, 'what Mr Coleridge intended, but I don't believe I know more than a line or two of Mr Wordsworth.'

'Oh,' said Fanny, who did think knowing about Wordsworth mattered, but with this apparently casual monosyllable gave Elizabeth the chance to change the subject if she preferred.

As Elizabeth chose not to do so, Fanny continued eagerly: 'Mr Wordsworth has determined to write in homely language of the daisy and the salt sea wave. No, not simultaneously – be fair to the gentleman! But Lord Byron now – who may delicately "walk in beauty like the night" at one time, at others, bears a resemblance, from what I have heard of his career, to some of literature's most exceptionable personages. It's a curious fact that the destroyer of Clarissa, Lovelace – I have sometimes wondered whether Mr Richardson did not intend by that name 'loveless' – is also a family name of the Byrons, or so I understand. Mr Richardson certainly cannot have known any thing of that. If it is true, the coincidence is disquieting. Yet I am glad that Mr Richardson's memory is still green with select readers –'

'– and,' said Elizabeth, 'the work of Byron is not altogether out of fashion – as distinct from the ostracised lord himself (what deplorable reports about him from abroad! I trust Darcy will not cross his path) –'

'Indeed,' agreed Fanny, 'though it is the young and volatile who are at risk from such writings.

'I was hardly supposing, ' replied Elizabeth tartly, 'that my husband could be "at risk" in that particular way,' but then continuing with kindly affability towards Fanny, 'though Darcy may sometimes be precipitate. No, no – no – he's not one to be impressed or affronted by poetry. Certainly, he wouldn't fall a-quoting on first acquaintance, Fanny.'

'You're referring, I take it, to our own unsatisfactory encounter with Sir Edward Denham?'

'Yes,' said Elizabeth, 'and to Miss Clara's account of her walk with the gentleman. Though there may have been some self-deprecation of her enthusiasm – it is difficult to be sure in one so young – I fancy she does admire the gentleman.'

'That is not unnatural,' said Fanny, 'he has a pleasing manner when he finds a suitable object for its application. But, even in the small matters of ordinary discourse, there is a kind of performance about him.'

'I agree,' said Elizabeth. 'For example, can he really have read with any attention the bulky old-fashioned books which he seeks to impress upon our minds?'

'I fear,' said Fanny, 'that the manner in which Sir Edward engages with these writings – to which, as you know, I also devote my time – is more arresting than my own.'

— Elizabeth feeling a lack of tact on her part, given Mrs Bertram's devotion to the old writers, was about to change the subject; but there was no need.

'It is very likely, 'continued Fanny, ' that he has merely read some indifferent abridgement – for this kind of production my profession of literary journeyman has to answer. Certainly, Sir Edward has not modelled himself on the good Sir Charles Grandison.'

'I observed,' said Elizabeth, 'that he did not embellish his discourse to Miss Clara with gems from Richardson's account of Grandison's virtues; even though the Clementina, from whom this man of virtue has to disengage himself, is a verbose vehicle for the female passions.'

'But isn't the disengagement nobly done?' cried Fanny. 'And the lady – she is noble too.'

'Yes,' Elizabeth agreed, 'she is noble, but still she is a mad Italian – just as' (with apparent lightness) 'Darcy is a sane Englishman.'

At which point Fanny, as if halted by a dark premonition, becomes silent and searches for some other topic of conversation. But that proving hard to find, they return to Wellington Terrace. As they enter, the smallness of the rooms and the proximity of the sea's sound and action seem to relocate them once more to a rocking carriage; either that or some cubicle in a bathhouse. This correspondence of ideas entertains them. They see the congruity of it. This is their 'rural cot' – an appropriately pastoral dwelling in the age of 'romantic' poets for a stay of restorative character in a sea-bathing place.

✷

Mr Thomas Parker, with the clicking Mr Wingfield safely installed, lost no time in bringing out a revised version of his visitors' list.

JANE AUSTEN OUT OF THE BLUE

SANDITON, SUSSEX

altissima quaeque flumina minimo sono labi

RESIDENTS

Gentry, Clergy and Professional Persons
Thos Parker Esq, Trafalgar House, New Sanditon
Sir Edward Denham, Childe Harolde Cottage
Rev Balm, Old Sanditon
Mr Wingfield, surgeon & physician, specialist in sea-water cure

Shopkeepers and Traders
Mr Jebb, Haberdashery
Mrs Whitby, Library & Stationery
Mr Woodcock, New Sanditon Hotel: *apply at the bar for –*
Woodcock's Billiards Saloon
Mr Stringer, General Provisions

Principal Visitors, June – July 18–
Resident for the Season: Mr Wingfield, surgeon & physician: *apply Mr Parker or Mr Woodcock*, also for the sea water cure

Sanditon House
Mr & Mrs Geo Knightley
Mr Woodhouse
Mrs J Knightley

Trafalgar House
Miss Heywood

The Terrace
Mrs Griffiths & Party
Miss S Lambe
Miss C Brereton

Wellington Crescent
Mrs Darcy
Mrs Bertram
Mrs Brandon (arriving soon)
Mrs Ferrars & party (do.)

New Sanditon Hotel
NB Inquire of Mr Woodcock daily.

NEW SANDITON

Mr Parker stepped back to ensure that the notice was upright, raising his hat to passers-by with a view to drawing them in to a close scrutiny of his handiwork. In that he was successful. He raised his hat again, and moved on to the next location where he would repeat the process; his eye alert for expected or unexpected visitors.

*

Two or three days at Norland had been quite enough for Elinor and Marianne, who wished they had stayed content with their memories, had not risked those being confused with scenes so disparate and, to their minds, so incongruous. Some of the stately timber had gone; gravel paths had appeared in dubious taste across the turf; the ha-ha had been filled in to extend the pleasure grounds, which (for the cattle in consequence no longer kept to their allotted space) were now circumscribed by an ugly fence; and a Folly – a Moorish accretion attached to the house – now occupied the site where formerly a few stones of the old cloister had been visible. The two ladies were united in their opinion that the changes to their old home were conducive neither to utility nor to beauty.

With a lightening of heart, therefore, they had made their departure from it. It was a relief to them to find that *this* Norland was not only not their home, but never had been; and that, once the 'improved' Norland was out of sight, their father's old Norland was given back to their inner eye.

'The end of a chapter, or perhaps we're in some *entr'acte* – orphans expelled from the family home once more,' said Marianne, turning to glimpse their older children's carriage as the road curved behind them.

'Indeed,' said Elinor, 'though the John Dashwoods were all politeness.'

'More so,' said Marianne, 'than becomes a gentleman and his lady with their sisters. True, John Dashwood – though our father's heir and representative on earth – is merely half-brother, but half as much polite stiffness would have been too much. He has never been dear to us nor have we to him, if the truth be told.'

'Certainly,' said Elinor, 'he acted ungenerously to our poor mother, when he wrenched her from Norland, her only home, and replaced her with that –

'With,' said Marianne, 'with your own dear Edward's dreadful sister – Fanny Ferrars. I mean no disrespect to your husband, of happy memory, when I say that the Ferrars are a strange family. Why, for instance, was Robert Ferrars not to be mentioned at Norland? Why their cool avoidance of him, their deafness to our few, but honest words, about his visits to us? He is very good with Brandon – why was I not permitted to tell them so?'

'We know too well the story of his unfortunate choice,' replied Elinor. 'And something of his escape from that snare, one which he laid for himself. And they must know that we know. Whatever the reason, I don't believe it was consideration for the memory of my poor Edward that made them avoid the subject.'

'I suppose they still do hold Robert Ferrar's marriage against him,' said Marianne, 'and that he has not tried to put things to rights by re-marrying.'

'If marriage it was,' said Elinor, 'But we should not inquire – the important thing is that the party is without question dead. And as to his marrying or re-marrying, I dare say Norland would applaud some grand alliance were he to make one. Unfortunately, notions of family duty for gentlemen with large resources seem out of fashion – particularly for the likes of Robert, for all of his play with our offspring.'

'Yes,' said Marianne, 'but he *is* good with Brandon. As for Norland and the John Dashwoods, we have no need of them. I fancy they are deeply disappointed by such independence – not that they are generous people. On the contrary – but they'd like the sense of power. For similar reasons, they would be sure to dislike and be uncomfortable with Robert.. Who as an uncle, as I say, has his points…Nevertheless –'

NEW SANDITON

Elinor felt her hand squeezed to indicate their agreed independence from Robert Ferrars, too: from anyone – their security residing in Marianne's inherited acres.

They rode smoothly on a short stretch of turnpike and played with the fingers and toes of the youngest children on the seat opposite. They were thus reminded once more of the old family home; as home perhaps to the next generation.

'So, yes – as you were saying, Marianne – the John Dashwoods may not have Norland in their grip for ever. Though, yes, they will continue to do their best – their worst – to disfigure it. We shall soon put them and it out of our minds. It will be soon enough to think of them if their unpleasing child does not survive, or survives and needs to marry, ten years on. At which time who knows who might be able to set the place to rights –?'

'Yes, our own little healthy darlings will be real beauties and beaux,' agreed Marianne, completing her sister's thought.

It was a warm afternoon and they were now jolting down the Sussex lanes toward the coast. Elinor and Marianne, the two little children and an attendant; the others still keeping close behind, with the rest of the holiday household.

The two vehicles slowed to descend one of the many hills and a figure on horseback passed them, raising his hat, but not catching either lady's eye, for the one was distracted by a child and the other holding on hard against an expected jolt. This part of the journey, short though it was, was not a comfortable one, but the children and their mothers were in good spirits from having escaped not only the constraints but now the very thought of Norland.

Soon, within sight of the sea, the land began to yield its characteristic herbal scents to those of fresh and standing brine. Arrived in the two ladies followed the bright finger post to New and there inquired the direction of Wellington Crescent, where they had taken by letter two large adjoining apartments. With difficulty the coaches ground their way up the new-made road cut into a headland.

'See the view of the bay, children,' cried Marianne, leaning out of the coach window so as to include the children in the rear coach in her exhortation. The children responded to this invitation by their mother (or, as the case may be, by their aunt) with a cheer; the horses halted; the drivers got down. Everyone else being occupied with the prospect of the sea, Elinor directed her attention to the immediate surroundings: saw at once that all was half-completed works and noisy bustle.

A perspiring gentleman, who having intelligence of their sudden approach, had hoped to intercept the carriages with soothing words at the foot of the hill: he introduced himself as Mr Thomas Parker. To which information Elinor, amidst the noise of building operations where peace and repose had been expected, responded coolly. There was correct instinct in this, as Mr Parker did not propose to take these ladies fully into his confidence.

(Unable to resist an unexpected tenant as grand as Mrs Darcy – though Elizabeth had looked to be unrecognised – he had transferred one of the two Wellington Crescent properties intended for the ladies from Norland to the mistress of Pemberley.)

Mr Parker had nevertheless hoped that the finishing and fitting and furnishing of further lodgings would have been complete by the time their parties arrived. In this Mr Parker had been frustrated. Worse, he believed some of the materials required for railings and paths and the like had been purloined by that rival sea-side place dismissed in his leaflet as a 'brackish settlement'.

'A thousand apologies, ladies,' said Mr Parker. 'I had thought you were to have remained a day or two more at Norland'; which was true and not denied by Elinor and Marianne who had had no wish to extend their stay at their half-brother's house. Mr Parker saw in their faces that this was the case, and so continued:

NEW SANDITON

'May I propose, ladies – given your early arrival – that for the beginning of your stay in New Sanditon, Mrs Brandon takes the completed apartment here, which I believe you will find affords handsome and convenient accommodation. During which time I do assure you your personal tranquillity will not be intruded upon: work on the nearby property which would have been complete in a day or two, will be halted and will resume only during those periods of the day when you and your party are out of earshot taking the air. There will be no disturbance' – he glared at the workmen who continued their labours in a more subdued manner.

Mr Parker was now able to make himself heard without raising his voice: 'For Mrs Ferrars I can offer a delightful lodging in a select development on a lower level, which we call Ocean Prospect' - he gestured vaguely, 'nearer to the sea' – making clear that the ocean was his to command –'I will just see if – that is, ladies, if you will excuse me, I will determine which of them is most suited to the requirements of your party.'

He bowed himself away and ran down some steps which led to a row of half-finished gimcrack houses. Elinor and Marianne looked at one another. Even if the accommodation were satisfactory, which looked improbable, to be separated was unfortunate; yet a return to Norland was not to be thought of.

Mr Parker had not returned, so the two ladies were still standing irresolute by the side of their still-loaded coaches, when a cloaked figure on horseback bore down upon them. He was muffled like some heroic apparition from the works of Mr (now Sir W) Scott. Such was Marianne's thought as she felt herself seized, and allowed herself to be whisked with reassuring words back into her carriage. Elinor had no other recourse than to do likewise. With an air of command and his person still concealed, the horseman next ordered the children to join their mothers – young Brandon happy to lead the way – and the drivers to drive, to thunder round and out of the crescent past the frantic Mr Parker (who had popped up from a second set of steps), out onto a chalk track which took them hazardously across a cliff top and down into the next bay.

Shortly after these events the friable nature of the coastline to which Miss Heywood's eye and Sir Edward's foot had drawn attention became evident to all. The rough road along which Elinor and Marianne had been driven was severed by a landslip. Mr Parker – though much exercised by the departure of the two families – regarded this development in sanguine fashion. No one dared to suggest to him that Sanditon was cut off from Brinshore, for who would want to go there? – And, after all, it was only right and proper that the exclusiveness of Sanditon should be confirmed by geological separation. All in all, Mr Parker rejoiced that communication between the two places was rendered even less practicable – the cliff top route having always been a rough one.

Mr Parker's habitual cheerfulness was magnified by the late June sun wherein Mr Wingfield and his patients acquired sunburn and a habit of clicking their fingers, in the afternoon; and an Arcadian glow and gooseflesh in the evening. The sea reflected the sky, as seas will; the high clouds echoed the ribbed sand left by the withdrawing tide, which was now on the turn. Miss Beaufort was collecting shells in the name of education or duplication, while Arthur Parker, grown bold, held that lady's parasol and gave barely a thought to the evils that cockles could wreak on his digestive system. Three bathing machines were drawn up in the precise position agreed upon by Messrs Wingfield and Parker on the very best medico-topographical principles. Mr Parker looked at his watch, at his brother, and then at the sea again, in his capacity of comptroller of the tides or man in the moon.

'Once it's over that steep sand bank,' he declared, 'the bank which separates the bather at Sanditon from all danger and difficulty, the water will be very quickly in position for us.'

Mr Wingfield made an obliged and fricative response. This proprietorial self-satisfaction awakened Sidney Parker's sense of mischief:

'Tell me, Mr Wingfield,' said he, 'man to man,' – true, he spoke quietly but loud enough for everyone to hear – *'à propos* dipping and drinking, is there not a tendency to overrate the former because of its very nastiness? After nerving one's self for a small ordeal and coming through it successfully, there is bound to be a heightening of the spirits. Would not some other unpleasant task – walking barefoot through a stubble-field, for instance, be equally efficacious?'

'No sir,' said Mr Wingfield, with great civility but rather less assurance, 'the practice of dipping is greatly on the increase all along the coast.'

'Indeed,' replied Sidney Parker, a twinkle in his eye showing his willingness that his question should be perceived by those present to have remained without answer; especially leading as it did to a second assertion:

'Dipping aside, I had heard that fashion and science were both against the practice of *drinking* sea waters.'

Mr Wingfield looking easier now, took on a well-versed air: 'Sir, sea water contains the bicarbonates of magnesium and calcium, both highly favoured minerals as partaken by royalty and nobility at Aix-la-Chapelle or Vichy. The sulphates of magnesia and of calcium are found in the German spas – also at Sanditon in this fine blue ocean. As for your sodium chloride, sea water is rivalled only by the inland waters of our native Droitwich. The total draught being beneficial in cases of scrofula, chronic exudations, chronic exanthemas, rheumatism, infiltrations, hepatic affections, chlorosis and gout.'

Poor Miss Lambe, facing in a little while her first dip, was alarmed at this catalogue of sad ailments. If sea water was the treatment for such fatal infections, and she, Miss Lambe, was to be subjected to sea water, then it followed that she must be threatened by the likes of scrofula, exudation and the rest, and was as good as dead – even if the shock of immersion did not make her catch her death of heart failure. Miss Lambe's seemed the one sickly constitution in the bathing party. She was rich and puny, with great brown eyes and sculptured cheek bones; the chubbiness of youth – she was only seventeen – seeming to have been all eroded away.

Miss Diana Parker who had come with Mrs Griffiths to hand over Miss Lambe safely to the bombazined dipper-woman, to see that every care was taken of the heiress (or to guard against her escaping), added to Mr Wingfield's list for Miss Lambe's reassurance: 'Also, general debility and dyspepsia.'

Charlotte Heywood left the group with a little distaste. Possibly because she thought Mr Wingfield disappointing – it seemed to her he talked and twitched by rote; equally possibly because the space at Mr Sidney Parker's elbow seemed to be taken up by the silent – the almost always silent – Miss Esther Denham.

Charlotte turned first to her right, then to her left – in the opposite direction from Arthur Parker and the cockleshell-picking, in which with rare energy, he seemed to have joined, the parasol being stuck upright with its point down in the sand – the two like children at play, with Miss Lettie rather superior (the younger acting older) at a little distance doing something fancied scientific with a miniature hammer and an awkward piece of rock.

Soon, walking quite quickly, Charlotte had left them behind. This, now, was the loneliest part of the beach. Charlotte followed idly the rippled sand. All at once, after the example of the famous Mr Crusoe, she noticed that her footprints were falling amongst larger barefooted ones. No one was to be seen ahead. The footprints continued, not in a straight line but in great curves and meanderings, with sometimes the top or outside of the curve devoid of prints as if at that point their maker had been walking in the waves.

Now there were scribbled writings in the sand, made with a stick picked out of the sea it was to be supposed. Charlotte walked crabwise to make them out, which was not easy, for the direction of travel of the writer being elliptical, but mostly right to left, he scorning orthodoxy, or not disposed to change his way however much the trouble, had written thus:

NEW SANDITON

'/ – notererB aralC ssiM naht reriaf diam yna em wohS'
No easy task that's certain/
'/ .EBMAL EIHPOS ssiM eb tI / ,ma I taht relfirt ,sselnU

The footprints were evidently Sir Edward Denham's. As for the verse – if wit was intended – it was wittier than Charlotte would have expected. She was interested to hear of this admiration for Miss Lambe, which seemed to be recent in origin and might be guessed by the uncharitable as a safeguarding passion in case the Denham inheritance proved not very favourable to the Denham fortunes. All young ladies like to be admired and Charlotte had enough self-knowledge to realise that her view of Miss Lambe was at the moment coloured by the verses' lack of reference to herself; or of preference for Miss Brereton, her protégée. Sir Edward had formerly been very attentive. Charlotte had perhaps, in seeking to put him down, not been certain that she had meant to put him off. She recalled yesterday's conversation.

No doubt Sir Edward had today intended to demonstrate that the highest art is the cryptic, private and self-effacing sort; that unheard melodies are best written on sand or some such notion. But, being not a very practical man, he had misread the direction of the tide and written on sea-washed sand rather than that which was about to be overtaken by it. In this way his verses had achieved a longer period of possible public view than he realised. True, they would be erased when the tide turned, but not from the notebook where Charlotte gave them covert permanence.

A little further on was the stick, thrown like a dart into the ground. Charlotte was sorry that there would be no more poems, unless he had chanced to find another stylus. But there was nothing further. Though at one point it looked from marks in the sand, as if he had either encountered a shod Man Friday or dropped his own footwear. Presently the trail led to a spit of land, behind which she guessed Sir Edward had left his clothes. He was doubtless somewhere out in the bay spouting like Leviathan in the Atlantic or Lord Byron in the Hellespont, spurning the medicinal aura of bathing machines.

✻

Mr Woodhouse was content. Confused by the long journey to Sanditon, he was at first uncertain of his whereabouts – he knew he was not in his usual place, but his recollection of Highbury and even of Hartfield had of a sudden grown insecure.

The late Lady Denham and he were of the same generation; and, though his disposition was much the sweeter of the two, their tastes and outlook were not dissimilar. The portrait of Mr Hollis in its dark corner, for instance, was deemed a familiar one. In it Mr Woodhouse fancied he saw in it an old friend of his uncle's whose likeness he was glad to see again.

'I had thought it was lost,' said Mr Woodhouse eagerly. 'The frame, too, is, I believe, the original and always counted a fine piece of work' – continuing into a long account of the person who had fashioned the frame, whom, indeed, he did remember very well.

The change of location, then, far from sending him into some frenzy, had settled Mr Woodhouse's spirits, but also confused his understanding. Mr Knightley was not unhappy with the transformation – being greeted by his father-in-law not now as an interloper but as the gentleman in the portrait, whom he had taken along with the house. Contrariwise, Mr Wingfield, for his own credit, was anxious that sea-water should restore the old man's mind to such remnants of clarity as it had previously possessed.

For this purpose it was unfortunate that Sanditon House, in common with other rationally-located old dwellings, was situated a mile and a half inland with a tricky descent to the shore for anyone wishing to give up the warm land for the cold sea. It was agreed therefore with the physician that since Mr Woodhouse could not safely travel to the waterside each day, the tide must be made to flow uphill to him.

Like some variant on the well-known tale of Canute, sea was brought to Mr Woodhouse by the bucketful. ('Fresh? – with the motion of the tide still upon it,' the prestidigitatious Mr Wingfield reassured Isabella.) Mr Woodhouse, anxious to follow the ways of what he still supposed to be an antique relative's household, took his draughts of salt-water with equanimity. In Isabella's opinion Mr Woodhouse recognised the potent medicinal qualities of the beverage, but Emma judged from his polite but unenthusiastic downing of the bumpers that he supposed it to be some cool Frenchified soup.

Neither could be sure: Mr Woodhouse agreed quite genially that it was doing him good, asserted that unlike so many things which no longer had any savour for him, the liquid did have 'some taste to it at least'.

The inner workings of the potent Sussex brine were thus far efficacious. It is not to be supposed that he realised that the fluid into which his exterior was plunged daily had the same origins – he might otherwise have believed it his duty to drink the hip-bath dry. Wrapped in an old night-shirt as if that would protect him against the ague, he would, when extracted from his diminutive ocean, be covered by hot towels and stowed before a roaring summer fire until his face was as pink and his eyes as protuberant as those of some ancient crustacean prepared for the table. Mr Wingfield personally supervised much of the ritual, taking portentous notes.

5

Sir Edward Denham was an excellent swimmer, but it got him no income; the salt-saline solution, chloride of sodium etcetera – on his face and all about him gave the illusion of cutting through an ocean of tears. Sir Edward, kicking, applied the thought as a similitude to his life and savoured it. He swam like an amphibian not a fish, admitting to no coldness of the blood. Indeed, the glow of exercise and the temporary sense of freedom and control in the lachrymal element – a sea of feeling – brought him a rare kind of excitement; an excitement added to at that moment by the recollection of Lord Byron's lines:

> Know ye the land where the cypress and myrtle
> Are emblems of deeds that are done in their clime,
> Where the rage of the vulture, the love of the turtle,
> Now melt into sorrow, now madden to crime!

The Bride of Abydos suited well both the mood and the propulsion of Sir Edward: a flurry of foam at the caesura and an exhalation at the end of each line. He had almost decided to be very much in love with Miss Lambe. Lacking the purse and retinue of a traveller, but with a taste for (he thought) foreign skies and sensational events, Sir Edward felt that Sophie Lambe, whom he hardly knew, was as exotic a creature as he was likely to meet in sleepy Sussex.

He was halfway across the bay, he an unsinkable Leander with Hero or Clara or Sophie or – confound her – Charlotte Heywood on the further shore. Way out from the beach, but in sight now of the bathing machines, he chose to wheel towards the shallows, suddenly curious to catch a glimpse of his shadowy Bathsheba,

Miss Lambe. Subduing self-accusations of arbitrariness and importunity, he bridled at the very notion of un-gentlemanly prurience. Circumspect behaviour was a convention only, to be faced and stripped away as firmly as if Sophie Lambe were old Giaffir's daughter:

> Woe to the head whose eye beheld
> My child Zuleika's face unveil'd!

Sir Edward made his way quietly towards the sandbar.

*

Sanditon,
25 June 18–

I trust my dear parents you are well. I need to assure you, in case of rumours, that I am not the party so nearly drowned today. My writing is not at its best, but it's not like the hand of a drowned thing – or even a nearly drowned thing – I think? Mr Parker, by the by, is particularly anxious that the news of this unfortunate happening should not get about, as – he thinks it could redound to the sea-bathing place's discredit. I fancy, though, it is merely a question of mismanagement by the resident medico; and hope Mr Parker will not prove too determined in his support of Mr Wingfield – at the expense, even, of his fair Sanditon.

Mr W– is the surgeon newly here, whose lustre is already a little dimmed. Though all that was amiss, in the view of Mr Sidney Parker, was the positioning of the bathing machines. They need to be a little further in-shore, he says. 'Where,' as Mr Parker puts it, *this* Mr Parker, Mr *Sidney* Parker, 'the high tide will certainly come to the bathers, thus saving them the trouble of going to it.' (Mr *Thomas* Parker is reluctant to accept this good advice. Which I think is good advice. Mr T is unhappy that bathers should be deprived of a walk across his low-tide sand to his sea. Lacking that, they would arrive at the bathing-place deprived of the pleasant phase of traversing the strand – with no more to remember than their short sharp struggle through the shingle at the top of the beach. Mr *Sidney* Parker believes that they will have to accept this roughness of passage and ameliorate it by laying board-walks Unfortunately Mr Thomas is unable to acknowledge any such necessity. It is an article of faith that every inch of Sanditon's foreshore consists of fair, smooth sand.)

You used to call me a water sprite when I was a girl – and that because of swimming in ponds and rivers (in some ways more difficult than sea-bathing, they say) – so I was not a likely candidate to be dipped by a butter-fingered fisherwoman dressed in black. I have bathed at higher water and privately; probably shall do so again. Have no fears for me – I am stronger and (alas!) older than Miss Lambe. Yes, it was she! Mr Wingfield still expresses doubt as to the cause of her being laid so low. Yet to the layman, it seems obvious enough that fear of drowning, and sickness from swallowing too many pints of life-giving sea water would account entirely for her present prostration.

I had returned with the turning tide from a deserted part of the foreshore. Joining the beach party, I could see that the water was well up to the machine's steps: a little high perhaps by then, there having been some delay because of difficulty in persuading Miss Lambe to venture in.

I fear a short lesson in geography is necessary. On the right hand side of the bay, that is the west, the cliffs fall away into a sand-bank which stretches out as a species of headland, becoming slighter and in any case submerged, but still existing right into the centre – or almost so. Mr Parker has me well schooled in Sanditon topography, as you may well believe. On the other side of the bank, on the further shore of what is virtually estuary, is despised and muddy Brinshore. I have mentioned previously, I believe, the recent cliff-fall on the rough road from Brinshore to Sanditon, as Mr Parker insists that no one would have made the journey in the opposite direction – an assertion not quite borne out in practice as the episode of the disappearing ladies from Norland shows – but I must return to my geographical – my hydrological drama.

At Sanditon, the tide makes slow progress up the beach; but when the water has acquired a certain depth, it advances with sudden rapidity. Mr Parker makes a virtue of this fact – certainly it allows several hours' access to the best sand, but the shell collector needs to keep a wary eye seawards. However, once the tide is well in, the sunken sandbank or bar makes of the Sanditon inshore a sort of lagoon, calm and safe for bathing. As I may have said earlier it is Sidney Parker's view (and mine) that Sanditon must learn to bathe at a higher tide, though it will be harder on the feet – for the proportion of low-tide shingle does not decrease, though Mr Parker urges (and has it scoured away) daily.

To return. No sooner has the already frightened Miss Lambe entered the water and is emerging (a struggling, tawny Venus) from of the foam of her first immersion, when over the protective sandbar comes a heavy ocean-wave! (It was said afterwards that there is a standing flow or tidal bore from the river which is a trouble to the fishers at Brinshore but has not been known to break so far east as Sanditon). The said wave pops *Miss Clara Brereton*, who had been quietly wading, neatly back onto the beach – as if nature had a special care of her – you will recall that in my foolish way I have speculated if she (not I!) mightn't be a born heroine. More on that head would, I suppose, become apparent if Lady Denham's intentions – did she ever commit them to paper? – were to be known. Miss Lambe is less lucky: spun clean out of the brawny arms of her attendant who is sent reeling against the machine which is itself rocked and shaken, and – when the wave recoils – carried half insensible out to sea!

That would have been the end of Miss Sophie Lambe I do not doubt, had not – as luck would have it – Sir Edward Denham, a strong swimmer, chanced to be, unknown to all, near at hand beyond the sandbar. He catches her in his arms, rides on the waves like a dolphin (this I clearly saw), returns her smartly to shore, says a few solicitous words, then calling for robes, emerges from the water like some old Roman god – Neptune? – in a toga. So he is a hero: though the rescued lady is, to my mind, no heroine – too colourless (for all her seeming sunburn). Nature after all played false here: Miss Clara Brereton needed to be the object of this gallantry.

These are stirring times indeed.

In haste,
Your affectionate daughter,
Charlotte Heywood.

✷

Sir Edward could not but be sensible of the advantages of being, *vis-à-vis* Miss Lambe, both a very gallant gentleman at the present moment and – God's will be done – a rich widower in the not too distant future; the latter prospect becoming a likelihood were Miss Sophie to persevere with her sea bathing when matrimony should have taken something of the cleaving edge from her husband's swimming arm. On the other hand, Mr Parker privately took the view that the coast of Sanditon could give rise to no condition which needed heroism to counter it; while, publicly, he maligned the poor dipper-woman (at some damage to his reputation for good nature), since, as he put it, while there was no detracting from Sir Edward's meritorious and highly serviceable act, the offence of the wave had been quite small by comparison with the attendant's weak grip and lack of fortitude. For his conscience, and to quieten any protest from the woman, Mr Parker paid her a tidy sum to stay away from the machines and resume her mending of nets.

Sir Edward's feat called for self-effacement of a heroic kind from the hero. His behaviour necessarily became tender. He could neither answer, 'Yes, I was noble, was I not?', nor could he confess to the idle and perhaps reprehensible curiosity which had caused him to be so close at hand. Yet it went against his nature and seemed discourteous to Sophie Lambe – who might now live or die, but who without aid would have had no chance of the former – to say simply, 'It was a convenient chance', as if the suffering heroine were some toy dropped from a passing boat.

What could Sir Edward do, then, but transfer the proffered admiration of the rescuer to the fair creature rescued? – 'Of all ladies in need, whom better to aid so fortuitously than Miss Lambe, who (it was common knowledge) despite her vivacity and youth, needed every preservative, and preserver, that was to be had?' – and like nonsense; which display of sensibility added to Sir Edward's credit: people immediately putting it about that were the poor lady only to be spared then a most happy and convenient match would undoubtedly ensue; she so weakly and so rich; he so strong, but poor. What medicine for general benefit could be more confidently prescribed?

Much, though, still depended on the Denham inheritance. If no will were found, it seemed likely that Sir Edward would receive *Something*. But the size of any portion and the length of time to wait for it were equally imponderable. Similarly, the necessity or otherwise of marrying Miss Lambe: who might well have time enough to marry and to die before Lady Denham's lawyers had done their business.

These were the thoughts of others rather than Sir Edward (he had disappointed Lady Denham by his incapacity for fortune-hunting). Now that Miss Lambe did preoccupy his mind, it was not on account of her gold. For him, she was an exotic plant – such as would beguile a modern botanist; or a Sargasso Sea becalm an ancient mariner. His attentiveness to her was the subject of much discussion.

On the one hand, as Miss Diana Parker put it, 'were a will to be found and Sir Edward inherit, would he not be throwing away his title and manner on one who – riches apart (which he would not then lack or need) – has nothing or nobody to call her own or to acknowledge her?'

'Why should he not take her?' said Sidney Parker. 'To do so would display a proper caution – not rashness. He is not sure of receiving any thing from Lady Denham – and, indeed, if her will is not found, might die himself (although a young, strong man) before matters are determined. As things stand he has barely enough to feed his dog, let alone to support Miss Esther and live like a gentleman. As to the possibility of his having sufficient resources without turning to Miss Lambe, the argument does not impress me. Sufficiency has no determinable bounds. Additional money during a lady's life and much more on her departure are enough to make a man a very loving husband. And Miss Lambe would have her money's worth during the time left to her. There remains the hope, too, that some part of the estate will enable Miss Clara Brereton to be relieved from her association with this meagre seminary.'

Miss Diana, sensitive still of her miscalculation of the seminary's summer enrolment sought to deflect this slur upon Camberwell by paying compliments to Clara's prowess in the school room. Mr Sidney knew his older sister was no fool, was aware of her own stratagem. He wished her to know that he, in his turn, was just as aware that his teasing words had had their effect:

'That,' said Mr Sidney, 'is not the point at issue. A charming young lady, with the capacity to make herself very useful. And, yes, I suppose I am glad to hear that she has a congenial little pupil – a

Miss Wentworth, you say? Yes, indeed, but – to return to Sir Edward: he should look to Lady Denham's life for instruction, if he cannot get any money out of her. He may, I'm afraid have derived disastrous notions of marrying for love from Sir Harry's side of the family. He would do better – would do very well – to follow his late aunt (and possible benefactress) in the pattern of her conquests. Marry money as she did. Look to the old aunt, there was strength in her (though – as I found in some dealings of my own with her – not much good will; but that quality he has in excess). Besides,' he concluded in a departure from his former logic, 'it would serve the old woman right.'

Mr Sidney refused to be drawn by Miss Diana and Miss Susan into explaining what he meant by that final comment, why he had taken so against Lady Denham. He would say no more. Mr Parker was not present and Mr Arthur ineffectual. Perhaps this young gentleman's mind was on contingent matters: he excused himself with a view to seeing whether the Miss Beauforts – so distressed for Miss Lambe – had need of his support in lieu of Mrs Griffiths who was at the invalid's bedside.

Miss Lambe had had a restless night. Mrs Griffiths, whom both duty and policy bound to extremities of discomfort before as many witnesses as possible, cradled Miss Lambe's tossing head all night long. When the young lady fell out of bed, which she did quite often, Mrs Griffiths became an extension of the mattress; when she rolled back again, the bosom of Mrs Griffiths gave additional amplitude to her pillow. By morning, the nurse was so nearly ill herself as to seem to have drawn off, as fresh meat can draw venom into itself, much that had been wrong with Miss Lambe.

To the extent that, when morning came – and with it expensive additional physicians from all along the coast and the principal inland towns – Miss Lambe's fever had much diminished and, by mid-afternoon, it was kept going only with some difficulty.

Mr Wingfield, who was certain to have been blamed for Miss Lambe's demise, was much fêted for her recovery: if Sir

Edward was the sea-borne hero, the physician had proved the *deus ex machina*.

'Credit where credit is due' was the general cry. Credit, however, needs its counterbalance; some loss to set against so much gain. That loss was Mr Parker's. There were some who chose not to lay the blame for the unfortunate occurrence on the fisherwoman-scapegoat. Some who quietly piled it upon the still-broad shoulders of Mr Thomas Parker – upon the low-tide sands of Sanditon, even.

✳

Six Days between June and July: a disjointed record made by Miss Ch*rl*tt* H*ywd, one too old at twenty-two for diary-keeping**

Invalids having been frightened from shore, I – in health – walk there. With me Mr & Mrs Parker and dog, who hope (esp. dog who is optimistic of finding rabbits in the sea-sand) to restore confidence in Sanditon. A gust of wind or dog's excavations (Mr P scolds) sends grit into my face and eye. Bo bo bo. Poor dog. O, foolish – I fall to the ground, sand to sand, ash to ash. Recover myself at the Terrace – an awning flapping. Cosseted. Despatch to Trafalgar House. Tedious evening with light curtains drawn and a night fretfully active.

Mr Wingfield in attendance. Obliged to sit upright in chair. Then required to lay throbbing head, side down; he placing something over my ear. The sounds of many distant seas overwhelming, the cries of gulls. 'Vertigo,' proclaims Mr W. in dolorous tone. His apparatus a sort of funnel (I first wrote 'funeral') – not, as I suppose because of the sound of seas, as from a sea shell.

Am I a healthy person who is (after all) sick? Or a sick person, who supposes she is some times well and will recover? Mr W makes his sharp snapping as a fanfare for his favoured medicament, salt sea. Am possessed by fear that he will pour his saline brew into my head where, so says my sick fancy, tiny spiky fishes will breed in the crannies of my skull – filling me full of roe and worm. Now, as with the letter-writing heroines of old, people come to take away my papers. I hide my writing beneath the blankets, shawls and wraps which weigh down upon me.

Find more paper. Mr W. prescribes (would he not?) sea water. Mouth averted to deny him. Tut-tuts Mr W, tut-tuts Miss Diana P. Nothing palatable. Can drink but little – and only sweet water. Cannot stomach their remedy – for sickness not for health – though some smack their lips over it, I'm told.

Fretful still.

A prisoner here in this chair or bed a long time. Upbraid myself for inactivity. Waves – but not of the sea – swill about me. There is a pain behind, between, eye and temple and I am sick: and against this I am offered an emetic! It is too dark to write, though I'm told it's broad day. Kind lady in attendance – Clara Brereton, as though she and I were at the bottom of a pond; between us float purple flowers and mauve fishes – I perceive them above this paper: they force me to lean back from my page and write blind.

A little rested. But for Mr W.

Bright day. Head clear. Mr Wingfield solicitous. Pretends to a salt-cure of me. Mr Sidney Parker arrives. Bears me up – my spirits. Miss Esther with him, silent. I say to Mr W – 'Sir, I am grateful for your attention, but do not make an *invalid* of me, for I am not like that.' (Meaning like Miss

Lambe, hum hum; and I think he understands.) Mr Parker (Mr Thomas Parker, bless him, unaffectedly) shocked at my condition. Mr W. – yes – prates about Miss L. (who serves as testimony to his powers and NB to his self-interest). I retort (Mr SP being of my mind too) to this effect: 'Sir, you claim sea water as a universal panacea – how, then, that Miss L. should be half dead from a generous dosage of your remedy?' Ingeniously Mr W. enumerates known medicines which are poisonous, but when taken in small quantities (in subtle measures known only to physicians) provide benefits. Thereby he owns (to my thinking) that his saline restorative is a canker and a bane. I rise in health and wish him good morning.

I meant to foreswear diurnalism. I have been a keeper of diaries and also of hiatuses – and much that was in them (diary and hiatus) both painful: the latter, that which was withheld, the more so. All the more reason to suspend the practice now. Let other pens &c.

*

Mr Woodhouse's first immersion in the imported tide having taken place in a corner of the library (where they had found him sitting at a moment when Mr Wingfield judged his condition right), the old gentleman would not thereafter suffer his ablutions to occur elsewhere. In consequence, certain old volumes on the lower shelves, though many of them were worm-eaten or coverless, were having to be removed. The books had, in any case, already been carelessly handled by lawyers searching for Lady Denham's will.

Emma, aware of Fanny Bertram's interest in such old things, asked that those books which had been cleared from the shelves should be set aside for her inspection, in case there were matters of use to her. Fanny was pleased at this offer, but suggested that Sir Edward Denham and Clara Brereton – as relatives of the late great lady – should have an opportunity of looking over the ejected material (though there was no knowing whether they would have entitlement to any of it in the future) prior to its despatch to a lumber room. Covering the shelves with hangings had proved ineffectual. Mr Wingfield always favoured immersion rather than mere anointing, and Mr Woodhouse's entry into the water provided a spectacular demonstration of Archimedes' principle.

Fanny arrived at the agreed time; and, Elizabeth being obliged to rest, Charlotte Heywood accompanied her; with Clara Brereton and Sir Edward, as already mentioned, completing the party. Unfortunately for the purposes of Clara's visit (which included the society of her cousin, Sir Edward), Mr Woodhouse – in his chair in the damp corner where his bath was habitually placed demanded her attention as a 'sweet child'. Fanny good-naturedly accompanied Clara – though she loved battered heaps of old tomes such as these; left the interesting pile upon a table and on chairs and the floor in favour of Mr Woodhouse and his dull corner.

Dust, literary interest and a kind of caution characterised Sir Edward and Charlotte Heywood as they inspected the volumes, putting some aside, referring to each other as they did. They became absorbed in their work. After some time it became clear that there was no immediate chance that Clara and Fanny would join them: 'not now, until father's bed-time, I'm afraid,' the two Mrs Knightleys had intimated, fussing first about the books, then about Mr Woodhouse, whose every move confirmed that the whole attention of two daughters and two other ladies was essential to his comfort. As time passed and the quartet remained occupied with Mr Woodhouse, Sir Edward and Charlotte ceased to work, took more their ease, began to talk of things literary over some of the books which they had selected as worthy of preservation.

At Charlotte's elbow were several novels by Fanny Burney (now Mme D'Arblay), by Sir Edward's some of Richardson – since none of the more licentious of the great man's followers were to be had.

'Miss Heywood,' said Sir Edward, 'I am put in mind of our earliest conversation.'

'About writers, Sir Edward?' said Charlotte.

'About what else, have we ever had an opportunity to converse?' said Sir Edward, with a studied rueful look, 'And even on that topic I have a feeling that you have thought my recollection (lacking the support of a book) to have been at fault.'

Charlotte blushed, an old-fashioned blush (a heroine's blush too young for her? Or self-consciousness at being so well understood?); and had no ready answer: she had underestimated Sir Edward, but did not wish to tell him so.

He went on without reference to her confusion:

'On the occasion to which I refer, I remember your own words exactly: you told me that our respective taste in novels was *Not at all the same*. How can it be – as I believe is the case – that there are certain novels we do both admire?'

Sir Edward answered himself, continuing, 'I think you hold the view that what I take from the best books is based upon a misunderstanding of their purpose. To that I would retort that authors – even the best of them – do not realise that the intention of their works is not always what they suppose. You have Miss Burney's work before you; I have some of Mr Richardson. Neither of us need rely merely on memory, why should we not put our taste and understanding to the test?'

Charlotte Heywood, not un-amused by the idea or without confidence in her own ability (without which a lady ought not to accede to such a proposition) accepts the challenge.

'Very well,' says Sir Edward with a courteous nod, 'What says the lady?' (by which he meant Miss Burney).

Charlotte intimates that she would prefer to see first what Richardson has to offer.

'Very well,' says Sir Edward, 'I would like to draw your attention to this spirited passage from *Clarissa*, the most uplifting of works – I suspect we would both agree so far. But is this not nobly said by Lovelace?–:

...I cannot bear the thought that a woman whom once I had bound to me in the silken cords of love, should slip through my fingers, and be able, while my heart flames out with a violent passion for her, to despise me, and to set both love and me at defiance.

Charlotte Heywood blushes for Sir Edward:

'No, sir,' she says firmly, 'it is not nobly said – you forget the acknowledgement by Lovelace that Miss Harlowe, with great good reason, despises him. '

'Very well,' replies Sir Edward, evenly enough, 'then what has Miss Burney to say that is equally noble?'

'I have no need,' says Charlotte, 'of Miss Burney to refute your perception of the point of the work and its interest.'

She takes up another volume of *Clarissa* and searches its pages.

Charlotte hands it to Sir Edward, marking a passage:

To say I once respected you with a preference, is what I ought to blush to own, since, at the very time, I was far from thinking you even a moral man; though I little thought that you, or indeed any man breathing, could be what you have proved yourself to be. But indeed, sir, I have long been greatly above you; for from my heart I have despised you, and all your ways, ever since I saw what manner of man you were.

'I grant you,' says Sir Edward, 'that Clarissa, too, is capable of nobility, because of her tragic conjunction with Lovelace: she – see here – writes from her heart's blood:

NEW SANDITON

How much more lively and affecting... must her style be, her mind tortured by the pangs of uncertainty (the events then hidden in the womb of fate), than the dry narrative, unanimated style of a person relating difficulties and dangers surmounted....'

'I observe, Sir Edward,' says Charlotte, 'that certain parts of this passage are obscured by your thumb and fingers. First, it should be noted that this is a man speaking (though not an incorrigible like Lovelace) and second, that even he is primarily moved by 'her patience and resignation' not her distress. When Clarissa writes, gives voice to her own thoughts, freed from the prison house and the drugs which were the unmanly means employed by Lovelace to subdue her, she speaks with both wit and a just sense of the illogic of the villain's – yes, the villain's – position. This is a man – no, let us keep to 'villain' – untrue even to his own villainy. Let me see, Sir Edward. Here, for instance; first imprisoning, rendering unconscious, forcing a fine lady; and then beseeching her to marry him. And her answer:

... to declare with fervour that I think I never could deserve to be ranked with the ladies of a family so splendid and so noble, if, by vowing love and honour at the altar to such a violator, I could sanctify, *as I may say, his unprecedented and elaborate wickedness,'*

'Lovelace has put himself in a position where it is clear that by his own actions he has made it impossible for a great lady such as Clarissa to accept entry into the noble family of Lovelace: she cannot permit him to legitimise his infamy by allying himself with the object and evidence of his crime. He has, Sir Edward, disgraced himself and his family and has deepened the disgrace and offence by his ignorant and coarse proposals of matrimony.'

There are movements on the other side of the room. Whether Sir Edward is able to respond or not to Charlotte Heywood by adducing other passages in defence of Lovelace cannot therefore be known. There is time only for Sir Edward, invigorated rather than abashed, to cry:

'Well done, Miss Heywood. You are a worthy opponent. You fight on equal terms – or, I admit, a better than equal in some of your perceptions. Let me shake your hand –'

Charlotte, liking his openness, and seeing he does not aim to flatter accedes; at which point she becomes aware of Clara Brereton's anxiety for their proceedings.

Mr Woodhouse, having risen from his chair with the help of attendants, there is a short period of quietness before the detailed difficulty of his ascent to the bedchamber (he refuses to sleep downstairs for fear of interlopers). It is a moment for all to say good night to him, but also one in which the glances towards Charlotte Heywood made by Clara Brereton convey (for such a sweet child) something more than the anxiety which she has hitherto reserved for whatever image of Miss Lambe is fixed in the eyes of Sir Edward.

Part Three: SPECULATION

1

Now that Miss Lambe was out of danger, and Mr Wingfield's credit restored, Mr Parker had hoped that the mishap to Sanditon's reputation for safe and salubrious bathing would once again be high – higher, even, for had not the element which had injured Miss Lambe also restored her, as some had suggested? (Mr Parker was immune to satire of his sea-bathing place.) Charlotte Heywood, too, after benefiting from Mr Wingfield's services – had suggested sea bathing could more safely take place (doubtless meaning 'still more safely'!) nearer to the shore at high tide. Mr Parker, finding this proposal more acceptable from her than from his brother Sidney, had agreed to shift one of his three bathing machines, by way of trial – but the sharpness of shingle in the new position meant that the handful of visitors who still trusted themselves to the waters preferred not to take off their shoes before reaching the firm sands of low tide.

    Mr Parker was pleased to meet Captain Wentworth (known previously only for his reservations about New Sanditon) when he and Mrs Wentworth called one day to collect little Agnes from the Seminary. Or rather, Mr Parker was pleased to test the quality of the captain's telescope. It proved to be a finer instrument than his own; but neither from the elevated Trafalgar House nor from the last spit of Sanditon sand could he discern... that which he could hardly put into words: the mystery of the tidal wave. Mysterious as to its causes, that is. Mr Parker had no doubt of its Brinshore origin. Even had the direction of the offence been indeterminate, Mr Parker would have seen the offender as likely to lurk in this ...culpable place that he would not normally refer to, let alone visit. But, since the lay of the land prevented telescopic inspection of the settlement – if that was not too grand a name for the place – visit it he must.

He regretted now that the cliff fall had made the upland track inadvisable if not impossible, for he would have preferred to follow the route taken by Mrs Brandon and the other equally disappointing lady from Norland. He had given little thought to these defectors owing to the aquatic drama of Miss Lambe. Now that they entered his head again, he knew – if he did risk the road they had ridden, he would enjoy looking for clues as to what had happened. Wrecked on the road? Carried off by highwaymen? Stolen away by gypsies? Mrs Parker urged caution, to his un-admitted relief. So he agreed to travel tediously inland and out again – the latter part coinciding with the route the ladies would have taken, if they had (as Mr Sidney suggested) looped back to Norland Park. His circuitous journey would take him to Hailsham and almost back to where he had started from, latterly over bad roads – all that Brinshore deserved. Formerly the lack of a bridge over the river Bryn, which necessitated the detour, had afforded Mr Parker a certain malicious satisfaction; Brinshore being thus confirmed in its westerly isolation, cut off from main routes and amenity in general. But today he could not help regretting that his visit to the butt and foil of Sanditon was not more direct and easy. It would take him all day.

In her brother's absence, Miss Diana Parker did her best to replace his excitements and computations with her own: the energies which she devoted to urban illness were, in this abode of health, diverted to domestic busy-ness, with much hemming of curtains aided by Mrs Parker and Miss Susan.

Mr Arthur's support was not to be had: he was as busily engaged in fortifying the Miss Beauforts as if he would defend them from siege. The recuperative Miss Lambe still had Mr Wingfield, Miss Esther and Mrs Griffiths either in attendance, or going to or coming from her day bed, or meeting one another in so doing, with incidental mention of their own assiduity and (in Wingfield's case) professional pre-eminence. Sir Edward's visits had been less constant since the evening when he and Charlotte Heywood had studied Richardson together at the Knightleys.

SPECULATION

Today he was obliged to meet Lady Denham's lawyers, taking along Bosun, his dog, as witness.

A less explicable social gap was caused by the sudden and indeterminate departure of Mr Sidney, who had gone off, apparently without a word to any one. Certainly not to Charlotte, who, finding herself without an escort, took herself to the grandly-named Circulating Library.

Meanwhile, as Agnes Wentworth was required by her parents for a family visit, Mrs Griffiths had pompously granted a little free time to Clara Brereton, whom she intermittently thought of as a possible heiress. Thus it came about that Clara, too, took herself to Mrs Whitby's premises, and there encountered Charlotte.

At first silence had been natural enough as they looked over the shelves and, properly, did not wish to disturb the few other readers. But now those few readers had left and Mrs Whitby had gone round to Mr Stringer's shop. He was a widower and she a widow, so it was likely that she would be absent for some time. A few remarks and a sigh had passed between the two young ladies, but the conversation had fallen away, though neither seemed willing to leave.

'You are more silent with me, Miss Brereton, than you were wont to be. Please forgive me, if that is through some fault of mine.'

'And you, Miss Heywood, for you are the senior, had use to call me Clara.'

'Very well, Clara; so now that we have sensibly adjusted each other's salutations, we are equipped to own in friendly fashion that a most unfortunate awkwardness has arisen. I am convinced that it need on no account come between us; for it is nothing – nothing that cannot be resolved, and quickly too.'

'Perhaps it has, Miss Heywood; but, given (and I thank you for it) your assurance that it is nothing, there remains only an uncertainty that we mean the same thing. I am otherwise very happy.'

'I can't have that otherwise, Clara, nor can I any longer be Miss Heywood to you. Call me Charlotte, please, and then, I believe, this uncertainty, this awkwardness will at once disappear.'

'I'm happy and honoured to do so, Charlotte,' said Clara, her eyes brighter, 'I intend to take these two volumes. What do you think?' (Charlotte gave her opinion) 'In that case I shall look forward to reading them very much – and perhaps we might compare our impressions of the work?'

'By all means, Clara... But, since it seems we may have some time to wait for Mrs Whitby, let us not avoid what has been our first misunderstanding – let us return to the difficulty, only a small one now.'

'To the awkwardness?'

'There need be nothing of that kind, if we look to our precedents,' said Charlotte. 'Let us play the propriety game.'

'THE PROPRIETY GAME,' smiled Clara, 'why, what's that?'

'I meant,' said Charlotte, 'only that we could emulate Mrs Griffiths in her school room – but I'm sorry, Clara, I forgot that you face too much of that –'

'I have faced only a little of the school room as yet. In any case, Miss Agnes is the best sort of child and I have need of practice,' said Clara stoutly.

Seeing that Clara either meant what she said or was happy to proceed as if she did, Charlotte continued: 'Very well, suppose us no longer in Mrs Whitby's, but searching about in the school room for some educational toy – a means of approaching an unapproachable subject (of approaching it irreproachably) – if there is no such means to hand, let us invent one.'

Clara playfully, assented.

'So, Clara; henceforth you shall be My Clara,' said Charlotte. 'If there were such a school room game what would it consist of?'

'Why,' said Clara brightly, 'why, a set of cards or some such, with Topics, you know, or Subjects inscribed upon them and –'

'And it would be called Oracles,' said Charlotte. 'And its necessaries would comprise another set of cards or (as you say, my Clara) some such, with Questions printed upon them, or engraved.

SPECULATION

You think engraved? Let us suppose the set of Subject cards and the set of Question cards complete – engraved nicely by some practised hand. What is our first subject to be?'

Clara looked down and did not answer, playing with her book mark.

'Well, Clara, my Clara, let us suppose that one of our unapproachable Subjects (except by means of these invaluable cards) were to be –'. Charlotte paused dramatically, opened the book she had selected for herself, closed her eyes, pointed a finger, placed it firmly on the page, opened her eyes, looked down, called out the word, she'd found '– you think I dissemble, Clara, but the word, the Subject, is *Gentleman*.'

Clara chose not to reciprocate Charlotte's assumption of girlishness. In doing so – or, rather, in not doing so – Clara became momentarily the senior of the two; was emboldened:
'A Gentleman and his Preference,' she said firmly.

'That is understood, Clara,' said Charlotte, re-establishing control. 'But we need further cards, another pile – let us have them differently coloured. Now these cards might be used to attribute Qualities to the Subject – in this case, A Gentleman.'

'Handsome,' suggested Clara, 'Handsome Gentleman?'

'I think not,' said Charlotte, 'that is both too general a description and one concerning which opinions may differ.'

'A Gentleman Possessing A Fine Reading Voice,' tried Clara.

'Very good,' said Charlotte, 'but I feel that form of words is a shade particular, and not altogether within the spirit of our educational toy. Suppose we settled for *Titled*? You agree, Clara? We may now play the sequence with our invisible cards: Titled-Gentleman and his preference for... we lack something – an Object for his Regard.'

'The *Lady*,' said Clara.

'Very well,' said Charlotte, 'a lady. A *Lady* with the attributes of Twenty Two or a lady with those of Eighteen?'

'Twenty Two,' said Clara, allowing precedence, and preferring (bad though that would be) a positive answer here to a negative one against the lady of eighteen.

'So,' said Charlotte, 'we play the cards: Titled Gentleman Prefers Lady of Twenty Two... We cannot proceed.'

'We need some means,' said Clara keen for the outcome, even were it to be chastening, 'some means to indicate an answer: Yes or No.'

'Yes,' said Charlotte, ' Why don't we add to your *Yes* and *No*, such terms as *Perhaps* and *Doubtful?*'

For a moment Clara pondered – then registered her agreement.

'Very well, Clara,' said Charlotte, 'now put your question to the Oracle.'

'Is it really my turn?' asked Clara doubtfully. Charlotte insisted that it was. Clara sighed. 'So – then, I'll do it: Titled Gentleman Prefers Lady of Twenty Two? That is a query to which the answer would seem to be an indubitable Yes.'

'No,' said Charlotte, 'I believe the honest answer to be Maybe or Doubtful.'

Clara, who had risen, sat down suddenly. She leant forward in pleasure, but then, seeming to see some damaging proviso to the Oracle's answer, drew back again.

Charlotte had no purpose of exercising the power of dubiety; sought clarification:

'So, Clara (you appreciate that this is a topic for inquiry, not a statement): Lady of twenty two Prefers Titled Gentleman. We need an answer don't we? – and at once.'

'I think,' said Clara, 'for you are my best friend, that I can bear the answer – your answer – whatever it is.'

'Why, it's a No, of course, you goose! May I call my dear Clara a goose?'

'Of course, my dear Charlotte.' Clara professed her delight at being a goose; the two ladies resolving to be friends for ever and a day.

Mrs Whitby returned, smiled at the two firm friends, packaged their chosen books, saw them off her premises with a –

'With a sigh,' said Charlotte, 'did you notice Mrs Whitby's sigh?'

SPECULATION

The mention of a sigh in a lady of fifty did not have its intended effect, a smile. Clara sighed – no, she assured her friend, it was sighing of quite a different order from that which had given rise to their colloquy in Mrs Whitby's shop. They talked together as they walked to Mrs Griffiths' school room in the Terrace.

*

The ugly room was empty, for Miss Lambe whom Clara saw merely as an example of Sir Edward's bravery was in her bedroom with Mrs Griffiths; and the Miss Beauforts in the latter's absence were walking with Mr Arthur. Charlotte was struck by what a horrid place the school room was, but Clara – who in any case had seen it enlivened by little Miss Wentworth (and sometimes by Bosun when Sir Edward had visited) was not sure that she deserved better.

Charlotte tried to make a reassuring reply, reassuring to both: 'And, my dear Clara, when I consider your prospects – fine ones – only to find myself thinking of myself, of my own...' Then sought to change the subject. Clara looked at her. For a moment Charlotte did not know why:

'Am I too sighing, Clara?' began Charlotte, 'your look seems to tell me so.'

Clara Brereton blushed and regarded her work:

'*I* have become very used to sighing, Charlotte, and must suppose myself surprised to find I'm not the only soul who breathes not only in but out! – though I cannot help thinking that, unlike others, I give back more in sighs than I take in from the air around me. I can excuse myself only by my fear that I have cause to sigh and shall have more before long.'

'I think you do have reason to sigh,' said Charlotte kindly, but countering exploration, 'yet I fancy any sigh of my own must be at Sanditon's expense. I sometimes think it does not suit me here. But please do not tell Mr Parker that. For you, my dear, things may soon be settled.'

'Whatever happens,' Clara burst out, 'I hope you don't and won't think me grasping or a hypocrite.'

Charlotte began an affectionate word or two, but Clara barely listened, being determined not to lose the gist of her appeal:

'Lady Denham showed me rare favour; but died at an advanced age and was not perhaps the most loveable of great ladies. Should I be given up to grief and prostration? Would it look well or make good sense? Would you, Charlotte, like me better for harrowed looks? Yet I am grateful and shall always remember what has been done for me here not only by Lady Denham herself, but by Mr Parker; by you, dear Charlotte and others – I have tried to resist any display of repining, for fear that what passed for grief might look like regret for lost benefits; might seem an exercise in fixing my face into desolation and dreariness as a suitable mask for the receipt of largesse or the denial of any thing further. There will be nothing further – or very little further, of that I am sure. Why should there be? ... Having said which, I should wish to dissolve, to be any where but Sanditon, leaving you, dear Charlotte, to tell my tale; and the very smallest gap for you alone to notice.'

'You are too severe, Clara,' said Charlotte, smiling, 'upon both yourself and me. You really are. Let us be business-like, describe our situations as we see them, and set down clearly the hazards which we both must face.'

Yet for all her apparent cheerfulness, and that it was she who had made the suggestion, Charlotte could not quite catch her breath.

'Sighing is said to be a sign of being in love,' said Clara tentatively.

'School rooms and sick rooms,' said Charlotte boldly, 'are much the same, don't you think? It might be that I am in need of air. But,' catching herself again in some thing that was not a yawn, 'that is what they say about sighs; what has always been said. So, Clara, in spite of what passes for our education, we have recourse to traditional sayings for the conduct of our affairs. Much as if we were – say, muttering bits of weather lore – like some ploughboy relying on doggerel for the best time to sow.'

SPECULATION

'You are right,' said Clara. 'Where shared experience may be helpful, let it be the experience of you and me, not of a ploughboy. I will make a tapestry and hand it to Sanditon as a parting gift. It shall hang in the lobby of the hotel as a warning of the effects of the air of these parts.'

'You may be right about Sanditon,' said Charlotte, 'but such observations are best put on paper. No need to worry, though, for paper may be torn up, the fragments burnt, and the ashes of those fragments buried.'

Clara assenting, they got themselves pen and ink and sat at a table.

'Let us formally head up our useful document,' said Charlotte. 'What, Clara – for I want you to be the heroine – do you suggest?'

'*Our Sad Fate*?'

'Good, but insufficiently elaborate,' said Charlotte. 'Let us settle for "The Diminishing Prospects and Sad Fate of Two Young Ladies of Sussex" – really, this is excessively girlish – but, if we go through with it, by the end of our inventory we shall either have found out something about ourselves or frightened it away. So, Item. To be an Old Maid, Yes?'

'Yes,' said Clara bravely.

'I'll write it then, thus.   There, is that not a pretty hand?'

'Excellent,' said Clara, smiling. 'Should we leave every thing to the end or try to collect our thoughts as they come to us?'

'I think we should take each point as it occurs. And, if we are to do so, we must begin by asking ourselves whether this first proposition, to be an old maid, is so very shocking a thing,' said Charlotte even more bravely than Clara – for the four years' disparity in their ages meant that Charlotte was considerably nearer to this condition than was the young maid, her friend.

Clara thought back to the late great lady – that other Miss Clara Brereton of fifty years ago:

'Lady Denham was twice married,' she began.

'– And Miss Diana Parker never at all nor likely to be,' replied Charlotte, 'Look on this unpleasing picture –'

Clara shuddered at the remembered dead visage. She could not bring herself to utter an outright condemnation (for all that she wanted Charlotte's good opinion), but was able quickly to leap into antithetical praise of Miss Diana:

'– And on this one, of a lady full of unselfish energy and care for others!'

'So, since there are worse lots than to be useful and benevolent, let us agree not to fear those qualities, if they may be part of such a prospect, then,' said Charlotte, deleting item one.

'Quite correct,' said Clara, 'but do strike out that first item very *thoroughly*. To be an old maid if it leaves open the possibility of being like Miss Diana Parker is not so very unfortunate, but to see old-maidenliness set down in one of our hands, to have it written so, and for someone perhaps to piece together the torn and partially burnt fragments –'

'I agree that being rich and possessing a husband or husbands does not necessarily damage one's character beyond repair,' said Charlotte. 'So, soberly, it would be preferable for us both to marry, if marriages of affection and convenience are to be had; but if not, let us resolve to be useful and cheerful. What else awaits us?'

'Employment,' said Clara as lightly as she could. 'If I'm not too stupid for such a position, I have hoped that Mrs Griffiths, having accepted my present small help, might find me a permanent place.'

'She might do so, for you are, of course, more than equal to any demands which she could make on you. But it would not be an enviable post. Miss Lambe, for instance, is pampered and very typical of a certain class of pupil with whom you would have to deal. You could not but be uncomfortable situated as you would be between Mrs Griffiths and one or more sulky heiresses who must not be offended. Like a cushion you would be pummelled into shape (or out of shape) by either party as a demonstration of their power. What is worse you would be the only means by which the Mrs Griffiths of this world and the heiress-pupils could pummel one another, as they would need to do frequently.'

SPECULATION

'I fear you do not exaggerate the unwholesomeness of the prospect, but I have no other. Set it down.'

'But you do have other prospects. Certainly, you do. Let us not exclude all hope from this our list of fears. We'll write the entry out as "Employment or Fortune". For myself, I have occupation enough at Willingden and think before long I must return there to it.'

Clara looked anxious at this intimation.

'Though it is to be hoped,' said Charlotte, 'that there will be tidings before then from the lawyers about Lady Denham. Ah, yes, that may take years. Well, if it takes years, I'll try to be with you for that necessary interlude – though I cannot extend my stay with Mr and Mrs Parker indefinitely. But when you're a married lady – oh, yes, my dear Clara, I'm sure that marriage – your marriage – will very likely be the first thing that comes between us. And proper that it will be so – we'll stay together until then, Clara. Now, supposing things were not to turn out fortunately for you so soon – supposing there was an interregnum – then you must come with me to Willingden.'

'There is nothing I should like better,' said Clara, touched, 'and I shall not pretend otherwise. I should – and I dare say shall – be happy to accept – fond as I am of Miss Agnes –'

'Oh, she would visit us,' said Charlotte enthusiastically, 'and her mother and father. I like Mrs Wentworth and the captain very much.'

'It would be lovely, though to be with you at Willingden in the circumstances you describe, would be but to postpone the time when I should become the foot-stool of Miss Lambe – or of some creature her successor much resembling her.'

Neither Clara nor Charlotte cared much for Miss Lambe: she was an alien presence on the Sanditon shore and the object of disproportionate attention. Poor Miss Lambe lacked position, friends, and health; but she had money, a frail beauty, and the assiduous Wingfield; and also Sir Edward – perhaps more attentive than his politeness or her indebtedness required.

Charlotte, sensing danger, began to talk of all that Clara and she would do together at Willingden: there was a little horse, for instance, that Mr Heywood would certainly let Miss Clara call her own. But, after a while, the conversation lagged and the eyes of both young ladies were drawn to their two items again: 1st Marriage; 2nd Employment or Fortune.

'As I have said,' began Clara, breaking the silence, or quietness – for the ladies had drawn together, rather than been parted by the absence of talk, 'I should certainly like nothing better than to stay at Willingden, but I have wondered as an alternative, it's no use pretending that I haven't, whether my cousin – our nonsense about a Titled Gentleman aside – mightn't be able to assist me,' she broke off and blushed.

'Sir Edward Denham,' said Charlotte, ' seems to me a very well-meaning gentleman; and, provided he were to inherit –'

'No,' said Clara, 'I mean as he is as the moment; that I should describe to him my difficulties and ask him to – to assist me – in the matter of employment, that is. Nothing further.'

'Ah,' said Charlotte carefully, 'and when you speak of *nothing further*, you mean you would not go so far as to think of putting yourself in his care – of becoming his dependant, his possibly ambiguous "ward" or companion (if only to dismiss the idea) – for that is something unthinkable? Remember that Sir Edward does see himself – or speaks as if he saw himself – as Lovelace; and Lovelace's purpose was to prey upon women.'

Clara flushed, almost angrily, but did not answer. After a short silence Charlotte continued:

'Whatever in the end is the upshot of his undoubted regard for you, for the moment it is safest that you convey to him no more than the sense of esteem – which he himself merits and conveys – of cousin for cousin.'

'Esteem for my cousin,' replied Clara with some bitterness, 'is a form of words that, I confess, does not quite fit, does not quite square with my thoughts. But it will nearly do; so nearly do, that I must thank you without irony for teaching me the phrase. Time and discretion will doubtless enable those outward words and what I can only call inward events to make a more exact accord.'

'Alas, Clara, my caution is a dismal doctrine. That I know, having been myself a victim in my youth; but now I'm older –

which in itself is much to be regretted. When I was your age, dear Clara, I made a big mistake, but I learned – a great deal from it – and very painfully too. So I have given the only advice I can offer.'

'I know you mean well,' said Clara, ' and I am grateful for your concern, but Sir Edward...'
Clara was not sure what she intended to say, so Charlotte spoke for her: 'Sir Edward, being kept on so tight a financial rein by Lady Denham, has never been permitted to learn through small mistakes. I fear, if he were given his head through access of money and power, that an accumulation of previously unmade small errors might manifest itself in some disaster. He is an active and energetic man, rendered ineffectual. His notions are passionate, his designs large and generalised. I cannot help doubting whether fortune, which would enable him to support others, would be seen by him in that light; or even whether it would be conducive to the development of his sensible and manly side.'

Clara had borne all this:

'He is very brave,' she replied simply and stoutly.

'I do not doubt it.'

There was a silence: this time it was a true silence at first rather than a quietness. But the silence returned to a quietness and then the quietness was quite softly broken:

'Clara,' said Charlotte, 'dear Clara, I hope you are not wounded by what I have said.'

'No,' said Clara, 'for I can believe, Miss Heywood –'

'Miss Heywood! After all we have gone through together, Clara, are you going to formalise me into some distant acquaintance or a maiden aunt? We know too much of one another.'

'I can believe only too well, Charlotte ("Charlotte", gladly) that if I knew the state of my heart, I'd choose to be a thousand miles away from Sir Edward's house than go there for sustenance.'

'Yes,' said Charlotte, 'but you need not – should not – strive to be altogether cloistered. Day visits to Miss Esther at the cottage ornée - unless Sir Edward finds a tenant for it – would do very well. And Sanditon House – if he inherits it – would be exactly the place to call, for it is your former home. In Sanditon itself you have many friends. I only ask you to be guarded against a *rich* Sir Edward, if it should come to that: left poor, if he could forget the hurt done him by Lady Denham, he would be a good man.'

Clara looked up, greatly relieved:

'Forgive me, Charlotte,' said she, 'forgive my lingering jealousy.'

Charlotte took her hand: 'Have no fears there, Clara. I said as much in our game, and said it in earnest. Fond as I am of Sir Edward, his opinions and mine run counter, if enjoyably so. I am not in favour of marital bickering and teasing. Besides –'

'Besides, Charlotte?'

'You tell me, my dear, what besides: we know each other's hearts better than we know our own.'

'Let me guess, then, though forgive me if I am far from the mark. In some sense, Charlotte, you have no heart to give.'

'That is true, Clara, for I know you are not accusing me of having a hard heart, albeit sometimes a heavy one.'

'Far from it, Charlotte: you have – as your concern for me has shown – the kindest of hearts.'

Clara is looking at Charlotte: 'the most easily lost of hearts. For all your quick wits, for all your care, you can't keep your heart to yourself. It is plainly visible, when you're in health; which explains why you sometimes seem to fade, almost to grow fainter...'

Charlotte hears the young voice as both outside and within her – making, as it were, comparisons – and feels again for herself, that damaging first love, recollected now, as by someone near to death; as if someone, some dear person, were changing the coverlet, trying to avoid hurting as the invalid has to be turned.

It is only Clara, concerned, chafing Charlotte's hands.

'How kind of you, my dear,' murmured Charlotte. 'I am recovered. From that condition you say some times afflicts me... I cannot but think it is this place, Sanditon, this unhealthy place –'

SPECULATION

'But it has possibilities of health!' said Clara.

'Yes,' said Charlotte, 'and – for you – of love. I do believe that.'

'I know, dear Charlotte,' replied Clara, 'that you would not tell me things which you thought were beyond all possibility. Your friendship is a most happy chance for me, but' – her face falling – 'what lies ahead for you?'

'For me, who knows? Regard perhaps, mutual regard. That happy state, for my head tells me it is a middle way which avoids unhappiness, may be enough. Why should I look for any more than that? Let's now leave well alone: we're done with Topics. Let us return to the record of our transactions.'

So Clara took up a pen and wrote between the title and the blotted-out old maid reference, so as to make it clear that this particular hope depended on that fear:

'Not to be altogether forgotten by persons unnamed.'

She then passed the paper to Charlotte who endorsed the addition, writing at the bottom of the document`:

Agreed. *This paper for secret retention by Miss Cl*r* Br*r*t*n and, subsequently, destruction in the approved manner.*

2

Charlotte Heywood and Clara Brereton returned to the Seminary on the best of terms after their colloquy. No one else was there.

'For the first time,' said Clara, 'this feels like a happy place to be.'

Fortunately she had spoken quietly, for immediately Mrs Griffiths was upon her. The Seminary mistress had returned from being the necessary companion of Miss Lambe – having been replaced by an obliging baronet.

Clara bit her bottom lip bravely when she heard Sir Edward's name mentioned in this connection, which Mrs Griffiths chose to interpret as indicating an unwillingness to work. She therefore began to heap tasks of a menial character upon the young lady.

Charlotte was about to offer to help when Clara's eye – its sparkle dulled – caught hers. It was clear that Clara saw what she had been requested to do by the mistress-in-charge as hers to do alone, for was she not a hired minion? As Mrs Griffiths showed no signs of discomfiture before Clara's friend – simply instructing Clara to get on with what was required – Charlotte had no option but to leave.

As Charlotte walked away with a heavy heart, it crossed her mind – and her heavy heart – to wonder what part Mr Sidney Parker might have played in their game of Oracles. What answer would she have made if Clara had thought to ask a searching question or two? (Clara was young and had played the game with herself centre stage – as heroine.)

Was leaving Clara to sweep the floor like Cinderella the sole cause of her want of spirits, Charlotte asked herself. Or was it the recollection of some thing unsaid and best left unsaid? Her lips moved. 'Over and done with,' she heard herself saying. What was over? Sidney Parker had disappeared – what was that to her? Had his *presence* been so significant, so real, then? Had there not been – for all his conviviality – some awkwardness when he had been present? Some sense that she and he were too many or too few? Some sense that their situation had to do with making up. 'Making-up', not as in reconciliation; nor 'making-up', as in invention; but making-up, in the sense of filling in, augmenting, being a fourth at cards? Making up for an omission. Charlotte felt an anticipatory hurt, flinched inwardly at the new injury she might have seemed to invite; but it was only – only! The old injury that spoke to her, the old mistake.

Mr Sidney Parker and the way they had fallen into of talking to one another – pleasurable in itself – had always carried with it a residue of pain, because of a certain resemblance to what had transpired when she had been so badly mistaken. Charlotte was glad – sad – to find her heart assuring her, convincing her, that it was the reminiscence of things past, the awakening of previous error (though mightn't it have found a new voice with which to torment her?).

Back at Trafalgar House, Charlotte brightened – realised she had made no new mistake, and was stronger for that realisation; was caught up rapidly in Miss Diana Parker's refurbishment. What she, Miss Susan (when not too fatigued) and Mrs Thomas Parker were undertaking was ambitious and they wanted it in place before Mr Parker returned.

'*Not*,' said Mrs Parker with a smile, 'that Thomas will notice whether we have new curtains or old. The salt has got into the others *so* – and they still quite new – that they are good for nothing.'

'No,' agreed Miss Diana with a chuckle, 'though he'd spot soon enough would Thomas, if it were some bran new device – some knick-knackery rod or runner – even if its only purpose was for suspending curtains!'

SPECULATION

All three ladies agreed that once the change had been pointed out to Mr Parker he would be appreciative of their efforts, though not keen to own that salt air could do any thing but fortify and preserve curtaining, a paradigm of its effects upon human pipes and ventricles. All three worked diligently – but the task, even with three pairs of hands (though little Mary occupied half of Mrs Parker's) was taking longer than they had thought. There was no sign of Mr Sidney; and Mr Parker himself was making a long day of it, so they lived in hopes of completing the task before their return.

They need not have hurried. A message arrived shortly by a rider who had risked the cliff-top road, saying that Mr Parker's horse had gone lame, that he had had to make do as best he could in Hailsham, that he had been forced to put up for the night with Squire Hargreaves of Brinshore Hall; also, whatever he had found or hoped to find at Brinshore might detain him further.

Charlotte Heywood had some curiosity about what might have occurred. Had a sea monster been sighted? Had there been a shipwreck? These were girlish matters of speculation which she hoped would restore Clara Brereton's spirits, when they next met.

So, the curtains complete, Charlotte resolved next day to rescue Clara from Mrs Griffiths if she could. Arrived at the schoolroom she found a coach, an excited little girl and friends delighted that Miss Charlotte Heywood had arrived. They had been about to call at Trafalgar House with a view to carrying her off on an excursion.

✱

Old Mr Hargreaves said it was a happy accident that had brought Mr Thomas Parker to his door again… He inquired, as a fellow spirit, about the Parkers' good Old Hall and land. Mr Parker reminded the old gentleman (with little of his usual rhetoric) that he had left and let the family home, and spoke only restrainedly about the glories of the Sanditon sea-bathing place.

Mr Hargreaves said that he could make but little of the speed with which old ways were being set aside, and that he rarely went beyond the bounds of his property. Did not need to do so even to shoe a horse, as Mr Parker would have noted. Not that his horses wore out many shoes, he added; which was why – he said – he had observed little of Brinshore. When pressed, he conceded that there were quantities of 'navigators'. Mr Parker who would have observed ships passing through to Brinshore, had there been any (in spite of the headland), decided that this was a confused old gentleman incapable of speaking less than he knew; and did not press him for more. A little repetitious information, however, continued to be dispensed:

'Yes,' said Mr Hargreaves,' I don't mind telling you that – very busy, the navigators.'

Mr Parker took his leave as early as he could from Mr Hargreaves, purposing to call in on his return and perhaps spend a further night at the hall. Leaving by the stable-yard, as directed, he came upon an overgrown lane which took him onto a back road which led him directly to Brinshore.

Mr Parker's first reaction was to rub his hands at what he saw. Nothing medicinal: no bathing machines, no apothecary, no marine equivalent of a Pump House. The place had a stupid air of thoughtless health, whereas he had striven according to the best precedents to establish a community dependent on invalidism and hypochondria.

Mr Parker was relieved that such was the case. As he peered at a distant building site he thought he could make out a pile of gravel chippings and a heap of slabs which he irritably assumed to be the very material which had delayed the work on Wellington Crescent and thereby lost him the party from Norland. But he took comfort in his mental picture of Sanditon as against the prospect before his eyes. Brinshore – whatever its malignant power of inducing tidal waves – still had none of the essential attributes of a seaside watering-place; no cliffs, no clear views, no uncluttered sand.

In short, Brinshore had few scenic advantages compared with Sanditon and was unlikely to acquire any now save through some unprecedented cataclysm: but as yet the Downs showed no signs of filling in Brinshore Haven with molten chalk to transform its Dutch-ness into commanding heights. Such were the thoughts of Mr Parker, as he strode diagonally down a steep shingle incline – the banks of the Bryn at high water – in search of its bore or tidal wave. Had there been any thought of converting this stretch of water to a place of pleasant resort, Mr Parker was pleased to be assured that there would be many difficulties in doing so.

He noted with a malicious sense of confirmation: first the mud at low water; then, that the long and twisting track to the hazardous ford had to be cleared of shingle after each tide; that low-lying though the spot was, great mounds of cobbles and banks of shingle cut out all marine views until one was right at the water's edge. But, when Mr Parker did on this occasion come within sound and sight of the conjunction of sea and river (being of a mind to rebuke it for recent Brinshore-like tricks), something very strange came upon his ear and eye.

Men were at work at the river mouth, shovelling great quantities of cobbles into barrows, pushing them when loaded along planks, emptying them and returning for more; others were driving stakes into cleared areas; yet others, excavating for foundations. Stripped tree-trunks, buttressed with cobbles and mortar, stood up to their ankles, up to their knees, up to their shoulders in the sea.

Mr Parker was jubilant: Brinshore had gone mad, had run amok; was destroying itself in disfiguring the only distinctive quality it possessed, its frontage onto the River Bryn, by erecting some kind of ridiculous boundary fence; growing a hedge, as it were to cage in the wild birds – or, to keep to itself its damaging tides and currents! Then a dark suspicion came to Mr Parker with gloomy menace: here was a clear and distinct change in the contour of Brinshore's coastline at the very time when neighbouring Sanditon's civilised sea departed from its decorum. Was this wall of timber, then, less a device on the part of Brinshore to keep its wretchedness to itself than a ruse to divert dangerous waters, heavy seas, in blameless Sanditon's direction? – With despoiling effects not only on its still lagoon but in swirling away its impeccable sands to leave shingle in their stead.

His brother Sidney, who had travelled abruptly to the county town, with worries of his own and a commission for Mr Thomas, could have told him more. He had rapidly picked up news which (though not of the best) he was keen to communicate. He hoped the speed with which he was acting would enhance his brother's view of him. He had need of some such because of other emerging matters which were likely to lose him that gentleman's good opinion. Having missed Thomas in Hailsham, he rode like fury to Sanditon, found fine new curtains but no Thomas Parker nor Charlotte Heywood; whereupon, having said enough to perturb the ladies, he leapt upon a fresh horse and got it to pick a dangerous way over the cliffs to Brinshore.

Meanwhile Thomas Parker's inquiries of the labourers were proving unsatisfactory. He could get no more from them than they were building a breakwater or jetty: so much his eyes could have told him. As to why they were building a breakwater or jetty (information which his eyes could not supply), the workmen did not know, or did not choose to tell: they were simply glad of the task, for the payment was good and the work no harder than that to which they were accustomed as canal builders or fishermen.

Mr Hargreaves had spoken in puzzles, in so far as he had spoken at all, about what was going on under his nose, so Mr Parker's best recourse proved to be the keeper of a little shop who knew not much, but (Mr Parker proving a good customer) was more than willing to tell what little he did. The word 'harbour' was mentioned, 'seaport' even. Mr Hargreaves – did the squire, then, dissemble? – was said to be well pleased: money had come from someone or somewhere; work was progressing; a road was to be

SPECULATION

cut to meet the jetty – and that was all the information with which he could oblige. He only wished it were more, and thanked Mr Parker warmly for the purchase of unnecessary goods.

Mr Parker returned to the jetty and spent further time walking up and down measuring timbers with the eye, guessing at the total wages for the labour, making rough and ready calculations for the cost of the materials – and rougher and readier ones concerning volumes of displaced water, reduction of flow to soughs or outlets, pressures per square inch, sustainable water-jets and the like.

At midday he rode inland by the main road in search of refreshment and encountered further droves of navigators or 'navvies' moving to fresh work positions or seeking to be hired. So much for Hargreaves' stories about seafarers! Had the old fellow's wits begun to turn? If he was still capable of having a purpose, was it senile amusement ? Or crafty concealment?

After a good lunch and talk which appeared to confirm that Hargreaves knew something – indeed, had a stake in what was going on – Mr Parker resolved not to return to the old gentleman's hall. Instead he sought something to calm his mind; turned to his practice of making comparisons favourable to Sanditon. Climbing away from the estuary's cobbles and shingle, his eye was on a level with what passed for the Brinshore beach. Who could possibly want to visit Brinshore? *Floreat Sanditon* and the Devil take Brinshore, for no one else would want it.

This comforting observation was interrupted by a sudden opening of the doors of the one decent house on the Brinshore front. From them emerged a great many little children – seemingly none of them in need of saline restoratives – who ran in an unregulated manner onto the foreshore carrying little nets and balls and scullery shovels. Attendants followed carrying kitchen chairs for the two ladies, evidently their mothers.

Mr Parker took off his hat (not out of politeness but so as to escape observation) and crouched below the bank of shingle, puzzled at the behaviour of these people. Taking a glass from his pocket, he observed them more closely. It was, he saw with great irritation, the Mrs Brandon and Mrs Ferrars who had left Sanditon so quickly, so rudely, so hazardously by the cliff top track.

His worst fears were confirmed. He had been sufficiently confident that they were going to return to Sanditon at what had been their originally expected day to leave their names upon the Visitors' List. He had preferred to believe they had taken the cliff track merely to save turning the carriages round, then re-joining the road which would bring them back to Norland Park. Their behaviour was, and felt like, treachery: compounded by the fact that the cloaked man observed in Wellington Crescent whom he had supposed to be a hired protector or outrider now began to take on the identity of an accomplice. Mr Parker's irritation at these considerations was augmented by the fact that the party was evidently enjoying itself at Brinshore.

Life at Sanditon was dedicated to other higher-minded purposes, to be sure, but some of the pleasure of the children, he had to admit, had an unfortunate resemblance to that which is gained in being usefully occupied. The desert neatness of Sanditon's strand could not offer the ragbag of flora and fauna which these children and their mothers seemed to find so instructive in the untidy rock pools and swathes of seaweed which were the principal features of the sea edge here – as, indeed, Mr Parker's pamphlet had scathingly indicated. The tide wrack of Sanditon was minimal – hence the purity of its medicinal waters. Who would want to sup such a sea-porridge as would be spooned from this murky basin?

Yet these people had come to Brinshore and had not yet left it. Moreover, someone, an accomplice, had conducted them here. He thought hard about the muffled man who had whisked the party away from Sanditon. Thinking back to that figure, that *muffled figure*, Mr Parker was suddenly presented with such another.

As he watched, the mounted figure – *un-muffled* – drew nearer, nearer; then, dismounting, approached the ladies; a figure which resembled, indeed exemplified, indeed incorporated, not only the mysterious accomplice, but more than all or any of that: this man was, as the villain of Wellington Crescent had been, Mr Robert Ferrars, whom Mr Parker (having had dealings with Norland Park)

SPECULATION

knew by sight; and as one who had at his disposal financial resources which outreached any thing available to himself at Sanditon.

That Robert Ferrars wanted to spend time at Sanditon's rival resort was bad enough, that he might have some financial stake in the strange Brinshore construction – while it would explain much – would be far worse. Yet if so – or even if not so – it seemed unlikely even to Thomas Parker that the sole purpose of so much labour would be to cause freak waves at Sanditon. And if Ferrars was investing in Brinshore why would he back a Brinshore causeway to nowhere rather than Sanditon's handsome water front? Was he biding his time? Waiting perhaps until he had a new turnpike ready and complete? A road which might isolate Sanditon – which would remain approachable only by twisty inland lanes or the crumbling edge of a cliff.

As it was, even now, even with the cliff top route recognised as dangerous, even with its slow and twisty approach roads, Brinshore was attracting more than its fair share of visitors – and attracting them at Sanditon's expense.

More people were arriving! It was as if the tidal wave had driven people away from Sanditon; driven them here to Brinshore – though, plainly, a pair of horses had effected the conveyance of, of – his telescope answered him: why, Miss Charlotte Heywood (by all that was disappointing!) and a companion whom he assumed was Mrs Wentworth of whom Charlotte had spoken.

The carriage drew up outside the Brandon-Ferrars house. Another child was added to the happiness on the beach, all staying together for a little while. Then, the adults left the children with their attendants to care for them, gathered together for a little discussion, walked into the house together, and closed the door.

Mr Parker, much agitated, but glad to be able to emerge from his station unobserved by adult eyes, left the shingle bank, retrieved his horse and his petty purchases. He was both disturbed and confused by what he had seen. The only consolation as he passed areas cleared for new construction work was the hope that his brother Sidney might have better news to report from his inquiries in the county town. If not, then it would be the Parker family's turn to be leached by the law – a whole clutch of lawyers would be needed to protect Sanditon.

*

The journey had given time to reflect. It would be difficult, he conceded, to prove that Brinshore's waters and currents had begun to impinge upon what was territorially, aquatically, Sanditon's; and, even if this could be done, Mr Parker was not sure that it would constitute trespass – and, if it did, might he not be placed in the absurd position of taking out a writ against the very waves? It was the sort of pitiably impossible pass to which an unscrupulous lawyer could reduce an honest man. He did know that it would cost more money than he possessed; more than he could find guarantors for.

Money: the Denham inheritance became of new importance to Mr Parker. There was money due – for someone. For whom? Sir Edward? Parker felt this gentleman might be malleable, gullible.

It was as if Lady Denham, who in her life had rendered all those immediately about her mean, was now from the grave extending her grip to include generous Mr Parker. He needed money. True, he wished to spend money rather than hoard it, but in order to get it, he would hoard if necessary. His eye gleamed greedily as he thought how he needed money. Sir Edward must inherit and he, Thomas Parker, must work upon the baronet's bounty. It would be for Sir Edward's benefit too; he already had a small stake in Sanditon – let it be a larger one! Best not the law, if other means could be employed. Better more manly measures: tear down their jetty? Mr Parker was too law-abiding – besides they would build it up again and a reputation for Sussex brawls would not enhance the reputation of Sanditon. No: he became possessed with the idea of jetties and counter-jetties of his own. They would serve to spill back the rough waves and associated mud and shingle whence they came.

SPECULATION

✱

Meanwhile, Elizabeth and Fanny had discovered that Charlotte Heywood and Clara Brereton were out for the day with Mrs Wentworth. They had called instead at Sanditon House, but had left when Mr Wingfield arrived to attend to Mr Woodhouse; this to the surgeon's evident chagrin: a lady as influential as Mrs Darcy might have provided valuable testimony. The day being fine, the two ladies elected to walk back to Wellington Crescent and to call at the Hotel on their way. Several letters awaited them. There were some literary matters for Fanny to deliberate upon and for Elizabeth a package with enclosures from Longburn, the family home where Mr and Mrs Bennet still lived. They sat outside under an awning to consider their correspondence.

'Certain booksellers have in mind the possibility,' said Fanny, looking up, 'that the work of the late Miss Austen might be included in the British Novelists series. I hope this may come to pass, though some will say that the idea comes either too soon or too late. Were you a subscriber to her novels?'

'I'm afraid not,' said Elizabeth, ' though I believe I did some years ago have one or more from the circulating library. If the works are still available, though, I would be interested in seeing them...' Her voice indicated less attention, with no intention or consciousness of impoliteness. Suddenly she blurted out:

'Here's news – indeterminate news of my sister Mary. Please forgive my self-absorption: my father's handwriting has in his age become crabbed. And what promises to be a very dull missive from Mary herself. Jane and I were always close, as you know. Perhaps we did not give enough time or thought to Mary. Whatever the reason she took to earnestness and speaks in apophthegms. I regret to say that I cannot bring myself for the moment to complete the reading of what she has to say,' concluded Elizabeth as if to offer her friend her whole attention, fearing Fanny sensed some rebuff.

Fanny, though she had little direct sense of her own importance, always had things more important than herself to show; was sometimes a little quick to show them:

'Isn't there,' she replied, 'some implication in Mary's practice for us all? The moral commonplaces we tread among (and tread so for our own good) may be found in the pinafore-primers and educational toys used by the Mrs Griffiths of this world, to choose an example close at hand. And they make their mark upon us. Have you seen – excuse me – these, or this sort of thing?'

Elizabeth stayed from her correspondence, happy enough to cast her eye over what Fanny had to show: Mr Bennet's handwriting was exacting and, if there were to be any surprises amidst the probable dulness of Mary's communication then their dénouement would be a keener pleasure if deferred.

'These engraved cards, Elizabeth,' said Fanny, 'comprise – some might think incongruously – one hundred sentiments derived from the prolific writer we were discussing earlier; Mr Richardson, whom Miss Austen (if I recall right) preferred to all others.'[†]

Elizabeth touched the smooth cards which felt cool to her finger-ends. They had such headings as *Pride*, *Prejudice*, and *Persuasion*. She glanced at front and back; pausing at the paradox on the Pride card about 'haughtiness in submission'. Darcy's unwilling first declaration of his love for her came to mind. She smiled at the ridiculousness of the figure he had cut, at the recollection of his 'in vain have I struggled', but winced at her own prepossession in favour of worthless Wickham, which had much to do with her initial condemnation of Darcy as suitor.

Fanny, noticing that some thing had caught her attention, leaned forward in expectation, but Elizabeth had no more to say than that the cards were pretty, if old-fashioned.

'Thank you, Elizabeth,' said Fanny, putting them back in their cover. 'I confess that I like receiving such things in the post – though possibly I overrate their significance.'

[†] There is only one footnote placed by Jane Austen herself in the published novels. It refers to Samuel Richardson. Mine does so similarly. See items 2 and 4 of end notes.

SPECULATION

Here Elizabeth murmured some thing supportive, at which Fanny continued brightly: 'There is a suggestion that the cards, together with other old papers might comprise a small educational volume, partly historical in character with some reference to Mr Locke's views. These playing cards, now, are things of some ingenuity. Their various maxims, which have to be got by heart, have (I fancy) some bearing on the books of Miss Austen. I wish she were at our elbow to ask whether she played with them as a child. But since she appears not to be, I doubt I shall undertake the work, knowing nothing of children, or of their needs.'

'While I,' said Elizabeth ' know every thing there is to know – about *daughters*.' Then recovering her countenance, 'But I must not repine. I have been reminded in reading this letter from my old home, how my friend the former Charlotte Lucas died in childbed some little while ago. A fate I have so far survived. Miss Lucas, I'm afraid,' looking down to her letter again, 'made an unhappy match with an egregious clergyman called Collins, a distant relative of my family.'

Elizabeth was still trying to establish the relationship between the various enclosures and to separate the more legible sheets from the less. She began again:

'So much for an obscure preface from my father – now my sister Mary's letter begins. She and he seem to have purposed that I should read what they have to say in a particular sequence, for neither of them – while asserting that there is a point to this bulky communication; an important point, indeed – quite manages to come to it; my dear father going over ground about the family entail, a matter of regret still for him, but one to which by now he surely might have become habituated.

So back to poor Mary. She would have *liked* to become a governess, she says. Send her your packs of cards and primers, Fanny! This ambition to join the tribe of outcasts – the unfortunate Clara Breretons – seeking to instruct and,' with a shudder, 'restrain the manikins and ladykins to whom they are indebted for their daily bread has been rendered impracticable by good fortune (to her chagrin!) by – as she reminds me here – the Bingleys and Darcys who etc etc , dutiful stuff –'; at which point Elizabeth dropped the

141

letter and wiped her eyes, whether from grief of pleasure or some combination of the two was not clear to Fanny.

'What's this paper I am being led to? An ominously familiar hand and style!'

Elizabeth read out loud the following:

'Mrs Darcy, Madam,

'Honoured lady, I trust you will not set this communication aside without its thorough perusal, since it comes to you through the medium of your worthy sister Miss Mary Bennet. That I, your kinsman, have not elected to address you on an important matter except via Miss Bennet is indicative of the distance between us, and makes no reference to your treatment of a former sincere regard, as that was many years ago. Since which time my wife is dead and you have become in law, though not in blood, niece of Lady Catherine de Bourgh. You will, I trust, recognise and respect my continued legitimate concern for your family's fortunes and property.

'It is with such self-effacing motives and personal satisfaction that I request your felicitations for an impending event. Miss Mary Bennet conjoins such intellectual distinction as can be achieved by the fair sex with a proper and chaste attachment to my own person. Miss Bennet has in consequence agreed to become the second Mrs Collins, from whom I hope to obtain...'

'Oh dear, oh dear,' interpolated Elizabeth, 'here's the rub:

'...the son and heir which was denied me by the unfortunate demise of Charlotte Collins, your former friend, who expected to hear from you more often, but feared you had become proud.

SPECULATION

'I bear no person malice. Mr Bennet understands that there are certain property benefits as a consequence of the union, though on Mary's part it is a love match, and one in which mind seeks mind.

Yours &c
Wm Collins'

Elizabeth, caught between wince and chuckle, returned to the point in her sister's letter where the necessity of reading the one from Collins had intervened. She read on quietly, then handed to Fanny the closing words from her father which she had slowly made out.

Fanny held the sheet close to her eyes:

'So Collins is to be my son-in-law in the end! The man's an ass, but since he takes Mary off my hands, then it seems all's fairly done. It grieves me still that on my death he'll inherit – though he would have done so in any case – that he'll come and put his feet under my table – the entail, you know, is no more congenial than it ever was. But mercifully nothing can happen while I'm here to see. I mind much less that his son, if he and Mary should have one, will in due course succeed such a father. This child will be my grandson, your nephew, after all – so great things may be expected of him. Our family doesn't seem to produce lads, does it? But perhaps this time will be right for you, dear Lizzy.'

✱

Mr Parker had worked himself into his habitual good humour by the time he got back to Trafalgar House and, having soothed Mrs Parker ('Sidney, my dear, seems to have spent the day missing, but he has little else to occupy his time and will be none the worse for it

– and should he have no news for me, he'll find I have some for him'), was about to read to his wife and sister a pamphlet or short prospectus which he had drafted when the Wentworths appeared at the door with Charlotte Heywood.

'Excuse me, sir, she said pleasantly, 'I have been taken to a place where I did not intend to go without your permission –'

'You mean Brinshore,' said Mr Parker, pleased with her frank disclosure, but a little shame-faced about his own peeping and peering at the company there, 'Why, my dear young lady, you shall go wherever you want. But I hear certain things are afoot at that benighted settlement; in consequence of which, I make the following proposals. He cleared his throat and read:

> '"To bring Art to the aid of Nature, a protective boom or jetty to be constructed to the west of Sanditon, at a cost to the community of approximately – "

'(which has yet to be determined, you appreciate) –

> '"to enable that favoured but select sea-bathing place called Sanditon to enjoy, as its invulnerable right, the smoothest tidal water on this fair coast. Mr Wingfield, one of the foremost medical men of Sussex, is in daily attendance and can attest to the restorative power of sea-water taken from this tranquil foreshore...

'(Then a little something to the effect that unprincipled detractors who, through envy, speak of a drowned lady, do so out of malice and shall answer for it.)

> '"The proposed jetty to afford a healthful promenade at the end of which the breezes will be more truly those of the ocean itself than from any existing head-land shaped by nature's hand alone. A rustic bridge will span the chine; high levels will be linked with low; there will be a covered walk or Colonnade below the cliff and – here – by the jetty, a low dam or sluice to withdraw water from each high tide and retain it conveniently during low water."

'What think you of that, Miss Heywood? I already have working drawings in process. Trafalgar House, after all, took shape from just such sketches as those – that is fact enough.'

SPECULATION

Charlotte, though surprised at the reference to Miss Lambe's bathing, recognised this flight of fancy as all too clearly as characteristic of Mr Parker. Concerned for its effect upon Mrs Parker, she replied:

'The project is imaginative, sir, but – if I'm not mistaken – not an easy one for a private gentleman to carry out. Forgive me, I may be mistaken. I know little of such matters.'

'You're not mistaken,' he chuckled, 'you're not mistaken. But I fancy, with the coadjutor I have in mind, Sanditon will be a nonpareil. Though, as is only fair, there will still be room in the enterprise for the small investor. If your respected father, Mr Heywood, now, were to soften his insistence on working back his income into his existing property, then – but I fear from your look that you are not of my party in this matter. No, Sanditon will not refuse to accommodate, for instance, Sir Edward's mite – or his main, should he prove to be Lady Denham's heir.'

'Sir Edward,' said Charlotte carefully, 'with his feeling for unfettered waves and breezes will doubtless be able to represent those visitors to Sanditon who enjoy good health –'

'– As distinct from my sisters,' replied Mr Parker who, having worked himself into good spirits, refused to be shaken out of them, 'who, some say, enjoy *bad* health!'

The two ladies referred to barely looked up from their hemming useful curtain remnants: the modern seaside house having such quantities of windows overlooking the ocean (unlike fisherman's cottages which, with the sagacity of their species, turn their backs upon it) as to provide salvageable sections un-soured by the sea.

'But my point, Mr Parker, is that I am not sure,' said Charlotte, 'that Sir Edward would wish the ocean to be tamed (as it might seem to him) to the extent envisaged. Wildness and solitariness have become very fashionable.'

'Ah,' said Mr Parker, 'but it would only *seem* to be tamed. For those who like the elements wild, the wildness could be enjoyed with increase in actual safety, while those who like them safe could take comfort in their being so, no matter how wild they appear.' Charlotte could not altogether follow Mr Parker's line of thought, but spoke briefly of the dangers of damaging the seclusion which Sanditon afforded.

No, Mr Parker said – but with less conviction than hitherto – he did not want Sanditon to become another Scarborough, but he did want it to have a rustic bridge and a jetty – had Miss Heywood not heard talk of the proposed iron *Pier* at Brighton? – and an oceanic lake and a colonnade – and all would be managed so as to please everybody – and no, it would grow to a point where the size was 'just right' and not beyond that mark. All that was needed was the backing – and was Miss Heywood quite sure that Mr Heywood might not be chagrined at being omitted from the chance to join the speculation? Well, no matter, it would not be Sanditon's loss, for – with the vast wealth of his principal (he was not yet prepared to divulge his name) – Sanditon was fully provided for, no matter whose fortunes were made or undone by the Denham inheritance.

But then Mr Parker began to fret: Where was his brother Sidney? Why had he not returned? Yes, no doubt Sidney had been put to some inconvenience by having missed his brother in Hailsham – he gathered – and then because of foolhardy riding across the cliffs, while he himself took the inland route – a tedious journey, but one which he would choose again in like circumstances. Nothing would persuade him otherwise.

Nothing but his own enthusiastic impatience. For, when by the next morning there was neither sight of Mr Sidney nor any message from him, Mr Parker leapt on his horse and, ignoring the pleas of his frightened wife and sister, departed for Brinshore by the cliff-tops; where he arrived in a short space of time.

✱

At Brinshore he saw Sidney soon enough – in the inn-yard, taking his leave of Robert Ferrars. Mr Parker allowed that gentleman to depart, then confronted his brother with a concentrated anger, which derived from the depredations of Robert Ferrars, from

SPECULATION

Brinshore, from tidal waves, from mishaps in Hailsham, from lack of news overnight, from grandiose schemes the morning after, from lack of money, from dead Lady Denham, from their unnamed powerful coadjutor.

'You villain,' cried Thomas Parker. 'You have deceived me. What is it that you have been keeping back from me, sir?'

Sidney Parker hung his head, then, recovering himself:

'I confess, brother, that I *have* withheld something from you. I could not help doing so, for the honour of a lady was concerned – and remains so.'

'Honour of a lady? Which lady? Miss Heywood is, as you know, under my protection. I meant to have a word with you about freedoms in her company, but thought them of no more significance than Sir Edward's foolishness – besides, she seemed in command of herself. What would you have me say to her father? Have you been indiscreet?'

Sidney Parker reflected for a moment before being able to reply:

'Indiscreet, yes; Miss Heywood, no – or, I trust not. I hope and believe she understood the basis of our discourse. I'm sorry, Thomas, but you'll oblige me if I'm not required to name the lady. Much previously hung upon her incognito, some thing of that remains still.'

Mr Parker would not be satisfied with so little of the story, so Sidney was pressed into continuing:

'Perhaps foolishly, I acted as a witness to Lady Denham's will – I know of one other person involved, a lawyer's clerk, now dead. No, I do not know where it is to be found. No, I do not know whether it still exists. Nor do I have the least idea of its contents.

'I came to realise that the lady with whom I have an understanding was being tacitly threatened by Lady Denham: there were questions of residence, inheritance, lawyers' entanglements. Lady Denham knew only too well that I was short of money and relished the contrast between my pecuniary want and her own carefully-guarded superfluity. Because of what she insisted on calling the fee (always a derisive word with her ladyship) for my signature, she at one and the same time took power over me and made it clear (not that I had any claim – but she enjoyed clarifying my position) that, as a witness, I could not derive any benefit from the document; and made it clear that any wife of mine – no, sir, I have none – would similarly be precluded.'

Mr Parker evinced surprise and some impatience at what he was being told and what he was not being told, but urged Sidney to finish his account.

'I grant that this was ill-judged, but Lady Denham had another hold over me –'

'– involving the lady.' supplied Mr Parker.

'As you say, sir,' said Sidney. 'Lady Denham lent me money which I was willing to accept whatever her conditions. Indeed, she offered me money, having heard something of my dilemma – you knew nothing of it, Thomas – nor, I do believe – did any one of your household. However, Lady Denham as the great lady of the district, – not being the pleasantest of great ladies – had her spies, and was always fully informed of all that transpired. So, yes, I borrowed money from her – I had pressing need of it – but that, sir, is by the by, all's paid back. I could not approach you, sir, for I knew your own resources were extended because of the work at Sanditon. That, sir, is all I can tell and, I trust, every thing you need to know.'

Mr Parker looked more cheerfully on his brother:

'Thank you for finally taking me into your confidence. It might have been sooner. Provided I have your repeated assurance that Miss Heywood is in no way touched on by these transactions, you've no need to say any thing further about the present lady – or, indeed, your late pressing need for money: that wasn't some other lady – yet another – was it, you dog?'

No answer being forthcoming, Mr Parker dropped his waggish tone, but continued:

'I can see – beside the matter of the will – that here's another reason why you've kept these matters close. I mean what might have become an acknowledged understanding, which circumstances have prevented you from owning. Is that the situation?

SPECULATION

Sidney nodded.

'Because you had an encumbrance, is that it? But you say you have no encumbrance of that kind now? And you assure me – let's be clear about this – that the understanding you refer to is definitely not with Miss Heywood.'

'You have that assurance already: there is this much understanding between us only, that I have enjoyed her company in company – no more than that.'

'So, I am at peace with Mr Heywood of Willingden, then – even if I have no strong hope that he will venture any of his capital on Sanditon's behalf, though we are corresponding on this point. Talking of which – for I see you have avoided this issue which was my starting point – what have you to say to me, sir, about your discussions with Mr Ferrars at – indeed, I suspect, *on the subject of* Brinshore? What is this lurer-away of visitors to you, sir? You'd see Sanditon sink beneath the waves, would you, and transfer your loyalty to this ragbag enterprise?! If so, I am outraged by your behaviour – when I had supposed you to be engaged in sounding out that principal personage whom we do not name –'

'Hold hard, Thomas,' said Sidney, 'there is an adequate explanation also for this matter. Hear me out.'

How was it possible that Sidney Parker could account for his apparent consorting with the enemy, Robert Ferrars; when Thomas had supposed him to be with moneyed associates in the county – additionally urgent now that Sanditon needed to counter all the strange developments at Brinshore?

But Mr Parker did not wait for any answer, piling on further questions and querying observations. Receiving no answer – for Sidney did not know where to begin – he contrasted his brother with Charlotte:

'*Miss Heywood* was very frank with me,' he began, with a dark look.

'She's an amiable lady with many good parts,' replied Sidney.

'Come,' said Mr Parker, 'less of your counterfeit courting. I remember our old father having to talk to you about some such thing, don't I – don't we both? But, as I was saying, Miss Heywood was frank with me and I bear *her* no grudge for visiting this place. I assume she travelled with Miss Brereton and Mrs Wentworth?'

Sidney grumbled about Thomas's impropriety in invoking their father's memory, but agreed on the circumstances of Charlotte Heywood's journey.

'So far so good,' said Mr Parker, 'but what I want to know is – and, yes, I agree not to refer to what happened so many years ago again; yes, to stick to the here and now...But what the devil,' said Thomas, ' was Robert Ferrars doing at Brinshore?'

Sidney understood he was a business associate of Hargreaves.

'How can Ferrars associate himself with a man who seems not to know whether he's coming or going: I wouldn't trust Hargreaves to know the time of day. Or does Ferrars believe the old fool does know what he's at?'

Sidney had no information on that topic, but feared that Hargreaves might prove to be an old fox.

'And all these works and excavations?' waving his arms, 'Who's behind them? '

'Who, indeed,' said Sidney, 'who's a manufacturer with a mint of money?'

Thomas looked dashed: "Then Hargreaves maybe does know what he's saying?'

'Maybe he does,' said Sidney and – having bided his time – told all that he knew of the matter; conveniently confirming much of his brother's surmises about Mr Hargreaves, about Robert Ferrars – and the great manufacturer whose name they continued to leave unspoken.

All men like to be proved right, Mr Thomas Parker more than most, so what might otherwise have been construed as depressing news from Sidney restored him to Thomas's good opinion, and Thomas to good humour. Mr Sidney was slapped on the back, Thomas declaring that he *knew* it, and that Sidney was a good fellow in spite of every thing.

SPECULATION

But Sidney, hitherto too caught up with what he had supposed to be discovery of his amatory dispositions, was able now to give chapter and verse for a major revelation. He had learned by talking guardedly in the county town to those who know about these matters that, yes, Robert Ferrars, and – yes – in his fumbling way Hargreaves, and - yes - the great manufacturer (whom he now referred to as 'RH') were in – or out – of this together.

'What do you mean, Sidney, by this in-or-out?' cried Thomas.

'As I understand their position,' said Sidney, 'they are interested in investing in developments hereabouts. The question is whether for industry or art, Brinshore or Sanditon –'

'Art, too,' said Thomas, 'has its utility – though I cannot see that industry has any beauty. Besides, haven't they enough money for both? But come, Sidney, the situation is very different from what I supposed. Here's my hand, sir. I am delighted that you and Mr Ferrars parted on such good terms. We must speak with him further. I am even pleased that you are committed – at last – to some respectable lady: I'll keep my guess as to her identity to myself. But I must speak to Sir Edward – and even Miss Brereton in case Lady Denham's will should be found and prove favourable to them! At least – thanks to you – I know that the document exists.'

'We do not know that, Thomas, for Lady Denham was contrary enough to have destroyed it. Or to have produced a sham; to have made me put a supposed counter-signature on a piece of fine white paper with nothing written on it. It was folded under so that if her signature really was above mine it was invisible to me – and I dared not ask to see it. All this to show the power she had over me. But I am very glad that you and I are friends again.'

'Of course we are – we need to stick together in times like these. I shan't say anything to Hargreaves, for he doesn't know what he's up to half the time – and the other half, he does. That makes him dashed difficult to deal with. But Mr Heywood now, I'd like to put some advantages in his way – for if Miss Heywood doesn't marry she'll need to be looked to indefinitely, won't she?'

Sidney looked a little abashed at this observation, but made no comment upon it.

'Let's get back to Trafalgar House, then, Sidney...'

And they rode off: Thomas making excitable references to Robert Ferrars, as the one gentleman with assured resources, coupled with – to calm himself – a series of time-will-tells; which animation made Sidney fearful of their safe passage above the cliffs, but both horses proved sure-footed.

3

Have events taken a predetermined course? Had they ever promised different? Sidney Parker, leaving Sanditon with apparent urgency, had returned anti-climactically – safely, albeit with an altered manner towards, and noticeable by, Charlotte Heywood.

She had come to Sanditon almost heart-restored – her early, hopeless attachment securely in the past – had her interchange with Mr Sidney aided or hindered that restorative process? A prudent young lady, profiting by an early mistake, Charlotte had guarded against any awakenings of any thing like her first love, her great mistake. Even if she were to learn to think of herself in that regard again – or, crucially, to attach such a thought about herself to some other person, then – though she might stray into error – it would not merely be a repetition of what had already occurred.

She knew that a warmth about the heart carried with it the possibility of chill – and the more exclusive the warmth, the greater the danger. Charlotte was not a chilly young lady: some such warmth she had recently detected in herself. But it was not a warmth attributable to any one person.

She felt it with Clara Brereton; had felt it in Sidney Parker's apparent seconding of her thoughts (and the sense that something was being withheld: she had only misjudged the nature of what was unspoken between them). She recognised the warmth (with a chill beginning to predominate) in her increasing anxiety for her father, for she had learned that he had, after all, been approached by Mr Parker about investing money in Sanditon and was not certain that the proposition had been dismissed out of hand.

Mr Thomas Parker she had known for the enthusiast that he was from the first, but he had begun to bear down upon her spirits, to weary her; as she feared his excitable communications were bearing down upon Mr Heywood. Mr Parker's character and fortune were so bound up with Sanditon that, with its development at a critical point, some diminution of his scruple was not to be wondered at.

The Parker family being engaged in some further discussion about money, and Clara Brereton in the school room, Charlotte had only her thoughts for company. Her thoughts about the Parkers: Mr Thomas Parker, Mr Sidney Parker...and that other brother who began to put aside his invalidism and to spread for the first time his chubby wings. Mr Arthur, who had at first seemed merely foolish and gross, was now all single-minded devotion to Miss Beaufort.

Which of his two brothers, then, did Mr Sidney Parker, who was agreeable to a plurality of ladies, the more resemble? Charlotte sighed: what a question to find herself asking, and how strange to to find herself beginning to think of upright Mr Thomas, the eldest, as manipulative, and therefore less approvable than the youngest, Arthur – as an example for the Sidney Parker in the middle.

Mr Thomas Parker, though, when she thought of it further, was in his way just as constant as young Mr Arthur Parker. Thomas Parker, respectable family man that he was – was a true lover, a single-minded wooer of a most demanding mistress: the sprite Sanditon.

But was this mermaid of a little town worthy of the affections that were destroying what was good in him? Charlotte pitied Thomas Parker – and the place too, if it was merely a siren without a heart. She dismissed that idea as extravagant. Sanditon was a locality only, in which she was fixed for some little time yet – though she needed to talk to her father, to what effect she was unsure – for who was there to give unbiased advice either to him or herself?

Sir Edward Denham was both poor and unworldly – he could have nothing to say to her. Nevertheless, her heart lifted up at the thought of him. At first she had found satisfaction in putting down his arguments – had seen him merely as an embodiment of what were often poor enough opinions. But his frank enjoyment of her counters and sallies – there was a kind of humility in that – had raised him in her estimation. Raised him, she realised with relief, beyond any regard she might have had for Sidney Parker; yet raised him entirely safely for her. Though she liked his comradeship and admired his capacity for it, her warmth of feeling for him – and she recognised that she had this warmth of feeling – came to her through Clara Brereton: she experienced a kind of love through another's senses. So she knew there was no danger to herself no matter how often she encountered this latter-day Lovelace; and knew this was not self-deception.

By the time that Charlotte had reached, by the path which descended from the Terrace, a point immediately above Sir Edward's cottage ornée, her mind was once more turning over the problems of Sanditon. She resolved to persevere, using what moderating influence she might have on Mr Parker and on Mrs Parker too (if that lady could be persuaded to have an opinion of any kind); to do what she could to get advice for her father which might prevent any imprudence. Perhaps Mr Robert Ferrars, one of the wealthiest gentlemen in the county they said, who was often at Captain and Mrs Wentworth's – might be able to help.

    Then Charlotte caught sight of the cottage through some trees. She recalled now hearing of a further cliff fall, which had damaged the roof: she hoped Sir Edward and Miss Esther could afford to pay for its repair. Meanwhile Lady Denham's fortune lay with lawyers, serving only to pay their fees.

    As Charlotte grew closer, the voices of Sir Edward and some workmen could be heard. Turning in at the gate, she could not repress a cry of surprise: the immature garden to the right was largely buried in a cairn of stones fallen from the cliff. Scrambling upon which above her, using long wooden levers on great chalk or limestone boulders were Sir Edward and the men.

    Sir Edward turned his head:

'One moment, Miss Heywood. How good to see you here at the very point and pitch of discovery! Best not to approach nearer, though… until – there!'

A final heave had turned over and rolled clear the main obstruction to a newly-exposed cleft or cave mouth.

'As I thought, Miss Heywood, a cavern. How unlike, when one peers through its massy portals into its Stygian depths, how unlike indeed, to Sanditon's little grotto with its mortar and green seat! We shall prepare lanterns and explore directly. The house, you observe, has been spared on this occasion. Now we have unlooked for recompense in a measureless or, at least, unmeasured – cavern; where formerly, I flatter myself, a sacred river ran. A Xanadu of a place! But, while the expedition gets itself in hand, let us have my housekeeper make tea.'

Both cups and imaginations were stirred: the cave took shape in the mind. Said Charlotte, with a not altogether convincing air of banter: 'Sir Edward, you may presently find long-hidden treasure on your domains!'

Charlotte's fancies sometimes, for all she could do, derived from her early reading: she could not but think how happily and horridly a Gothick setting would lend itself to improvised fortuities: Sir Edward had full need of fortune; he should acquire it in a fashion suited to his adventurous spirit. An ancient tomb? A pirate's hoard? Lady Denham could then, without harm to him, leave all she possessed to Clara Brereton. Rendered rich, Clara and Sir Edward could make a marriage full of mutual love and property to universal acclaim.

'A treasure on my strip of property here?' said Sir Edward in reply. He was nothing if not gallant, save when he chose to be surly and Byronic, 'Do I not even now perceive just such a *treasure*? But forgive my saying so, Miss Heywood,' (Charlotte had lifted her chin, not lowered her eyes), 'I responded in kind – not that I don't always mean what I say – for I thought you spoke like a heroine – yet I know we have gone beyond that sort of thing, put it behind us, you and I.'

Charlotte blushed in spite of herself, at first out of a sort of chagrin, for she *had* spoken like a heroine – or the author of a romance – but then out of pleasure for his very pleasantness.

'But, no, Miss Heywood,' he said, putting banter aside, 'I'm seeking neither treasure-chests nor walled-in monks nor gibbering

SPECULATION

ghouls. The quality I seek is that best exemplified by a cave: a vast emptiness along with the elusive and distant plashing of underground waters. That will suffice...

'... But I see indications that all is ready. Shall we commence our adventure? – For, yes, I *do* – am I inconsistent? – concede that it is an adventure. Planks may be needed over the fallen stones. Yes, good, I see they have been supplied already. Bosun shall come too, if he is not afraid.'

The dog agreed with his tail that he was not afraid.

Now,' turning to the men, 'if one of you stay with me and the other guard Miss Heywood until we have made our first investigation. Yes. So, Miss Heywood, if there is any thing to be seen, depend upon it that you shall be admitted into its presence very shortly.'

'Take care, Sir Edward,' said Charlotte, who was in good heart. 'Beware the underground river.'

'That I will,' said he. 'Nor shall I trip over my pots of gold,' and he and his great dog stepped into the obscurity of the rocky portal.

Charlotte found it preferable to relinquish her own pattern of thought in favour of Sir Edward's at this juncture. (She is mortified to have been detected in the act of becoming once again, not only the heroine of a novel, but something worse, because doubly interfering and foolishly inventive: a narrator; one whose mind resembles so many pieces of paper to be filled with secondary impressions, internal sensations. She is grateful to Sir Edward for indicating that tendency, though she is really further gone in it than he is allowed to know.)

Charlotte's dulness of spirit, brought on by Mr Parker's unscrupulous reaction to the misfortunes of Sanditon, has been alleviated through Sir Edward. He has added imperceptibly to her stock of self-knowledge. Or, more probably, it is simply that the dank and gloomy prospect of a cave raises the spirits of creatures about to enter it.

Some minutes went by, after which Sir Edward emerged:

'I have found no treasure, Miss Heywood,' said he quite cheerfully, 'or any river either – though I fancy the cave must have been formed by water. A new entrance seems to have been made by the present cliff-fall into a very old cavern. There must be another more ancient entrance now hidden.'

(Charlotte finds herself again imagining a labyrinth which ends not with the Minotaur – for her girlhood reading had its preferences – but in a forgotten vault beneath Sanditon House, where Denham doubloons dating from the Armada are waiting to be claimed.)

But Sir Edward has continued to wax much more practical, not to say geological: 'The earlier entrance would probably have been higher up the cliff – collapsed, doubtless, long since under some landslip.'

Charlotte said that she thought he was probably right, keeping her romantic fancies to herself.

'More candles are needed,' he concludes. 'I have sent for as many as are to be had, which we shall fix about the chamber. Then you may wish to become its first lady visitor. I think you would find the rock formations noble and uplifting.'

Soon all the necessary illumination was accomplished and Charlotte was being helped along the planks and over the threshold onto – to her surprise – a pleasant sanded floor. The forms and colours of the rocks were indeed very fine. She congratulated Sir Edward on the chamber which was half the size of a ballroom with a natural graceful vault.

'I could be happy here,' he replied, 'in solitude – as a hermit in communion with the rocks and stones and sands of time,' and some other very feeling things about his simple material needs but lofty spiritual ones. Then, so soon, he was once more restless. First, gesturing that he was to venture into the darkness alone, he then cried in his fine voice:

'O, let me test that deeper shadow there.'

Charlotte did not blame Sir Edward for falling into blank verse; gave him credit for winning their old argument about spontaneity (because he did not perceive the metric). She watched in pleasant dread, as he took a candle in each hand and the shadow first gave way and then closed over him.

Another cavern it seemed or the mouth of one. Did the labyrinth begin at that point? Was Sir Edward about to claim an inheritance of ancient plate and priceless jewels? He was some time gone.

Charlotte, growing nervous, was about to send one of the men after him, when Sir Edward returned. Lighted candles were clasped against his bosom to the peril of his linen, for his arms were full of what he had found. Not gold, but bones.

'Alas,' he cried, 'what antediluvian giant is this? Did Adam have a navel? How futile our speculations! How petty our pecuniary needs and desires!' – and much more by way of exclamation over what looked, for all the world, to be the obscurer skeletal fragments of a cow – or, at best, a horse.

But whatever the bones were, they were of no interest to Bosun, the dog. There was nothing sniffable about them, no more relics of life than if they had been made of stone; and, to be sure, they were like stone to the touch.

The bones and Sir Edward began to disappear into the darkness, though all eyes had long grown accustomed to the dim light. That was not through any failure of vision or the coming of cavernous night; simply that the candles began to burn as low and doubtful as their owner's finances.

✻

The next day, Charlotte Heywood thought it best to allow Sir Edward to savour his solitude – or, if his stock of candles was not replenished, his darkness. Concerned for her father, Charlotte travelled to Mrs Wentworth's where, though Agnes was elsewhere, picnicking – as fortune would have it – she found, and was able to put certain questions to, Mr Robert Ferrars (who, appreciating her worth, gave her sensible answers).

Meanwhile, Sir Edward was still searching for candles; and his dog for better bones, which had traces of viands about them, so Esther Denham was alone. As she had no duties with little Mary Parker that day, she went to call on Clara Brereton at the Seminary. Clara proved to be out with Agnes Wentworth on her picnic, so Miss Esther was disappointed in that respect. Instead, she encountered Mr Sidney Parker, who had perhaps been seeking Charlotte Heywood. Whatever his reason for being there, he – who had seemed so dismissive of Miss Esther (excluding her in her absence from the novel in letters!) – seemed more attentive to her than hitherto.

The day went by, punctuated by appropriate refreshments. Save for Sir Edward: he had gone without his dinner to buy candles, which he was now using economically, one at a time, in the vast space of his caves. He played Hamlet to Yorick; then, entering into oneness with the bones, Yorick to Hamlet. Oppressed with the sense of mortality, he ran out of the cavern - his eyes dazzled by the sudden light – crying in a loud voice, 'I am such stuff as dreams are made on.' Admitting quietly to a passer-by: 'Sorry, wrong play.'

He smiled and blinked and, having no hat, raised a bone at Elizabeth Darcy, who – feeling the heat – was retracing her steps from a turn along the strand prior to calling on the Knightleys. Fanny had stopped to peer at something.

Elizabeth absorbed in herself, continued walking. Sir Edward who had heard something in the billiard room from Mr Sidney Parker about the absent Mr Darcy's Italian sojourn gave her departing figure, walking a shade awkwardly now as she started the ascent towards the Terrace, a sympathetic look.

Finding himself so doing, he felt a sudden surprise. If the object of man was to be universally seductive, particularly in decadent parts of Europe, then why shouldn't Mr Darcy follow Epicurus – do as he pleased? Further, wasn't the purpose of man, properly understood, to arouse within himself and those taken unto himself, the uttermosts of passion? Provided all was noble and open. In a natural (or a decadent) society there need be no petty constraints, ties or expectations. Sir Edward told himself that these reflections were for his own part a matter of faith, so why should

SPECULATION

they not apply to Mr Darcy? That gentleman had every right to enjoy the same amplitude in practice that he, Sir Edward, accorded himself in theory. But the image of Elizabeth walking alone, with difficulty, did not altogether square with these precepts.

'Come now, Ned,' said Sir Edward out loud to himself; addressing otherwise only his dog, who had returned boneless, 'come now, Ned, you're becoming insensate. Isn't the aim of life to trust to the sharpest and truest sensation without a thought for consequence?'

But again the image of Elizabeth impinged. Did this once comely – and they said vivacious – woman begin to waddle? Should a man turn her into a species of duck or broody fowl? But wasn't the point of manhood to be a hero – to dash and slash and thrill to the delights of all that is sensuous? Again, some of this discourse fell upon his dog's ears.

'No,' he cried suddenly, 'it is to be mortal! It is to conjoin. To generate. To get new bones, to keep together old bones.' And he retired to his cave like St Jerome with his revised opinions and his Bosun lion to shake his head over the house of Darcy.

✱

Fanny, too, had sensed something about Darcy and abroad – something less precise than Sir Edward had heard, but heard it she had. Elizabeth was fatigued and, Fanny trusted, too preoccupied in these later months, to pay much heed to what people were murmuring. But she seemed calmer in the Sanditon air and – Fanny thought – more hopeful that there would be no still-born child this year.

Elizabeth Darcy, showing her tiredness, was now nearly at the door of Sanditon House. One of the reasons that Elizabeth was calling upon the Knightleys was so that Fanny could take back to their lodging more heavy old books. She had initially had doubts about her current project. For all that Fanny Bertram had noted Sir Edward Denham's incapacity (as she and Elizabeth Darcy had concluded) to assimilate more than sensational gobbets of literature – and held to the impropriety of shortened versions of great works – Fanny had suddenly found herself approached for a projected abridgement of *Sir Charles Grandison*, Miss Austen's favourite work by her earliest-favoured author, Samuel Richardson.

Elizabeth whom she had consulted could see only the advantages of undertaking the work; which Charlotte Heywood, whom Fanny had next consulted, seconded that: 'Mrs Bertram,' Charlotte had said, 'there is a readership for one-volume versions – yours will be supported by taste and judgment. You should not give it over to someone less able than yourself.'

Fanny knew that there was no flattery intended in Charlotte's advice; so she had accepted what was said and set about the task happily; happily, for she had been coincidentally half-way through re- reading the long work; and now gave thanks that she was able to add to her income by doing something which was neither despicable nor disagreeable. In spite of Richardson's detractors, Fanny was finding the narrative lively enough.

She was at the mid-point of the story and reached for the later volumes which had been rescued from Mr Woodhouse's flood, which would complete the narration. In order to remind herself of the pattern of the work, she turned the many pages which still lay ahead, letting their cue-titles catch her eye. At regular intervals the illustrative engravings printed on card or board, stiffer in kind than the paper used for text presented themselves to Fanny; giving her as she regulated and released the edges of pages with her right-hand thumb a species of moving picture, like some nursery novelty.

A first image is of the good man Sir Charles Grandison, sword reluctantly drawn (for like the author who created him, he believes in the law of the land not deeds of blood): a wicked woman is turning archly towards a door, a wicked man ('her temporary husband') lies helpless before the power of good, though there is a threat to Sir Charles from the right. But all will be well. Grandison, pacific by principle not necessity, is skilled in all manly arts: *'I drew,*

SPECULATION

put by Salmonet's sword, closed with him, disarmed him, and, by the same effort, laid him on the floor.'

And here in the next engraving which stays the onrush of succeeding pages, is the noble Clementina. She stands before a classic temple, the crucifix of her Roman Catholic faith broad on her barely-covered bosom – which doubtless heaves, though the lady's ringlets peep in well- disposed order from beneath the chaste drapery that covers her head like a Madonna; her arm like some Roman senator's: all speaks of the noble lady that she is.

Ay, but she's mad and a catholic enamoured of Sir Charles who has his duty at home to the great protestant English lady Harriet Byron. Clementina, mad, catholic, noble, is observed in the Garden of Europe, the trunks and foliage of the framing verdure rendering the scene a very *Salvator*, a perfected landscape such as Mr Darcy is engaged in seeking.

And what else does Mr Darcy seek? Why, a son and heir. Fanny prays that Elizabeth does not again miscarry, that Mr Darcy has not become the 'temporary husband' of some Latin scion of nobility; has not found – such things happened in books, or were hinted at – a surrogate to bear the male child that his ancestry demands. What better – or worse – place to seek than amongst the ancient families of Italy?

Another engraving, a final scene. And here it seems to Fanny that Sir Charles strongly resembles the likeness of Darcy that she has seen at Pemberley.

The room has fine proportions: an apse, a dome, an abundance of Corinthian pilasters: there are two contiguous chairs and a door ajar. The Darcy figure seeks the left hand of the noble Italian lady, who turns her head away, gesturing temperately with her right arm but not withdrawing her left.

Darcy seems about to move forward from his chair, bear his weight down to his right, fall upon one knee. He will bury his face in her robes and cry:

'My noble lady, though my duty is at home, my heart is with you. When our son is born, I will give up my lands and my hall – you have your Villa D'Este we English have our Pemberley – and live here in your great house in its perpetual garden, with my line assured – what other title do I need than to be with you in this paradisaical land? '

'Noble sir,' cries the Italian lady,' her countenance still averted, 'and so you would renounce all that you have in your own country. Honoured sir – I cannot accept your sacrifice, better the disgrace for me of a fatherless child (though the blood in his veins be as good as any in Europe); such things are not unknown even in the noblest of families where the blood runs warm in our veins like wine upon a summer table.'

She paused: 'Unless,' and the lady turned towards him soberly, 'unless some dispensation regarding your religion could be effected. Your wife, remember, is not bound to you immutably in the eyes of our holy mother church.'

And to that end it is now apparent that a Roman Catholic divine is observing and listening at the open door cogitating on how best to approach his Holiness to secure a papal dispensation

Fanny looks up from the book; sees now Elizabeth Darcy, clothed also in classical drapery but fashioned from muslin with sprigs of English flowers interspersing its folds. She is as tall as the Italian lady, her eye as bright, her mien as fierce. In the background in an arbour lies Darcy's love-child. Elizabeth's garments are, as has been indicated, voluminous; and from them there peeps a dark curl from the head of a cherubic head – from the head of Darcy's legitimate heir. The proud Italian lady's eye becomes cast down; Darcy will

SPECULATION

emerge from a ruined portico, embrace his wife, acknowledge and rejoice in the heir to Pemberley – and all will be well.

Fanny is surprised at the way this narrative has grown within her. She has never laid claim to powers of invention. However, having found this faculty, she has no further need of it – Clementina's renunciation is there in black and white and ends the scene:

'O sir! Could you have been a catholic! God Almighty convert you, chevalier! But you must leave me. I am beginning to be again unhappy! Leave me, Sir. I will pray for composure of mind.'

And the poor noblewoman begins to ramble (though, unlike Mr Woodhouse, she has youth on her side and may recover). Grandison rejoices in the principle of Clementina's decision for all his admiration of her person and character. Both can suffer for their steadfastness to truth as they see it and find therein pleasurable satisfaction (joy, even). Grandison will arrive safely on his native shores and salute his bride to be, Darcy will do the like honour to his only wedded wife, Elizabeth; his renewed affection responding to her completed duty, as wife and mother.

✳

In the days of Richardson a young lady and gentleman would first set eyes upon one another at worship in the parish church; their subsequent demeanour to each other being determined by recollections of the consecrated precincts in which they first exchanged a look, a modest smile. Or so says the old author's precept (in practice, the personages of his stories may be obliged for their close acquaintance to an involuntary journey in a closed carriage, to a barred door in a disreputable inn, or worse).

For Miss Burney (Mme D'Arblay), such encounters between the sexes were managed by means of assemblies, presentations, dinners and sentimental toasts for the young gentleman and younger lady; routs and masquerades for the indispensable heroine and the expendable villain. For Miss Austen, young people would be brought together through such means as a house newly-taken in the neighbourhood, a day-visit protracted through an over-night cold, or a country ball.

All such mechanisms pre-date New Sanditon. In the Regency era – with its bow fronts and stucco, sea-side and Arabian halls – a lady and gentleman are as likely to get to know one another over sheets of calculations, speculative prospectuses, architectural fancies, estimates of costs, problems of inheritance; only literature and sick visits, of the older modes of discourse between the sexes, continuing to have some currency.

Sir Edward remained meditative at home, Miss Esther (more active than hitherto) took herself out, while Mr Wingfield accompanied Miss Lambe on numerous convalescent walks. Charlotte resumed her calls on the Wentworths, as did Mr Robert Ferrars, from whom she conveniently received further advice: a necessary counter to Mr Parker's influence and her father's malleability.

'Yes, my dear, sir,' Mr Heywood would be saying to Mr Parker, ' we do have to consider that our daughter Charlotte is not very likely to marry. What use is this poor old home to her when we are gone? We have her interests at heart – and are inclined to agree with you that seaside apartments – and the income from them – how many did you suggest the capital might build? So many? – such a seasonal return would ensure her comfort well into the middle age and beyond.'

Which Robert Ferrars would be countering, by saying to the future unmarried beneficiary of the sea-side speculation, 'I have been a madcap fellow, Miss Heywood, but luck has kept my fortune afloat. With your permission, I will engineer a conversation between myself and your good father. There is money to be made at the present time, but money attracts money, if I may speak so vulgarly. The skill is in the half-promise of investment in a venture.

SPECULATION

Yes, Miss Heywood, that does sound underhand, but I'm afraid it is the way of the present world. Those who know it know exactly where they stand – it is a matter of credit rather than the committing of hard sums.

'*That* your esteemed father must on no account do, for I fear he is unacquainted with the methods used by the principal players in these games. You say that Mr Parker struck up his acquaintance by spraining his ankle while searching the Sussex lanes for a resident surgeon? Some thing at least as plausible as that will, I'm sure, come to my aid in making his acquaintance.'

An opportunity, both plausible and fortuitous, did come to pass. Mr Parker was anxious to secure promises of investment from both Mr Heywood and Mr Ferrars, who consequently found themselves together at Trafalgar House. Found themselves there without either Mr Sidney or Mr Thomas Parker; being received only by Mrs Parker (cosseting Mary who had a cold, and hoping Mr Arthur might return from Miss Beaufort's), who presented the gentlemen with a scribbled apologetic note to the effect that the two elder brothers had been called away for urgent financial consultations – with whom, Messrs Parker were not at liberty to say, but Mr Ferrars knew well enough that it was a meeting with the great RH.

They agreed to wait a little while in the library, though quite aware that none of the brothers – or Mrs Parker for that matter – would return for some time. There they naturally fell to talking about that which in former times two gentlemen would have been reticent: money, family, expectations. Mr Ferrars suggested, with due delicacy. that it was premature to assume Miss Charlotte Heywood would remain unmarried; to point out, in any case, the fondness that he had on brief acquaintance found, the fondness in her for old homes and old ways – of one such old home, in particular, which Mr Heywood was planning to dispose of; and on her behalf!

Eventually the two Mr Parkers reappeared. Thomas was ebullient.

'Gentleman, forgive our absence – rest assured it was in all our interests, the urgent meeting called by our coadjutor – who, you understand will not as yet allow us to use his name in connection with this enterprise. His word is his bond –'

Mr Ferrars reminded Mr Parker that a word with no name to back it could not depend on the credit of that name.

'Yet,' said Mr Parker, 'I do know where I stand in this matter. The gentleman – and I think Mr Ferrars you may have an idea of his identity – was clear to the point of bluntness. If I – we, that is to say, though the definition of that 'we' remains incomplete – if, on this side there is the ability to match the sums, the very considerable sums at the gentleman's disposal, then the future of Sanditon is safeguarded without detriment to the very different destiny of Brinshore, as I now recognise. Much, gentlemen, depends upon the Denham inheritance: how providential that so great a fortune should be hoarded, the original settlements all still intact with great accumulations of interest, augmented through known economies – increased, too, by certain un-lady-like ventures, eh Sidney?' – but Mr Sidney made no reply.

'We must,' continued Mr Parker, 'rescue Sir Edward from his subterranean investigations and get him to think steadily about the use to which he would put the fortune if it should prove to be his at the last. For, yes, I believe that Lady Denham's wishes will be discovered,' again, he looked to Sidney, but that gentleman held his peace, 'for our unnamed associate would certainly, as I said before, match whatever funds are within our capability. Yes, to be sure.'

And Mr Parker relapsed into repetition, from which he was stirred by a more immediate piece of good news; that Mr Ferrars had spoken to his sisters-in-law who had both agreed to move to Sanditon for the rest of the season, it having been confirmed that the two houses on The Crescent were now both complete and available. Mr Parker shook his hand warmly.

'That, then, is agreed,' said Robert Ferrars. 'I shall arrange that Mrs Brandon and Mrs Ferrars transfer their effects in a day or two. After which they will call at Trafalgar House, I do not doubt.'

SPECULATION

Thus Elinor and Marianne and Elizabeth and Fanny became neighbours at the last. Similarly, Clara Brereton (when not needed in the school room), Miss Esther Denham (who had resumed her informal help with little Mary at Trafalgar House), and Miss Charlotte Heywood (coincidental to certain visits of Mr Ferrars) became closely acquainted with all four ladies.

Sir Edward Denham continued to avoid company. Mr Parker called on him every so often, turning the conversation to Sanditon's need for a great outlay of capital, urging Sir Edward to think expansively; this to a gentleman who was pinched to keep any sort of roof over his head. Unlike Mr Parker, he and his sister had not abandoned their family home out of salubrious theory, but because the house was falling down about their ears.

A storm in late Spring had broken down a further section of its roof and – Lady Denham proving inhospitable – forced them to regard their summer cottage as a permanent residence, with no possibility of letting it for the season. Fortunately Sir Edward's outlay on the cottage itself had so far been inconsiderable, the land having been given to him by Lady Denham in exchange for some family jewels which were to remind the late great lady of her dear dead second husband's family.

However, Lady Denham had persistently made it clear that she would see her nephew and niece put up at the Hotel (at their own expense) rather than give them shelter at Sanditon House. She had died without either of them spending a night there or even latterly meeting at her table – asses' milk she did continue to supply to Miss Esther for a small weekly payment. This was the extent of her bounty.

Alas, Sir Edward's one sound property, his cottage, seemed to show a regrettable likelihood of following Denham Court into dilapidation – the workmen having brought him a tale of further fallen stones.

Part Four: OUT OF THE BLUE

1

At Sanditon House, whose fine old roof had been denied to Sir Edward and Miss Esther, the Knightley brothers had gone to stretch their legs; Isabella, with some indisposition, to her bed. Emma and Elizabeth Darcy were alone with Mr Woodhouse. Emma's good nature had been tried in the past by the foolishnesses of various harmless people, but she now had to keep her composure in the face of the decline in her father whom she had always loved, and for, all his oddities, respected.

Mr Woodhouse had become uncommonly comfortable in Lady Denham's old house: he liked its low beams and its rambling gloom, its great many unread books and dusty hangings. Its shapelessness appealed to his half-turned wits, as if it concealed some inner order, provided some solution.

Emma was plying him with Wingfield's potion. He took a spoonful willingly enough, but declined another.

'The soup,' he said. 'The salt soup is well enough, but I do believe it is keeping us from the true thing.'

'The true thing, father?' said Emma looking to Elizabeth.

'The true thing,' he repeated, 'the true thing.'

'The true thing, for what purpose, sir?'

'To put me to rights, of course,' said Mr Woodhouse, stiffening his back as if to rise.

Emma put out a restraining hand, but there was no need of it: he hadn't the strength to raise himself from the chair.

'Perhaps, Mrs Knightley,' said Elizabeth, 'it is time to send for Mr Wingfield once more.'

'No, madam,' said Mr Woodhouse whose hearing was intermittently sharp, 'no, indeed, he can do no more for me. What is needed is –' and he grew silent as if forgetful of what was so essential.

The two ladies sat companionably by the old gentleman, leaving him to his thoughts.

Elizabeth spoke hers: 'I have to confess, Mrs Knightley, that you handle these matters better than I should.'

'It is kind of you to say so, Mrs Darcy, but such ministrations do not come easily to me. When I was younger, Mr Knightley – for he has known me since I was a girl – often used to upbraid me for my thoughtlessness for others. It was good that he did so.'

'I understand,' said Elizabeth, 'for my own character was guarded by angels of a different order. My father was and is a good man, but not – nor would he claim to be – free from error. While Mr Darcy and I did knock the rough edges off each other in the give and take of our courtship, it is to my dear sister, Jane's example that I owe the most. I haven't her sweetness of disposition, though I hope I have the honesty to realise that if it were, say, our mother Mrs Bennet, who needed the assiduous attention with which you support your father – and very commendable that you do – if it were Mrs Bennet who was declining here, I know that it would be her daughter Jane who would be her handmaid in extremity. I might to my shame be elsewhere – save that nothing would keep me from being with Jane if she were in difficulty; and, therefore, I should be with her with my mother, I conclude, after all. But where's the merit in that?'

'The merit, Mrs Darcy, is in your honesty,' said Emma. 'And I like you the better for it. It would have been easy for you to pretend with me, since I do not know the circumstances of your early family life.'

While Mr Woodhouse slept, Elizabeth told Emma something of life at Longbourn, and at Pemberley; sighing a little at Darcy's absence, creasing her brow (though saying nothing to Emma) over a rumour she had heard of what had transpired in Italy.

OUT OF THE BLUE

Mr Woodhouse stirred. He awoke, un-refreshed; awoke at the same point and with the same words as when he had last been awake:

'The true thing, my young misses, the true thing.'

'But what thing is this, father? Do you think perhaps I should call not for Mr Wingfield, but for Mr Balm, the parson?' This latter for Elizabeth's ears only, but Mr Woodhouse got the sense of it well enough.

'No parsons, no doctors, no anyone. Look for it: that is all I ask.'

'But, father,' said Emma, 'how shall I recognise this thing when I find it? What kind of appearance does it have?'

'Why,' said Mr Woodhouse, 'it's writing isn't it? So that's what it looks like. Something written down. And so what should it be written upon?'

'Paper, I suppose,' replied Emma uncertainly, 'and there is plenty of paper in this old house despite the attention which lawyers have not long since given it. Yet, father, none of this matter is to do with us. How can it be to do with us, sir?'

'How,' said Mr Woodhouse, 'how can it not be so? Is this not my old uncle's house?'

They had not the heart to deny his assertion.

— 'And was not my old uncle a great one for remedies? There are those in the family who say I feature him in that regard.'

The ladies rose and made some pretence of looking about the bookshelves.

'I don't find any thing, father,' said Emma, but Mr Woodhouse was engaged in repeating: 'They were wise men in those days.'

'Do you find any thing, Mrs Darcy?' — seeking to bring her father from his unhealthy self-absorption. Elizabeth indicated that she did not.

'No, father, neither of us seems to be able to lay our hands upon what you seek at present.'

Would you care to rest, sir?' And Emma gently touched his old hands with hers.

'No, daughter,' he replied, 'I do not care to rest at present. Look again, as I ask.'

So the two bustled about the room, glancing at Mr Woodhouse with hopes he would once again fall into a doze.

But his eyes stayed bright following the ladies about the room as best he could. At length, they returned to sit by him, defeated.

'Have you done as I say?' he said. 'If so, what have you found?'

'Indeed, sir, we have done as you have said and heartily wish we could put our hands upon what you call the true thing, the old-fashioned remedy that you seek, but neither of us can find any thing to the purpose – and, father, I am bound to say that I believe we are unlikely to do so. That is, unlikely to do so this afternoon,' she added, seeing the old man grow agitated.

A tear of chagrin started in the old man's eye and Emma found her affections moving her to act against her best belief.

'I'll try again, sir,' she said, and got up – but stood irresolute. Elizabeth joined her.

'The bureau,' said Mr Woodhouse, 'you have of course searched it?'

'Bureau?' said Emma, 'which bureau would that be?'

Mr Woodhouse pointed and sure enough behind a curtain in an alcove there was a bureau.

'It's there, you see,' said Mr Woodhouse, 'there where it always was in the old days.'

The two ladies exchanged bemused looks. Then went to the bureau. 'I would with the utmost willingness do as you say, father,' said Emma, 'but I do believe, sir, that it is locked. Besides I cannot believe that there is any thing in it to concern us.'

'Not concern us?' rejoined Mr Woodhouse. 'Don't I know my old uncle's bureau when I see it? And don't I therefore have some idea about what it contains? Come, ladies,' he said with a reversion to his old-fashioned courtesy, 'It always did stick a little: try again.'

Both of the ladies knew full well that the bureau could have nothing to do with Mr Woodhouse's esteemed uncle since the article of furniture in question was the property of the heirs of Lady Denham (whoever might be fortunate). Nevertheless, they did as they were asked.

'The lid is warped,' cried Mr Woodhouse, 'push down a little more firmly on the left, then pull on the right and it will move, I don't doubt.'

They followed Mr Woodhouse's instruction closely so as not to court his dissatisfaction; and to their surprise the lid swung outwards and down, as he had foretold.

'There,' he cried, 'what did I say? I believe you'll now have the remedy close at hand.'

But Lady Denham's lawyers had been equally successful in their approach to the stiff lid. The bureau's shelves and drawers were bare and empty.

'I'm afraid, sir,' said Emma, sadly, who had almost begun to believe in the cure-all remedy and its location, 'there is nothing in the bureau, after all.'

She lifted up the lid ready to close it.

'Not so fast, missy,' called Mr Woodhouse with rare energy, 'you haven't looked properly.'

'Indeed, sir,' said Emma with the beginnings of impatience, 'Mrs Darcy will support me in this; indeed, sir, I'll ring and have the piece of furniture brought to your chair-side so that you may inspect it to your own satisfaction.'

'No need,' rejoined Mr Woodhouse, 'no need. I can tell you what it's necessary for you to do. Look closely. You perceive the third drawer across from the left?'

'Yes, sir, I do,' said Emma with a sense of futility.

'Well,' said Mr Woodhouse, 'that isn't the one. Let me think. Yes, find the next drawer down, the one immediately below the one you've got hold of. You have your hand upon the drawer which I have described to you?'

'Indeed, I have, sir,' said Emma gloomily.

'Next,' said Mr Woodhouse, 'I wish you to open that drawer to its fullest extent. Have you done so?'

'I have father. I'm afraid, father –'

'You are telling me, daughter, that it is empty.'

'Sorry as I am, father to disappoint you, it is empty. Tomorrow early, we will consult Mr Wingfield about other remedies –

– Other remedies, nothing! Place your hand flat inside the drawer. Still you feel it is empty?'

'I have done what you say, father,' with increasing anxiety. Emma did not know what dark disorder might not follow this cogent interlude – 'and, yes, I'm sorry to say the drawer still appears to be empty.'

'Yes, girl, it appears to be empty. It would do. It needs to do.'

'Why, father, what do you mean? What do you intend? Mrs Darcy, perhaps –'

'Do you think,' interposed Mr Woodhouse, 'do you think I don't know my old uncle's bureau like the back of my hands?' and he gazed at the veins and mottles which made up the chief part of those appendages. 'Of course it needs to be empty to protect the remedy from those who don't know how it is to be found.' He paused with exultation piping in his old voice.

Emma, wishing to do nothing to cross him, nothing but what he had instructed, yet seeking for some means of demonstrating that there was nothing whatsoever to be found, inserted her palm flat into the drawer with a flourish and pushed it into each corner, probing; to communicate to her father that she really and truly was searching for something in whose existence she believed.

There was a small click. The two ladies looked at one another. Another click and something eased its way free. A third click and a half-round receptacle revolved into the light.

'And look what's here!' cried Emma and Elizabeth together.

OUT OF THE BLUE

'The very thing, the very thing to set me up for life,' cried Mr Woodhouse, falling into a swoon of joy from which he never recovered.

※

The secret which the hidden drawer contains is nothing so implausible as Mr Woodhouse's uncle's remedy (nor as superfluous now that the poor old gentleman has no need of it), nor as bathetic as the laundry list found by young Catherine Morland at dead of night in Northanger Abbey.

The document proves to be, as the reader may have surmised, the Last Will and Testament of Lady Denham: written and sealed by her self – to keep fees from lawyers (an object defeated by the cost of their search); hidden away, as if the Lady disowned any generosity which she has been obliged to have it contain.

※

Charlotte Heywood's first concern on hearing the news is for Clara Brereton's prospects; her second for Sir Edward, who – if he were to inherit would take Clara along with the other trappings of the estate, and take her – very warmly: Charlotte has learned to value the decency in him. But she worries still about Miss Sophie Lambe – feels the need to keep the West Indian heiress under Mr Wingfield's caring eye (yet how could she put that into effect? – and what business is it of hers?). If Sir Edward were to be disappointed by Lady Denham then Miss Lambe could mend and make his fortune – it being clear that she would jump at marrying a title.

Charlotte worries, too, at the way the discovery of the will has occurred. Not so much (she has to be honest about this) for the death of old Mr Woodhouse, Emma's father – for he had become increasingly a burden to himself and others), but the business of the secret compartment. Is this yet another instance of Gothick romancing on her part? And yet again, what is it do with her – how could she (not being at Sanditon House) have intervened? And if she had been at Sanditon House, hadn't the will been hidden by old Lady Denham. To be found or remain undetected? Who has caused it to be found? – Mr Woodhouse in his mistaken way, surely? If not he, then the same person who has made him say what he said, and placed it there to please him, sparing him the knowledge of what it was. The person who realised, in authorial fashion, that it was time to reveal Lady Denham's secret.

Charlotte having puzzled her head about what has gone on; sets herself instead to compose, to write – to write a letter. No more than a letter:

Trafalgar House,

Sanditon, 17th July 18–

It was your particular skill, my dear parents, from the time – as the old song has it – when I was but a tiny little child, to make something of a princess out of me: you taught me to have a belief in myself and my star; and were – still are! – so good and affectionate that I have been always much more cosy at Willingden than any princess in her draughty palace or castle. Not but that Mr and Mrs Parker, Miss Diana Parker and the rest have been other than the embodiment of kindness itself here, high above the bay.

Much has occurred during my time at Sanditon, some of which you are already apprised of. Heroic deeds have taken place; I instance the rescue from the waves of sickly Miss Lambe by the Byronic Sir Edward. Have you heard of his transformation into Gothick hermit?

Charlotte breaks off. Her pen has faltered. Every thing seems to stop for her decision. What mention shall she make of Mr Ferrars? How long might the lawyers be about their business? What will be the outcome of the will? What will become of the might-have-been hero or heroine – whichever does not inherit? Is Clara Brereton to lead a governess life? Sir Edward to live under an ever-leaking roof? Will Miss Esther ever marry? And what of the Sanditon speculation? Might Mr Parker some day return to his ancestral home?

First, the will has to be read, that much is clear. Charlotte Heywood resumes her writing.

✳

It is now a bright morning and the parties likely to be concerned directly or indirectly are to gather in the old hall of Sanditon House – this with Mr and Mrs Knightley's permission, for their Let has not run its course. The mortal remains of Mr Woodhouse have, with necessary despatch (though partly pickled in brine) been set upon the London Road for Highbury and burial. It is doubtful if the Knightleys will come back to Sanditon. Decisions have to be made within the family about the future of Hartfield once Emma and George Knightley have settled in Donwell Abbey, which his brother will now be vacating. In spite of all the distress and busyness, though, Emma has kept her curiosity about the Denham inheritance; Fanny Bertram and Charlotte Heywood being deputed to communicate what transpires.

Fortunately, the draughty great room, the oldest part of Sanditon House, has been cleared of lumber by numerous lawyers seeking a document which (until Mr Sidney Parker's disclosure of his role as witness) might never have existed. Thereby the old hall – no more than a cluttered thoroughfare in Lady Denham's time – has become available to accommodate all of them; together, now, with those other legal colleagues who are researching the claims of the deceased's complicated kin – themselves present and hopeful, down to fifth-cousins several times removed.

Amongst them, Sir Edward Denham, already restless. He has arrived far too early, thinking himself a day late, having grown impervious to the ticking of his watch during breakfast in his catacombs. In a paganly pious and stoical mood, he wants nothing, expects nothing; seeing his aunt along with the dubious bones from his cave as a mere instance of universal and enveloping mortality. Miss Esther by his side looks self-contained and likely to be fortunate. Charlotte Heywood has come to see fair play, and – by adroit management – to ensure that Mr Arthur sits next to Miss Beaufort.

Some said Miss Lambe had no business to be there, but there she is; as mended by Mr Wingfield, who smirks modestly beside her. Mr Thomas Parker is glad to see the West Indian heiress in attendance, because she has set him thinking: if she and Sir Edward were to make a match, he muses, then it would be tactful if she were to expire immediately after the ceremony (was this the formerly good-natured Mr Parker?) – From *painless* excitement, for he wishes her no particular harm. There would then be two fortunes which would together match the great manufacturer's resources, and thereby bring confirmation of his conditional promise to invest (as he understands it) munificently in Sanditon...

Mr Parker has sought to speak persuasively to that other possible successor to the estate, or some part of it, Clara Brereton. However, she remains monopolised by her aunt and uncle who seeing their poor relative possibly metamorphosed into a rich one, continually express the hope that she will not forget what they have done for her. They offer deference to the similarly deferential Clara, who makes generous acknowledgment of her indebtedness to them, while seeing small expectancy of being able to reward their good works. Becoming a governess, she says, is an elevated prospect for one who has thought only to have been fitted for a nursery maid. The uncle and aunt are thus alternately flattered to be placed so far above someone who has the air, if not the airs, of a fine young lady; then despondent that she seems unwilling or unable to promise them patronage.

Uncle Brereton is no fool, however. 'Depend on it,' he says to his wife when they are at last alone, 'Clara will get something, though perhaps not a great deal. She is a good enough girl who may have ensured through her compliant ways that the Breretons – not the Denhams – get the prior claim. The Brereton dowry of so long ago is our family's legitimate due: thirty thousand pounds with accrued interest represents a sum so tidy, as to leave very little for the Denhams – those people who contributed nothing but a name.'

What of the Hollises? Where are the relatives of the first husband with his picture in such a dark corner of his own former house? A number of people bearing his name have arrived – all of them in trade and wearing stiff new clothes. They could have little reason to love Lady Denham nor much expectation of any thing from her: if Mr Hollis had left every thing to his wife then, in doing so he had gone out of his way to leave them nothing – or had been excessively afraid of displeasing his spouse or recklessly confident of outliving her. These Hollises are of little account, out to make what they can from retailing to their neighbours the wealth and ostentation of their late great cousin whose marriage so injured their legitimate expectations.

This particular Mr Hollis had, to be sure, been affluent even before his marriage to the first Miss Clara Brereton. This was the Mr Hollis who stood second only to the most notable Hollis of all – to the cotton magnate Sir Richard Hollis of late fame for vast fortunes from nothing at all. The Sir Richard who has been dead upwards of twenty years; though his son and name-sake (and nephew to Lady Denham's first husband), brought up a gentleman but calling himself Engineer, is only in middle age. However, 'Engineer', the second baronet can hardly be expected to come to Sanditon: he is notoriously too busy a man to be seen to be present when he might be seen to be absent. He has sent along, as representing him, a sort of clerk: a gentleman, fallen on bad times, by the name of Fowkes. Mr Parker casts many glances in his direction, but the man has either been selected for his cool handling of information or his total ignorance, for he gives no sign that he is conscious of Mr Parker's presence.

The attorneys who have come from the county town seemed to offer fair looks to the Breretons, because of the second line of her memorial slab, inspected by many distant relatives:

> Lady Denham, of Sanditon House,
> born Clara Brereton 1746
> died 13 June 18–,
> Who liv'd a long life
> of active benevolence and utility.

Couched in such moderate language, imbued with transcendent authority (though of her own composition), and displayed on expensive-looking stone (paid for by the returns on asses' milk), the eulogy is well-judged. That the chosen words inaccurately represent Lady Denham's virtues is a thought which, if it occurs to some, no one expresses. Indeed, had her stone told the truth – 'Lady D–, by her tight grasp on the property and titles of three families, forced meanness on all her people' – everyone, save the most hopeless and absent of the relatives, would have professed, and actually experienced, a sense of shock.

Confirmation that the Breretons may be favoured, seems to come from the fact – said to be a fact – that the will bears a date near the time of the great lady's visit to London, when – because she could do no better – she accepted the hospitality of Clara's aunt and uncle; and agreed that Clara should stay with her at Sanditon House for a while.

But speculation and expectation are about to be ended. The will contains a modicum of benevolence in the clauses ' the continued use of Sanditon House, together with an income of £500 per year to any young lady or ladies of the name Brereton or Denham living under my roof at the time of my decease, the sum and property reverting on her or their marriage or death to my nephew Sir Edward Denham.'

So, Lady Denham's refusal to accommodate Esther Denham and her brother when Denham Court fell into disrepair is additionally mortifying – the phrasing of the will seeming to suggest that Lady Denham had thought to accommodate Miss Esther Denham only to reject the possibility; or – worse still for Esther's comfort – that the great lady might at any time have been about to propose to Miss Denham that she, in her turn, came to live at Sanditon House as successor to Miss Brereton.

How are the tables turned on Sir Edward! – unless the rest of the estate were to be his: that he should have to come cap in hand as a lodger to Clara Brereton who has seemed so powerless, so dependent; so *seducible* – will he not become, as perhaps he already has after his reflections on Elizabeth's maternity and on the antediluvian bones, no longer even the shadow of a Lovelace…!

So much for the great lady's benevolence: all else is utility and money-making. The remainder of the estate will pass ('to be used for what purposes he thinks best by the relative who may best make my money work for him; to one who has no need of working for money, but has never disdained it') to the second baronet, Sir Richard Hollis.

There is inevitable outrage amongst those assembled; save from Sir Edward who seems amused by the turn of events. Mr Parker, too, though greatly surprised is not dismayed. RH, the engineer, might now – mightn't he? – choose to identify himself as the backer of New Sanditon. Given the Parkers' assiduity in pursuing 'Engineer' Hollis, the sums that they themselves are able to invest in Sanditon – the mite of Mr Heywood (which he has withdrawn, but whom Mr Parker in his good nature still intends to afford a dividend for his past support), the middling of Hargreaves (if he is truly of their party), the assumed main of Robert Ferrars: Mr Parker is quietly confident that with the access of great additional wealth to Hollis from Lady Denham (from Sanditon's great lady), all will be well; all be assured. It is ironic, he suggests to Mr Sidney, that Lady Denham in seeking to take her money out of Sanditon has unwittingly directed it towards the development of that very place as a health resort, based on those principles which she foolishly opposed!

Mr Parker finally catches Mr Fowkes' eye. He sees the clerk select one document from two which are ready and requiring attention. Fowkes casts an eye over it, folds it crisply, writes a name on its obverse seals it, presents it to Mr Parker. Is this, then, the climactic avowal, the beginning of a historic partnership? Whether there would have been a different letter had the residual estate gone to the Denhams or the Breretons, Mr Fowkes cannot of course divulge, but this is the one which Mr Parker receives and, with much bitterness, reads:

For the attention of Thomas Parker, Esqr
'Sir,

'I thank you for your proposals concerning developments at Sanditon village, with which I regret my inability to be associated owing to heavy demands on my funds and time at present. You were doubtless led to honour me with your request through my known interest in this part of the Sussex coast. You and your esteemed associates are partially aware of my plans for Brinshore as a convenient and much-needed port for my produce, involving an iron bridge over the Bryn &c.

'Such work will, in my view, do Sanditon little or no harm. I am sorry that you should feel antagonism towards a neighbouring settlement whatever its character.

OUT OF THE BLUE

'I assure you, sir, your prejudice against Brinshore is not reciprocated. However, the growth or decline of Sanditon as a watering place is no concern of mine, for it cannot relate directly to my present enterprise.

'Believe me, I wish you well in your proceedings and am sorry not to be able to assist you further.

'I am, sir, your obedient servant,

           Rich. Hollis (Bt)

'P.S. I am with Hargreaves of Brinshore Hall for a very short while and can be reached there — if necessary: but cannot see that further communication about the present matter will serve any purpose for my mind is made up.'

It is dated clearly at the foot of the page (for neither Sir Richard nor Mr Fowkes has any truck with the novelist's practice of using dashes and blanks to evade what is real and necessary):

              18 July 1817

*

Charlotte's letter is still unfinished — barely started, though she seems to have been writing for a very great while. Much disappointment for the Parker family; much reassurance from Mr Ferrars who has gone to see her father. She meant to write something in her letter about Mr Ferrars but is not quite sure now what it was she intended to say.

It is mid-afternoon, a bare five hours since the reading of the will and the receipt of Richard Hollis's peremptory letter. The disclosures, taken together, have sent Mrs Parker into convulsions and dragged her husband (who already sees himself as well punished) and his sisters down with her, to the accompaniment of great clatterings and compoundings from spoons and pestles and phials and herbs and powders. From this unhappy scene of decline and excessive energy, Mr Sidney remains absent (though sent for): Mr Arthur does his best to conceal personal buoyancy and join in miserably.

Sir Edward has retired to his cave after defending Clara Brereton against detractors; Esther sits palely in the cottage as one fearing an avalanche – actual or in similitude; Clara has been left by her kin, all of them in anger and huff, save for her uncle who, as he left, had the grace to wish her well.

After a number of attempts, Charlotte has managed to get Clara into the heavy air: they are walking on the lawns of Sanditon House, together; both troubled, both neither rejoicing nor affecting to regret that some provision has been made for Clara. The day is fine if somewhat oppressive; it has rained during the night and thunder is not far away.

Charlotte turns her head to catch the eye of Clara; stops; makes to speak; spins round. No one. Nothing. Has Sir Edward come (spurning Miss Lambe) and carried off Clara in a sealed coach to a mock-marriage Lovelace-like? – Or to the Bosporus (*Giaour*-fashion on a charger?) – Or to his solitary cave? Where are the wheel-marks, the hoof-prints on the wet lawn? Where the footsteps on the sand? Charlotte is aware of the slipperiness (after the rain) of the turf beneath her feet: the lawn is a flat slime-covered rock. A cobbled path attained, it shades into an ankle-twisting shingle beach of steep acclivity. Limpets like corns. Stucco become white-and-tawny cliffs.

The bones and shells of myriad little dead sea-creatures ground into sand, and their flesh and juices carried off into salt water.

High cloud cracked like an old painting – the image separating, opening and coming apart in honeycomb puffs.

OUT OF THE BLUE

Sound as piercing as salt.   Cries of gulls and drowned sailors. Pounding lace, flints, salt sticky as blood, massive shuttling of shingle, white-dazzle, shallow darkness, arcs and secants of waves, volutes and consoles of water, cragged curling hair, seagulls near the breakers' tops.

Charlotte, the girl, the young lady, the dying woman, crawling in pain up the shingled beach.   Like a tossing snowdrift drifting; one wave becoming a gull lifting wheeling alighting, shifting patterns of the mind, shadows; so bright a path where there is nothing, the reflection between is nothing.   Contrast all the orderly waters, millponds and conduits.

A great voice like rabble at the execution of a king.   A shipwreck?

The strong thrust and attack of the waves; their fierce gathering withdrawal, drawing the sand and broken shells through toes. Fronds, grit, worms, slime.   Sea air? Charlotte sometimes thinks the air of Sanditon does not agree with her.   The tide is going out and night falling; falling in drawing in leaving wrack and driftwood behind.

Deep water. Salt, spray, mist, liquid smoke, seething, bursting star, fan shape, grey deluge, spires of water, plumes, coronets of seaweed, rise and release of waters.

Sir Edward, naked, grey and hard and smooth as a shark, catching her – or Clara or another lady – about the waist with one arm, by the thinning hair with the other.   Drowning stifling draperies in swathes and swaths.   Says he:

'You never doubted the reality of passion.'

And they swim. The ritual of bathing and dangerous masquerades. Her skin darkened like the sky.   A man's hands in her bosom.

Herself unclothed and on a great wave like the seagull and the seaweed. The view of all the land from the top of the cliff. Crashing down onto the scree: the blood from cut knees, sticky as salt.

No, there is something about the air of Sanditon. Another man. No doubt, no shadow of doubt, no drifting shadow over the shallows of the mind, of his motives. Another chance. The acquaintance has been short. Cut off by the tide.

Was it at Sanditon that they had met? Was it a past that could be controlled? Would time, discretion, erasing waters, death, make it well?

Says Sir Edward: 'The world, Miss Heywood, has been destroyed and has made itself again three or four or many more or an infinite number of times. The world was inhabited by mammoths, behemoths and giants, but not by man till the Mosaic period as is proved by the strata of bones found. The world will be created and destroyed, the meeting will be arranged and erased – but first, Miss Heywood, you must make way for the mammoths and behemoths.'

She flees his sensual clutches, naked feet crumbling the bare bones which splinter and lacerate. The cave, as she had fancied, seems to lead from the cottage ornée to the cellars of Sanditon House.

Feverish but relieved, she sits in its back parlour to get her breath.

*

The sound of a creaky gate followed by a sharp rap at the door; a slither of slippers on the floor – or of writing being slid away under other papers: Charlotte isn't clear whether she or the lady in the door was the source of that small papery sound. Is it all done by mirrors?

OUT OF THE BLUE

The lady wear a cotton nightdress and cap, her looks so altered as to be beyond the help of any conjuror or Sanditon cure. She has the air of a wrongly-coloured waxwork.

'Who are you?' cries Charlotte, rising in alarm.

'Never you mind,' returns the lady, no more polite than Charlotte; and in a voice too clear and firm to be that of a dying woman. She comes, and adds: 'I trusted you.'

Recovering her manners, Charlotte inquires as to the nature of this trust.

The lady looks at Charlotte very directly: 'I left you in charge, didn't I? – and all you've managed is death and disorder.'

'*I*, in charge!' said Charlotte, – ' in what sense, madam, may I ask?'

'After Chapter seven. Chapter seven of that book – so, naturally, you'd be able to keep on as far as Chapter twelve, wouldn't you?'

'That *book*, madam?'

'Yes, girl, that book. That book or piece of a book, about salt and water – about Sanditon.'

'*Sanditon*? Sanditon a book, madam? Chapter seven and Chapter twelve, madam?'

'You are repeating what I am saying. You may have no option but to be my echo, if nothing better has been given you to say. Chapter twelve. That was the last of it, all I could manage. But you were set to work as early as Chapter seven. You should have got your hand in with your letter home. That letter. Think about it, miss. Think about it. There I've done the repetition for you, so you've no need to follow suit.'

Charlotte sits down and thinks for a little. She is surprised to find herself saying, and more surprised to find herself believing, that what she is saying is the truth:

'Yes, you are after all, quite right. I did write the letter you said I'd written. Yes, you'd set me writing letters at the beginning of Chapter seven of *Sanditon* (did you say it's to be called?), and I wouldn't be surprised if I was still writing right up to – and even – after you'd finished with Chapter twelve.'

Charlotte hopes that might be the end of it; that the lady might be gratified to be proved so surprisingly right about the details of book and chapters, but she does not appear to be giving Charlotte the attention which agreement merits.

There is a long pause and then the lady begins again, tangentially:

'*I* didn't call it any thing, you know, those pages – chapters – chapters of a book, *Sanditon*. It still had no title. Not as far as I was concerned. Suppose I'd given it the name of one of the people in it. I might have done that, mightn't I? *Charlotte*, for example. I'd done that with that book called *Emma*. I always meant to make another heroine, after writing about the one who married Wentworth, Anne Elliot (how is she, by the way?), one called Charlotte; *and* said so. Did you know that? But I'm not so sure now. For one thing, missy, who'd want a heroine who has so many failures of will – who moons about; wilfully moons about, gets up, flops down – walks out of rooms, I dare say?'

At this point that seems a good idea to Charlotte:

'You must excuse me now, madam,' she says, trying to get up.

'Come, come,' says the lady, 'you'll not do that.'

'You mean you would force me to stay, madam?'

'No, no, young lady,' says she, 'I mean if you leave – *cease*, I must leave – cease – also; as, if you shut your eyes, I shut mine. If you die now I am killed (though I don't think it necessarily works the other way round). You – supposedly acting for me! – have decimated my clergy, cut back a whole generation of squires and over-provided for the next one, in a manner that should *presage* a fiction not preoccupy it. You have thought fit to provide by-play with dogs and children; borrowed inordinately from the works of Mr Richardson (whose prolix shade could happily be left to its rest); and, in your own person, bounded about one minute and fallen away with the vapours the next.'

Charlotte, disturbed by the realisation that she cannot tell whether it is the lady or herself who is in the grip of a sick fancy, has recourse to silence.

The lady, too, holds her peace for a long time.

'You see,' replying at last, 'what I mean. When you are silent so am I.'

(Which of them is saying this? And what way of telling, of being sure?)

'I don't know how to reply,' says Charlotte at length.

'Very well,' the lady resuming slowly – and then at a dash: 'I don't suppose, I *don't* suppose – that you'd expect *me* to know any thing about literary theory...'

'I know the two words separately,' admits Charlotte, 'Not the term. Is it cant? Does it exist?'

'Do you?' asks the lady. 'Do you exist?'

'In some sense,' says Charlotte, 'though maybe not separately. I begin to feel that what you think may somehow be passed on to me.'

'No,' says the lady, 'only so much as is appropriate for your personage. So *No*'s the right answer for you, in most cases. I always' – giving way to a chuckle – 'always described myself as *unlettered*. But *nobody*' – fierce about this – 'nobody ever said I was stupid. Did anyone ever say *you* were stupid?'

'I'm not sure,' says Charlotte, 'No, probably not. Not in so many words. Not until now.'

'I'm not saying you're stupid,' says the lady.

'Not in so many words,' says Charlotte boldly.

'No,' says the lady equably, 'not in so many words.'

'If you'd wanted to keep control, shouldn't you have stayed around? If you exist, that is,' says Charlotte firmly.

'Clever girl,' says the lady, 'though I made you *clever* – definitely not stupid. I made you a writer. A writer and you'll stay a writer, even now my hand is stilled – maybe when my tongue has rotted to the root. What I make you do – if I do make you – is what defines me. I make you what you are and you make me. So whether I'm writing about you or you're writing about me doesn't matter. Whether I'm writing in my head or off my head. I'm in no condition to put pen to paper, because I'm on a deathbed, in my coffin.'

'Does that explain why things keep fading away? If so, you shouldn't blame me.'

'It's your waywardness. I left you. I let you alone. I left you to write a letter, as we have agreed. I set down in my own hand what you

'No, no, young lady,' says she, 'I mean if you leave – *cease*, I must leave – cease – also; as, if you shut your eyes, I shut mine. If you die now I am killed (though I don't think it necessarily works the other way round). You – supposedly acting for me! – have decimated my clergy, cut back a whole generation of squires and over-provided for the next one, in a manner that should *presage* a fiction not preoccupy it. You have thought fit to provide by-play with dogs and children; borrowed inordinately from the works of Mr Richardson (whose prolix shade could happily be left to its rest); and, in your own person, bounded about one minute and fallen away with the vapours the next.'

Charlotte, disturbed by the realisation that she cannot tell whether it is the lady or herself who is in the grip of a sick fancy, has recourse to silence.

The lady, too, holds her peace for a long time.

'You see,' replying at last, 'what I mean. When you are silent so am I.'

(Which of them is saying this? And what way of telling, of being sure?)

'I don't know how to reply,' says Charlotte at length.

'Very well,' the lady resuming slowly – and then at a dash: 'I don't suppose, I *don't* suppose – that you'd expect *me* to know any thing about literary theory...'

'I know the two words separately,' admits Charlotte, 'Not the term. Is it cant? Does it exist?'

'Do you?' asks the lady. 'Do you exist?'

'In some sense,' says Charlotte, 'though maybe not separately. I begin to feel that what you think may somehow be passed on to me.'

'No,' says the lady, 'only so much as is appropriate for your personage. So *No*'s the right answer for you, in most cases. I always' – giving way to a chuckle – 'always described myself as *unlettered*. But *nobody*'– fierce about this – 'nobody ever said I was stupid. Did anyone ever say *you* were stupid?'

'I'm not sure,' says Charlotte, 'No, probably not. Not in so many words. Not until now.'

'I'm not saying you're stupid,' says the lady.

'Not in so many words,' says Charlotte boldly.

'No,' says the lady equably, 'not in so many words.'

'If you'd wanted to keep control, shouldn't you have stayed around? If you exist, that is,' says Charlotte firmly.

'Clever girl,' says the lady, 'though I made you *clever* – definitely not stupid. I made you a writer. A writer and you'll stay a writer, even now my hand is stilled – maybe when my tongue has rotted to the root. What I make you do – if I do make you – is what defines me. I make you what you are and you make me. So whether I'm writing about you or you're writing about me doesn't matter. Whether I'm writing in my head or off my head. I'm in no condition to put pen to paper, because I'm on a deathbed, in my coffin.'

'Does that explain why things keep fading away? If so, you shouldn't blame me.'

'It's your waywardness. I left you. I let you alone. I left you to write a letter, as we have agreed. I set down in my own hand what you were to do; left you to supply the details. Now tell me, what kind of tone did you adopt?'

'You are sent to punish me for my foolishness,' says Charlotte. 'I have let you down. You needed a heroine. Instead you got me – I have made matches. I have been speculative, directing and partial.'

'Nothing wrong with any of that – but what a botch you've made of your main business! Shouldn't you have married by now?'

'That's hardly for me to say,' says Charlotte.

'Indeed it is,' says the lady. 'Besides, you're not heart-whole. First love won't come again, which makes it easier for you. Oh, it does. Concentrate on second love. I left you a plentiful supply of suitors. You'll pick one out soon enough. For all that at times you act like a green girl. Did I make you like that?'

'I don't think *you* meant to make me like that,' says Charlotte. 'Not directly. It's my dear papa at Willingden who still sees me a child, in spite of my unfortunate experience of some years ago (of which he thinks me quite cured).'

And yet,' the lady continues, 'and yet at other times you behave like someone fully grown, who demonstrates, if you will allow me to say so, good understanding and judgment. Can you account for that?'

'I can only suggest, madam,' says Charlotte, 'that I was always a reader – influenced by the variety of things I read – till my father feared such concentration on the printed page would affect my eyes and cause me to squint. So I take care in his presence to hold my book at arm's length, even though I'd like it much closer for my own convenience.'

'I suspect,' says the lady, after some consideration of Charlotte's attributes, 'you're two ages in one. Some people are. Some seem to age at a different pace from others. I do still think you are marriageable – not too old, by any means – though some of the people about you are older than I recall…I'm pleased,' she added slyly, 'that – *where you've not killed them off* – they've found occupation after marriage, and various widowings.'

The lady falls silent, but noticing a movement of Charlotte's hands, is reminded of some thing:

'Ah, while I'm on the subject of mortality, what exactly was it befell poor little Fanny Price? Very well, Fanny Bertram – what have you done to her? And, if it wasn't you, made me do through you? I used to call her "my Fanny". Not any more, it seems.'

'Indeed,' Charlotte attempts to answer, 'I left her very well. I can't think that I've done her any thing that could be seen as harm …'

'I mean *done to her husband and her husband's family* don't I, miss? Ah, you do know what I'm talking about! If you won't tell me, show me! What's that you're holding?'

Charlotte is uneasily fingering a page or two:

'They were left out,' she says apologetically, 'it was thought best not to explain.'

'Not explain? *I* always explained. Show me!'

'I'm afraid this is all I have,' said Charlotte, holding – withdrawing what she holds.

'Let me see, miss.'
'Are you sure you want to see? They would have come in earlier, but as I say –'

The lady has lost interest in Charlotte and reads aloud with snorts some sections of the discarded narrative as follows:

OUT OF THE BLUE

...When ill tidings came from the Bertram estates in Antigua Sir Thomas Bertram was afflicted...
...natural that Sir Thomas's eldest son, Tom, should take ship there... In case of a recurrence of Tom's former delicate health, he was accompanied by his brother, Edmund...

A single letter from Edmund was safely delivered..., Tom had succumbed to a virulent tropical fever and would not live. Other tidings were no better: the plantation fire was indeed a ruinous one, but the brothers' inquiries had revealed some villainy – by known persons, though unnamed. Edmund was returning with what portable assets he had been able to rescue and documentary evidence with which to prosecute the malefactors...

'Humhum' says the lady sceptically, 'So much for the inhabitants of Mansfield Park... And I suppose the ship was lost with all hands?'

'I believe so, madam,' admits Charlotte.

The large eyes in the strange bronze face roll upwards:

'With your propensity for disaster, is it any wonder that I fear for Clara Brereton? She never looked consumptive to me. But if that's the miserable condition you mean to inflict on her, you've wasted the opportunity to mend it with milk of asses by despatching their mistress, Lady Denham. So don't allow Miss Clara to fall into a decline. Or have her catch her death in cold sea water. You nearly drowned her earlier. What is your intention? – *And*, I repeat, what have you in mind for yourself? When are you going to marry?'

'I know no more than Miss Clara Brereton does –'

'Nonsense,' says the lady, 'you're working it out. And *she* will know what she needs to know when she needs to know it – that's if you are really quite sure you're not going to have her die from an ague caused by leaving her too long near the cold sea.'

'*I* have her die – how could I?'

The response of the lady is sharp:

'I think that you have not altogether attended to what I have been saying. To speak plainly: let's have no more sicknesses, no more failures of spirit...You do know what I mean – in your half-life you do know. Come now, is that a bargain?'

Charlotte accepts that it is.

'No more deaths either – not at all the sort of thing to dwell upon. No more deaths?'

Charlotte looks up in agreement – she has now the energy to compose: she composes herself in several senses. As someone leaves by a creaky gate, the writer slides her work out from the concealing blank papers and settles to work in the parlour.

2

The recent experiences of Charlotte Heywood are best forgotten; yes, acted upon, but then forgotten. She summons up her energy to start things moving: to write, to finish her letter.

> You will, my dear parents have been much perplexed by the blow to Mr Parker's expectations. I trust the opportunity to disengage yourselves honourably will have been welcome – but I know very little of these matters; only what I have been told by Mr Robert Ferrars, by way of reassurance.
>
> I believe that you will have found his advice of service. I am writing partly to say that his recent role for you as negotiator and intermediary will have concealed rather than revealed much about him that is remarkable. For instance, that no man can be more entertaining. Yes, you may observe cautiously, 'when he wants to be' – but it does not take any effort on his part when the company is to his liking. Nor does it take any effort on the part of the company either.
>
> You used to quiz me – as I began by hinting – for my fancy that I was a heroine and for my way of living my life through books. Well, Mr Ferrars – does this surprise you? – has in his time been something of a madcap. There is much to commend a reformed scapegrace to a romantic young lady; and I own – for all my barbs at dear Sir Edward (yes, he is dear – much as his great dog Bosun is dear – and both of them reformed!), that I have that inclination still within me.

Much has occurred during my time at Sanditon, some of which you are already apprised of. Heroic deeds have taken place: cast your minds back to the rescue from the waves of sickly Miss Lambe by Sir Edward. Have I told you of his transformation into Gothick hermit? – An occupation difficult to reconcile with impending nuptials to Miss Clara. I think I may have referred previously to the dashing impersonation of a highwayman by Mr Robert Ferrars. For it was he (Mr R F) who, muffled and masked, carried off his sisters-in-law to Brinshore (wherein began a temporary misunderstanding with Dear Mr Parker).

Heroes can be heroes – can gain their spurs for some fleeting moment of action as described above: heroines need to be made of longer-lasting stuff. All of us young ladies, though by now I'm a 'younger lady' (which means an older one!), have had our special moments. Mine, as you can hardly not recall, were characterised by sadness. Sometimes still I fall into a melancholy fit, into an emotional valetudinarianism, but the affection of my family and the liveliness of my friends continue to sustain me.

You are, of course acquainted with the circle of Mr and Mrs Parker, but I don't believe you will have met my firm friends, formerly at Brinshore – now in Sanditon. I refer, firstly, to Mrs Edward Ferrars, relict of the brother to Mr Robert Ferrars. Mrs Ferrars was born Elinor Dashwood (of Norland) but now lives with her sister (Mrs Brandon – Marianne Dashwood, the second friend) at grand old Delaford! Mrs Ferrars would very much like to make your acquaintance. I believe she intends to call on you quite soon and will probably be accompanied by Mr Robert Ferrars – yes, again.

I must reassure you about the misunderstanding between Mr Parker and Mr Ferrars. The latter gentleman proved not to be an advocate of Brinshore after all; well, not in opposition to Mr Parker's Sanditon, at all events. The truth was more prank-ish than that – more heroic, or mock-heroic. Mr Ferrars, recognising the ladies and seeing them undecided where to lodge, swept them away simply because he knew of a house which would suit. Yes, the house belonged to Mr Hargreaves, but Mr Hargreaves' motives are so unfathomable as to be a mystery even to himself.

'My daughter means me to think well of this Mr Ferrars,' say my kind papa and mama. You have it in a nutshell – and has he not (I've said already!) been of use when the behaviour of Richard Hollis put all in doubt? Mr Parker means to economise and to eschew all that is grandiose, I am urged to tell; to prepare for you for some thing which, I believe, you will see as good news.

'And what is the topic of Miss Charlotte's next paragraph to be? Our daughter grows monotonous,' you may say as you read on. Though approaching the middle years, there is something boyish about Mr RF: the admixture is a congenial one for the younger lady, as defined by me above.

I am about to take leave of my kind hosts at Sanditon: for the date which Mr Parker proposed to you for my return approaches. Though he urges an extension, I believe we should keep to the original proposal, (if that is still convenient) particularly as I sense Mr Parker is about to make drastic changes in his daily life.

I will now – for I have held back from doing so! – finally say a word or two about Mr Robert Ferrars.

No, dear parents, I do not do so injudiciously – for I long ago learned my lesson. Mr Ferrars says that he is now finished with playing the highwayman and other such games and looks to more solid pursuits, occupation and responsibilities. What, then, are your daughter's feelings about this gentleman? The answer to this question resides in the fact that she hopes you will like his sister-in-law, when she calls, sufficiently to invite both Elinor and Marianne to Willingden. No more than that at present, but it may *grow into* a l*v* m*tch

I don't – I daren't – write the words remembering past foolishness – the girl who once accepted a suitor at supper and denied him at breakfast – and that young woman's *hurt*, of which I won't, can't, needn't say more. But if affection does grow from this present point, it will be not least because of the care and concern he has shown for my father's property – and, I sense, without any prying or importunity. But you will judge that better than I.

What I am able (at the advanced age of twenty two) to judge with a much better degree of certainty than any younger self is that my situation is not at all like my former distressing one.

I will say no more – save, you may have heard that Mr Ferrars had a previous wife. His openness with me about *his* past mistake has been reciprocated. That we are in this respect birds of a feather – and *know* we are birds of a feather – enhances rather than impairs my present (I will not spell it out, but, yes) h*pp*n*ss *No*, a HEROINE would never become the second Mrs Anybody! But there is a destiny which shapes our ends &c, including those of

Your loving daughter,
Charlotte Heywood

Her letter written, Charlotte knew that healing Time had had its way: the diversionary attentions of Sidney Parker and her literary duels with Sir Edward had not only left her unscathed, but had given her strength.

Already some things seemed as certain as things can be: Miss Lettie Beaumont would soon be Mrs Griffiths' only pupil –

for an announcement of her elder sister's engagement to Mr Arthur Parker was expected daily; similarly, Miss Lambe (both recumbent and upright) saw a great deal of Mr Wingfield – with little pretence of medical supervision, nor of the fact that Sir Edward's failure to inherit had had a bearing on her choice of companion.

Mr Wingfield's monopoly of Miss Lambe disencumbered Sir Edward, leaving him free to burrow, dig, excavate, and exclaim in his caverns. There he cried aloud of his foolishness in not having told Clara Brereton of his determined generosity towards her were he to have inherited: how could he now approach her – he with nothing, she with a sufficiency and the solid roof of Sanditon House over her head? Besides he had his sister, Miss Esther to support. Even Bosun who cost a lot in dogs-meat was a party to these melancholy reflections: he had no faith in a future where his master put so much energy into digging up stone bones. There was no abatement to Sir Edward's troubles – until the morning, a particularly fine morning, when Mr Sidney Parker called to disclose his long-standing attachment to Miss Esther.

*

Mr Parker had rashly undertaken further building work in the expectation that funds would be forthcoming. He was too much the gentleman to urge any contribution from Mr Heywood who had listened to the advice of Mr Robert Ferrars, who had likewise urged Mr Parker to stay his hand.

'I was warned,' said Mr Parker to Mr Heywood, 'and you. sir, told me of your decision.'

'Besides,' said Mr Parker, very cheerful by the next day, 'things will pick up. I see a good many visitors here. And, as for our residents, why here is Sir Edward with Miss Esther, looking light of heart.'

'Indeed, sir, I am much changed by Miss Esther's happiness and thereby with the prospect of becoming your brother-in-law; as well as to Miss Diana, Miss Susan, Mr Arthur (I have never been blessed with so many brothers and sisters!) – and, naturally, to the happy man himself, Mr Sidney!'

Mr Sidney Parker, having been clapped heartily on the shoulder by Sir Edward, stepped forward and took Miss Esther's hand. Sidney, as he did so, murmured some thing for Charlotte Heywood's ears by way of apology for keeping the understanding so close.

Sir Edward was of the opinion that secrecy had added spice to the engagement; an observation which he embellished with a few words about Lord Byron's penchant both for mystery and frankness: 'Now there we have both, don't you agree, Miss Heywood, Miss Brereton?'

Charlotte Heywood made a decision to hold back, defer to Clara Brereton, give her strength. Clara did speak up, but her first response was to shake her head:

'I would be equally open with you too, Sir Edward. I thank you for defending me – as I have heard – from those who envy me. At present it seems to me a sad enough choice – or accident – of the late great lady's. Would that your sister, Miss Esther, had been invited to live at Sanditon House, for then she would have had an unarguable claim.'

Miss Esther, obliged instead to Trafalgar House and the Parkers for the pin-money which care of little Mary brought, agreed heartily with Clara Brereton's sentiments, but had sufficient sense to see that no good would come of her speaking them out loud.

Sir Edward sought to prevent further dissidence by courteously acknowledging Clara's feeling and moving back to Miss Esther's nuptials. Clara, however – not intending to be distracted – asked Charlotte whether it would be practicable for her to renounce the bequest.

'But at such cost to yourself?' said Charlotte, 'my dear, I have often thought you were born to be a heroine, but of some domestic romance, not of a tragedy!'

She turned with a questioning look to Mr Ferrars, who could not but have overheard what Clara had said. Mr Ferrars' engagement to Charlotte Heywood was not yet known, so he was at

Sanditon to help Mr Parker with his affairs; not only those, but now Clara's:

'Miss Brereton,' he said kindlily, 'your sentiments do you great credit, but to renounce your good fortune – and I understand you gave Lady Denham more affection and service in her life-time than most, so the bequest has by no means an arbitrary feel to it – to refuse to accept what has been bequeathed to you would benefit no one. Certainly not Miss Esther Denham who, not being resident at Sanditon House at the crucial time, is precluded from any inheritance. No, it would benefit no one – except the residuary legatee: the person who has received the great bulk of Lady Denham's worldly goods. Were you to refuse to accept what is properly yours, Sanditon House and the fund which is to give you your income would be added to his vast resources. You mustn't think of it, Miss Brereton.'

✳

The sun shone, and the builders' bills were not yet come to Mr Parker, though he knew they would be arriving soon enough. Yet, as he said, there seemed plenty of visitors in Sanditon, so he trusted that the new properties – though they had begun to be available only late in the season might still be taken.

Mr Parker's reviving optimism smiled upon his companions at Trafalgar House during the next few days; during which Sir Edward and Miss Esther Denham, Clara Brereton, Charlotte Heywood, Sidney Parker and Robert Ferrars often walked along the shore and cliffs of Sanditon; and even made the journey together as far as the landslip, from which viewpoint they could now clearly discern the Brinshore jetty as it crept out like a sea serpent into the English Channel.

The three gentlemen and the three ladies walked and talked with no discernible pattern to their companionships. It was as if those of the six who were partial wished to diffuse their partiality:

all six seeming to find the other five congenial, severally, generally – and, even – particularly.

Thus, though Sir Edward, Sidney Parker and Robert Ferrars might all seem to court Charlotte Heywood at one moment; at another, their attentiveness would confirm that Clara Brereton was the heroine. All was open and good-humoured: for these six, there was less hypochondriacal oppression in Sanditon's ether and more concentration on the springiness of turf; or the bounce of the sand, firmed by the tide.

But invalidism was the preoccupying condition of most of the new visitors whom Mr Parker had observed. Mr Wingfield's luck was continuing to hold. It was advantageous to him, for instance, that Mr Woodhouse had succumbed to a spasm of excitement, as distinct from the depression of spirits for which he was being treated. Thus Wingfield acquired a reputation for curing whatever ailment you had, forcing you to die (if you must die) of some thing else; all of which was additional to his credit for restoring dead Miss Lambe.

The popularity of Mr Wingfield's regimen, while enriching that gentleman daily, was – unfortunately for Mr Parker – producing no new residents. Wingfield's patients were generally day-visitors, or repaired to cottages in the villages around, since Mr Parker's buildings tended not to be ready for occupation.(Mr Parker had seemingly learned little from the initial failure to provide accommodation for Mrs Brandon and Mrs Edmund Ferrars. Further ill-timed initiatives were committing him to expenditure without the surety of any income from them.)

Whatever the educational shortcomings of Mrs Griffiths' establishment, two-thirds of her resident scholars were proving betrothable: Miss Lambe, with her salt-encrusted interior and exterior, to Mr Wingfield; the elder Miss Beaufort, with her harp and telescope, to Mr Arthur Parker. There remained only Lettie Beaufort, though Arthur would have taken her too; and the young day-pupil, Agnes Wentworth, who was reluctant to attend now that Miss Clara had given up her work there. Consequently Mrs Griffiths, who had received two months' additional fees from Miss Lambe on her graduation from the seminary (fees larger than any paid by Lady Denham's late husband for his doctoring), declared that she would return immediately to Camberwell. Miss Diana Parker on hearing of this determined to do likewise.

So the school room fell vacant, with a further reduction of Mr Parker's income; and though one or two more of his new houses became ready for occupation, they remained empty. Meanwhile the builders' and retailers' bills continued to arrive, and ways of paying them had to be found.

One day Mr Parker looked up from some unsatisfactory calculations and said to his wife and Mr Sidney: 'My dears, I've been thinking a little about the old house and the garden produce – some of which is going to waste – whether it wouldn't be wise to reconsider the business of giving it up.'

'Yes,' said Mrs Parker, 'poor, dear old house – but there things stand,' adding with a change of dimension, 'we've made our bed and we must lie on it.'

Mr Parker was appreciative of his wife's loyalty, but said – and merely this: 'Not necessarily.'

'What!' cried she, 'leave Trafalgar House?'

Mr Parker made no demur, though he could hardly look her in the eye.

'Leave Trafalgar House,' cried she, sitting up and opening her eyes very wide, 'has it come to this? Leave Trafalgar House, when I had learned to bear it, when the plantation had begun to shoot up and fill out a little, and the winds seem not so rough of late. Oh, if we must move, if we are, forced to give up this house for a smaller, do not,' she appealed. 'Oh, do not let us build nearer the edge of the cliff or we shall go over – nor even cling halfway up it like Waterloo Crescent – nor on the shingle in some fenced-off area the tide is not supposed to reach – no, not on the beach, nor on a jetty. Oh, do not let us be nearer the sea –!'

'No, no, calm yourself, my dear,' said Mr Parker, sorry that his wife's very understanding seemed impaired by his past grandiloquence, 'What you fear is far from the truth.'

'Alas,' she replied, fearing one dismal prospect could only give way to another, 'are we then to leave dear Sussex? I don't think I could face a foreign clime, be turned all shades like Miss Lambe and have poor little Mary's fair hair singed and crimped by the sun. Are we, then, so totally ruined that we must make our home in the colonies? I trust it is not so!'

'It is not so. Indeed, it is not so. But you have suffered too much from my quirks and designs. Let us go back to what we were – that is my point.'

Said Sidney: 'Talking of which, Thomas…Talking, I mean, of Old Hall…'

Thomas looked at him.

'Yes,' continued Sidney, 'that's just what I was doing the other day. Talking…Or, listening, rather. Your tenant, Mr Hillier had asked me to look in (knowing my brother to be fully occupied with pressing affairs) for some advice, which I (for the same reason) agreed to give, though speaking for myself alone.'

'Occupied, I have been,' said Mr Parker, 'excessively so. It had quite slipped my memory, before your mention of his name brought it to mind, that Hillier's lease is due for renewal at the end of next month. How I came to forget such a matter, I do not know – or, rather, I know only too well.'

'It was to discuss the lease that I was asked to call,' said Sidney. 'To be brief, Mr Hillier is doubtful whether he and his family feel quite easy in a squire's house, which carries with it almost a squire's responsibilities; the household, for one thing, being greater than Mrs Hillier has use to manage – '

'Poor soul,' said Mrs Parker reviving. 'Yet it's a fine old place. For all the seascapes from Trafalgar House, the windows here will rattle when it blows, though perhaps that is preferred as poetical? But,' and for the first time in weeks there was comprehension, 'do I dare to hope? – that some arrangement has been made, whereby we may retreat from the seashore – go inland a little? How could I have expected it! – to Mr Parker's, old Mr Parker that was, to his dear Old Hall.'

'Yes, my love, you have the general idea,' said her husband, 'Hillier to his former house and functions and we to ours. Thanks, that is, to Sidney.'

'And yet,' said Sidney, 'this is but part of the tale. There will be some saving – as on fresh vegetables and on upkeep, but you will not have Hillier's quarterly payments –'

Mr Parker looked dashed.

'Nor if you abandon Sanditon – sell its freeholds and leaseholds to some Richard Hollis, for instance, for a fraction of their worth – will you have any income from that. So I took the liberty of discussing certain possibilities with Robert Ferrars, who, you'll agree, is a shrewd gentleman.'

Mr Parker urged Sidney to continue. 'But I held back from making any observations to you, Thomas, until you had taken a crucial decision, such as your present one to return to Old Hall. First of all, you require to let Trafalgar House at a good rate – and, yes, I believe there is some one who will come forward shortly to take it; secondly, there is the strong possibility that the school room will be re-taken at a rental higher than that paid by Mrs Griffiths, if you will entrust the negotiation to Mr Ferrars and myself. Thirdly – and this is the final and most important point: don't you think,' urged Sidney, but gently, 'that Sanditon would run itself –?'

Mr Parker, unable to acknowledge yet that he was so entirely dispensable, did not reply.

'I believe that I hear Mr Ferrars downstairs,' said Sidney gently, 'might he join in our discussion, do you think?'

Mr Parker accepted this proposition. Mrs Parker went to fetch him, her head reeling, but somewhat reassured. She saw Mr Ferrars up the stairs herself and then popped down again to make lists. If they were to move, then Diana must return – it was unthinkable that progress could be made without her needle and thread.

Sidney outlined the position to Mr Ferrars.

Mr Ferrars saw what needed saying at once: 'We should be clear from the outset, Mr Parker, that your brother had no intention to denigrate your fine work here. No one would –'

'Far from it,' agreed Sidney.

'I expect what he had in mind,' said Mr Ferrars, 'was merely that the letting and so on – well, I'm not sure that that's an occupation for a gentleman. Wouldn't you say it could be handled by a manager – Woodcock of the Hotel, if he's up to it? – who would probably pay you for the privilege if he were allowed to take a percentage of the profits.'

'Profit, profit, profit – where's the joy of that?' said Mr Parker.

'Ah but, Mr Parker,' said Robert Ferrars, 'if the income's there, and there securely, we can forget all about such things and occupy ourselves with our science, our art, or our landscape improvement. Let others find the money: it will come with little or no effort on our part, if the books can be made to balance – as I'm sure they can. Sanditon will look after itself and pay for itself very well quite soon. When it does, you'll find the Richard Hollises of the kingdom will want a part of it, will seek you out.'

'Yes,' said Sidney, 'Sanditon will prosper. Its beginnings have been promising and I doubt whether either the Brinshore jetty or bridge (neither of which will be much noticed) are a serious problem. I have come to know a gentleman who lives hard by, a Captain Wentworth, and to value his opinions. It appears that he was appraising the situation very shrewdly the other day when you looked through his telescope. His advice to Sanditon is that it should now be left alone, to grow more easily and slowly and less forcedly; in accordance with the wishes of not only those who come here (wishing to visit a little place in Sussex) but of those who choose to live in the vicinity.'

'For my part, I shall keep an eye on it,' intervened Robert Ferrars,' – an uninvolved, but eagle-eye – from my eyrie in this very house, if you accept my taking it off your hands at valuation. Trafalgar House, Mr Parker, shall not be without your own presence for very long: you, your whole family, shall come and enjoy its fine views as often as you wish. Thus, neither the new place nor the old place shall go to seed, depend on it!'

There was a great sense of relief. Mr Parker resolved to walk first on the cliffs with his family as far as the landslip and then back to Old Hall. He began to look with an approving eye on both New and Old Sanditon: his returning fondness for the estate of his forefathers leaving no room for rancour towards Brinshore: a place, which after all had proved what he had always maintained, that as a watering place it could not hold a candle to Sanditon. Let Brinshore be what it would; let Hollis make of it what he could, a port or whatever he chose; Brinshore had yielded up any fashionable pretensions. That was enough.

After their return to Trafalgar House the Parkers were left alone. Thomas surveyed the bay from his great bay windows a little wistfully, but Mrs Parker looked at him so fondly and cheeringly that soon they could not but be as comfortable with the decisions that had been made as they were with each other.

Soon it was their bed time: 'I didn't like to ask in company, my dear,' said Mrs Parker, 'for I know there will always be some things which I shan't understand at first hearing, but I don't repine that it is so. But I don't quite see why Mr Ferrars should want to take up residence in a good-sized family house.'

'No more do I,' said her husband, affectionately 'though I have an inkling. And I believe you have, too, my dear.'

*

'I knew I was not born to be a heroine,' thus Charlotte Heywood to herself (but happily) when Robert Ferrars and her father both meet her with open hands before she is to travel back to Willingden – for a stay at her old home of no great length prior to her marriage. 'Far better to be one of those sensible, managing ladies who help the heroine on her way – if she's lucky.' She tries to upbraid herself for smugness, but is unsuccessful: she finds herself happy, and why not?

The *Why not* consisted only of a need to give precedence to the heroine and where was she to be found? A heroine demands a hero; and the definition of both the former and the latter resides in this mutuality, their coexistence; which is a constant matter for conjecture and the very stuff of narrative.

A possible hero and heroine, in Sir Edward and Clara, have appeared. What of their future together – or apart?   Little or no time or space remains.   Perhaps just enough – if there is energy enough, too, to do it – to tell briefly or rather to foreshadow what will come to pass; to resolve things.

Sir Edward's seductive pose and florid airs had always been a thin cover for his respectability.   There was some principle there too: he could never have brought himself to marry a Miss Lambe, to hunt down capital coolly.   However, though there was no fortune to be had from it, Lady Denham's will was such as to make any thing but marriage between Miss Clara Brereton and Sir Edward excessively inconvenient. If Clara Brereton were to have Sanditon House until she should marry, losing it thereafter, and Sir Edward was to take possession of it thereafter, but lack it now, the one way in which both (and the heirs of both) could enjoy the property not only now, but happily ever after, was for the pair to make a match of it. And marry they did, just as soon as they had contrived the necessary number of conversations, understandings, and situations subterranean and terrestrial – by candle and sun-light, by wave and wind; over books and bones, on green benches, under awnings; and in the parlour of Sanditon House.

Such, then, was the outcome: a second union between the Breretons and the Denhams. Once more, there was a Lady Clara Denham, though she was neither rich nor domineering. Yet the former great lady's power had lain in her shrewdness, so it is possible that the first Lady Denham had been beneficent at the last: her legal provisions having ensured that the means of Sir Edward and Clara were small but adequate; and such as to keep the Lovelace and *Giaour* in their household to a domestic and manageable scale.

Sir Edward had in any case become notably quieter since the finding of the cave. After his marriage he left Denham Court to its creeping damp – his sister Esther had no need of it, being by then wife to Mr Sidney Parker who had taken a property no longer required by Mr Robert Ferrars; no longer required because this gentleman resided during the summer months at Trafalgar House with his happy wife, the former Miss Charlotte Heywood; and in a large warm house inland left him by his mother when the days grew short and cool. But whatever the weather or the geology, Sir Edward retained the cottage ornée, making the cave his regular occupation. Thus the adherent of sensational literature became for a time a species of showman, guiding parties of visitors through candlelit vaults, inventing legends and verse to account for the rock formations.

Later, growing philosophical, sensing science come upon him, he built a museum or cabinet of rarities – central to which were the bones of his alleged mammoths, behemoths and giants. The cave and the museum together became chief among the sights of Sanditon, though later they were leased to old Stringer, whose 'general provision' – now that Xanadu Caverns had been added to his stock – became the most comprehensive of his fellow traders. Together with the concession in bottled sea-water (which Mr Parker good-naturedly remembered in spite of his own troubles, and which Mr Wingfield promoted, subject to his own levy on each pint), the tradesman and his son whose livelihood had been threatened by Mr Parker's miscalculations lived to do very well.

As proposed by Sidney Parker, Mr Wingfield took over the former school room for what he called 'a tidal pump room'. The popular expectation that he would acquire by marriage to Miss Lambe a very great fortune was also fulfilled; but Sanditon, far from being the means of her premature demise, turned out to have a clime suited to her constitution: she lived, and proved a tartar. Indeed, far from Wingfield's becoming an enriched widower, Mrs Wingfield soon became a widow; one with wealth enough (and a continuing income from Mr Wingfield's enterprises) to mind but little adverse tidings from Antigua; coming to resemble Lady Denham in temperament and demeanour if not in complexion. An advertisement for her husband while he lived, she became a memorial to those skills which passed with him into the grave.

Miss Diana Parker (called back to re-curtain Old Hall) grew to like Sir Edward and Lady Clara very much; made known to them some new provisions of her will: which assurance of future benefits from Camberwell ameliorated the Denham's anxieties for the young family they were soon to acquire.

All three Parker brothers proved themselves constant. Mr Arthur Parker, who (along with Miss Lambe) represented Sanditon's best instance of a complete cure, married his Miss Beaufort and grew gentlemanly and slim. Mr Sidney Parker, in his conjunction with Miss Esther, who retained the placidity and quietness desirable in a child, perhaps sought the antithesis of certain worldly-wise female acquaintances whom he had been unable to acknowledge – in any case, he continued to supply in company fully enough talk for both his wife and himself. And Mr Thomas Parker's devotion to his Old Hall resumed from the point of its interruption.

*

As for Charlotte Heywood, who becomes Mrs Robert Ferrars, she marries a little too late (at nearly twenty-three) and as a second wife. She could not, therefore, ever have been seen as a heroine – and resists the idea that she has been a party to constructing a fiction with any such purpose, however tentative. She keeps faith, though, with her belief that being a heroine is exactly what a very few special young ladies are intended for, and that this is what they unaffectedly achieve.

Consider, for example, Elizabeth Bennet before she was twenty: whether any of her numerous daughters will follow in this heroine's footsteps still lies far in the future. Mr Darcy, too, has been a *hero* in his generosity and despatch. Being a heroine, being a hero are conditions associated with youth; though men are accorded more years than women for fulfilling such roles.

It is doubtful whether a happy lady of about thirty – as Elizabeth has become – can be other than a mother or a confidante; if unhappy, she can be little more than a victim – of her own folly or of some man's misdeeds. For it is permitted that a man of any age may be a villain.

*

No one was to accuse Darcy of being so much – or, his great name considered, so little. Whether there was any encounter with a Clementina in Italy or no, Darcy on his return kept his own counsel. Any thing that was unfortunate weighed little in the balance against a joyful turn of events: Elizabeth was able to present him with a healthy baby boy of the male sex.

He was pleased to know Fanny and interested to hear of the good use she had made of the time since all had turned unfortunate for the Bertram family. Fanny's short account of the reasons for the fatal voyage of her husband and his brother – for she made no parade of her loss of Edmund – brought Darcy to mind of a conversation he had had abroad with a fellow called Willoughby; a man who if not a scoundrel himself had a scoundrel's connections.

Further reflection upon what he had been told – Darcy's memory was an efficient organ, even when directed to matters to which at the time he had given scant attention – and inquiries among powerful friends put him in a fair way to being able to identify the malefactors behind the West Indian plot against the Bertram estate. There was the likelihood of partial restitution – if not by the villains themselves (though they would be brought to justice), then by parties who had bought goods and shares which were not the property of those who did the selling. If that were the case, then some who were innocent would suffer some disadvantage; for instance, it seemed likely that the great fortune of Miss Lambe – of Mrs Wingfield – would be subject to some diminution.

Darcy fell in love again with the mother of his son. His line established, he had nothing but kindly thoughts for Sanditon, the place where, to every one's surprise at the suddenness of it, Elizabeth had given birth one morning near the end of Summer.

While necessarily at Sanditon – his imagination still stimulated by Triumphal Arches and Aqueducts, by the Appian Way and Tivoli – he found a congenial companion in Thomas Parker, who, though never to travel further South than the Isle of Wight, was a true amateur of the arts and sciences. Darcy had brought great folios of engravings back with him, and together they scrutinised them.

Mr Parker made some sketches of a landscape bridge or two – one constructed of iron, which might do for Pemberley, as he no longer had any intention of inflicting his designs upon Sanditon. Darcy accepted the sketches happily, asking Thomas, as they walked about the Old Hall garden, his views on large forcing frames for exotic plants.

Darcy was anxious to be heading north; but, detained by Elizabeth's need to lie in a while longer, he visited Trafalgar House, when the newly-married Robert and Charlotte Ferrars were about to take up residence; heard from Mr Ferrars the story of Brinshore, decided to call on the great Sir Richard Hollis.

Sir Richard, though Baronet because of his rough father's doughty enterprise was sensible of the honour; for Mr Darcy, plain esquire, was heir to a Dukedom. They talked of art and construction, of motive power and beauty, of generosity and natural philosophy. Hollis, who had adopted brusqueness for business, was not an ignorant man. Indeed, so convinced was he of his own capacity and by Darcy's discourse on Art and Utility, that it was he himself who proposed operating the Hollis manufactories with (as it were) his left hand; reserving his strong right arm for the future Duke, as Gardener Extraordinary to Pemberley.

END

NOTES

1 Dates

Jane Austen worked on her last novel during the first three months of 1817. It was given the title *Sanditon* after her death, which occurred in Winchester on 18 July. That date is the only specific one in the present work.

But the clock has not stopped. It is seen as continuing to tick away for Jane Austen's characters during the remainder of their author's life, including the time she was able to give to *Sanditon*.

I have re-started stories from her other novels at points where an element of change or crisis seemed plausible; taken on *Sanditon* from the point where Jane Austen left it. The twelve short chapters of her manuscript are summarised in my letter home from Charlotte Heywood (page 30, above). Thereafter the story is improvised around possibilities Jane Austen provided. In particular, the continuation of her duel with Samuel Richardson – a writer who had been dead for fifty years, but whom she read and scored off as if he were her regular correspondent.

2 Sources

In the present work, I have avoided using Jane Austen's own words as far as possible. There are no more than a couple of sentences that I am conscious of directly quoting. However, as already implied, I have borrowed frequently from 'the father of the English novel', Samuel Richardson. In so doing, I have followed Austen herself – from her juvenile comic dramatisation of *Sir Charles Grandison*, and her finger-pointing footnote in Chapter 3 of *Northanger Abbey* (defending a female's right to fall in love unilaterally), to her 1817 view of Sir Edward Denham as 'quite in the line of the Lovelaces', and – most importantly – the way in which she took Richardson's sententious utterances and gave them an ironic twist.

Besides my (unattributed) polite collage of Richardson 'sentiments' in, for example, the meeting at Sanditon House after Lady Denham's death (pp 51-2), there are quotations from and references to his novels *Clarissa* and *Sir Charles Grandison* . These are authentic; as are those from the works of, in particular, Byron – including some very odd stuff.

Jane Austen herself makes no reference to Byron in the original *Sanditon* – though she does so in her earlier works. It may be that by 1817 Byron's activities abroad had made him too shocking for further mention, but I have taken the view that she was holding the most celebrated poet of her time in reserve. Accordingly, I have presented Sir Edward as not only in the line of the Lovelaces, but as spokesman for a not dissimilar Byronism.

I was led into this work by following Jane Austen's own habit of wondering what happened to the characters she invented. Many other writers have done likewise. Others, too, may have differed from her view that Mr Woodhouse lived for only two years after Emma's marriage to Knightley. But I don't know that anyone else has tried to address the whole gallery of characters. The narrative makes clear my acceptance that the shade of Jane Austen herself – and, by implication, purist Austen fans – might disapprove of what I, and Charlotte Heywood, have made of them.

3 Jane Austen Characters chiefly referred to in the present work

Northanger Abbey

Catherine Morland
(Mrs Tilney)

Sense and Sensibility

Eleanor Dashwood
(Mrs Ferrars)
Marianne Dashwood
(Mrs Brandon)
John Dashwood
Robert Ferrars

NOTES

Pride and Prejudice

Elizabeth Bennet
(Mrs Darcy)
Fitzwilliam Darcy
Jane Bennet
(Mrs Bingley)
Mr Bennet
Mary Bennet
Rev William Collins

Emma

Emma Woodhouse
(Mrs G Knightley)
George Knightley
John Knightley
Isabella, Mrs J Knightley
Mr Woodhouse
Mr Wingfield
Robert Martin
(who married Harriet Smith)

John Willoughby

Mansfield Park

Fanny Price
(Mrs Bertram)
Sir Thomas Bertram

Persuasion

Ann Elliot
(Mrs Wentworth)
Captain Wentworth

Sanditon

Lady Denham
Sir Edward Denham
Esther Denham
Clara Brereton
Charlotte Heywood
Mr Heywood
Miss Lambe

Thomas Parker
Mrs Mary Parker
Sidney Parker
Arthur Parker
Diana Parker
Susan Parker
Mr Hillier

Mrs Griffiths, the Miss Beauforts, Mrs Whitby, Stringer & Son, Mr Jebb.

4 Jane Austen's use of Richardson's Sentiments (Aphorisms)

The cards which Fanny Bertram shows to Elizabeth (page 140, above) actually existed. They were used for a sociable mind-reading act, which involved a selection of sentiments taken from Richardson. The game, if one can call it that, went through many editions over 25 years, before disappearing completely.

Jane Austen may well have used these cards at an impressionable age. A reconstruction of the game, including a working set of cards and an account of how it was played, will be published 2006/7 by the present author under the title *The Jane Austen Puzzle*.

The source of the sentiments on the cards would almost certainly have been the reference system to Richardson's huge novels which he himself made and published in 1755 as *A Collection of the Moral and Instructive Sentiments…Contained in the Histories of Pamela, Clarissa, and Sir Charles Grandison*. Two sections from this work are given opposite in the original format.

Consider what is being put forward there under the heads *Prejudice* and *Pride*. The cited volume and page numbers and the characters mentioned refer, of course, to Richardson's *Clarissa*. However, I am inviting the reader to look at this series of sixteen sentiments in the light of the attitudes and behaviour towards each other of Elizabeth and Darcy in Jane Austen's *Pride and Prejudice*.

When I first read these two lists many years ago, I could not help seeing this sequence of *Pride* and *Prejudice* sentiments as not only a possible source of Austen's title, but something approaching hints for the novel itself. There are other equally pertinent sections. This topic will be returned to in the forthcoming *Jane Austen Puzzle*.

NOTES

Sentiments, &c. *extracted from* The History of CLARISSA.

Prejudice. Prepossession. Antipathy.

EARLY--BEGUN Antipathies are not easily eradicated, i. 19. [20].

Those we dislike can do nothing to please us, i. 89. ii. 114. [i. 92. ii. 202].

An extraordinary Antipathy in a young Lady to a particular person, is generally owing to an extraordinary prepossession in favour of another, i. 108. [112].

An eye favourable to a Lover, will not see his faults thro' a magnifying glass, ii. 50. [142]

Prepossession in a Lover's favour will make a Lady impute to ill-will and prejudice all that can be said against him, *ibid.*

Old prejudices [*tho' once seemingly removed*] easily recur, ii. 314. [iii. 52].

To those we love not, *says Lovelace, speaking of Mr. Hickman,* we can hardly allow the merit they should be granted, vi. 1. [328].

Prejudices in *disfavour* generally fix deeper than Prejudice in *favour*, vi. 306. [vii. 233].

Whenever we approve, we can find an hundred reasons to justify our approbation ; and whenever we dislike, we can find a thousand to justify our dislike, vi. 256. [viii. 181].   [*See* Love.   Lover.

Pride.

PRIDE, in people of birth and fortune, is not only mean, but needless, i. 186. [193].

Distinction and quality may be prided in, by those to whom it is a *new* thing, *ibid*.

The contempt a proud great person brings on himself, is a counterbalance for his greatness, *ibid.*

It is sometimes easier to lay a proud man under obligation, than to get him to acknowledge it, i. 322. [ii. 13].

Pride ever must, and ever will, provoke contempt, i. 186. [ii. 13].

There may be such an haughtiness in submission, as may entirely invalidate the submission, ii. 72. [162].

A person who distinguishes not, may think it the mark of a great spirit to humour his own Pride, even at the expence of his politeness, ii. 73. [163].

Acknowledgements

I am much indebted to Jon Measham for his technical support, without which the work would never have been published in this form; also to Bill Berrett – designer of Staple publications for twenty years – particularly for his cover, based upon small details from picturesque engravings made by T Barber in the early nineteenth century.

D M